Copyright © 2018 by Lana Williams

All rights reserved.

By payment of required fees, you have been granted the *non*-exclusive, *non*-transferable right to access and read the text of this book. No part of this text may be reproduced, transmitted, downloaded, decompiled, reverse engineered, or stored in or introduced into any information storage and retrieval system, in any form or by any means, whether electronic or mechanical, now known or hereinafter invented without the express written permission of copyright owner.

Please Note

The reverse engineering, uploading, and/or distributing of this book via the internet or via any other means without the permission of the copyright owner is illegal and punishable by law. Please purchase only authorized electronic editions, and do not participate in or encourage electronic piracy of copyrighted materials. Your support of the author's rights is appreciated

No part of this book may be reproduced or transmitted in any form or by any electronic or mechanical means, including photocopying, recording or by any information storage and retrieval system, without the written permission of the publisher, except where permitted by law.

Thank you.

Cover art by The Killion Group

http://thekilliongroupinc.com

Hope the story holds you "captive"
Lana Williams

A KNIGHT'S CAPTIVE

FALLING FOR A KNIGHT BOOK THREE

LANA WILLIAMS

OTHER BOOKS IN THE FALLING FOR
A KNIGHT SERIES:

A Knight's Christmas Wish, A Novella, Book .5

A Knight's Quest, Book 1

A Knight's Temptation, Book 2

For information on new releases and special promotions, sign up for my newsletter. https://lanawilliams.net/

CHAPTER 1

SCOTLAND 1298

"To my dear daughter," Lord James Graham declared as he stood at the high table in the great hall and lifted his pewter goblet, wine sloshing over the sides. "And her soon-to-be husband. On the morrow, they wed."

Cheers filled the chamber while defiance filled Lady Arabela Graham's heart. She shifted to avoid the splattering dark red drops that stained the table linen. If only she could so easily avoid her wedding.

Her father reached down to grasp her shoulder. Hard.

She did her best not to grimace and looked up to find his eyes full of warning. Forcing a smile, she attempted to appear the adoring daughter, though that was far from the truth.

His grip eased while the guests who'd gathered for the evening meal continued to cheer, raising their cups. *"Slàinte!"*

Arabela drew a breath of relief as her father took his seat next to her, his attention shifting elsewhere. If this evening's meal was anything to judge the rest of her life by, she was in serious trouble.

Defiance was not a desired trait in a young lady. One of her many flaws, according to her father.

"Have you ever seen your father so pleased?" Sir Rory Buchanan, her betrothed, asked with a smug look on his face as he leaned close.

She braced herself, knowing what would happen if she moved away. The number of her bruises grew daily. With the same forced smile, she briefly met his dark, glittering gaze but didn't bother to answer. He preferred she didn't speak. He and her father had much in common.

Though a knight, Rory was anything but chivalrous. In fact, he couldn't be further from an ideal knight in looks or manner. A brute of a man with coarse features and pock-marked cheeks which left his dark beard spotty, he saw no purpose in treating others kindly. Stale sweat and garlic seeped from his body, creating a unique stench she'd recognize anywhere.

His claim of being an indirect descendant of Donald, the last Scottish king to have the honor of being laid to rest by the monks at Iona centuries ago, had brought him to her father's notice. Their shared hatred of the English finalized the betrothal.

Arabela held doubt as to Rory's heritage. When she'd questioned him, he'd been unable to explain his exact connection to Donald, the last ruler who'd truly believed in Scotland's full independence. Additional questions only angered him. She'd raised the topic with her father, who told her to leave such matters to men.

Her father had made no secret of his plan to place her and Rory on the throne of Scotland. With no obvious heir, division tore the country apart. An alliance with France two years prior had angered England, causing additional problems. Her father was certain Rory's tie to Donald would convince the people that he was the rightful king and unite the country. And if it didn't, her father intended to see Rory and her become king and queen by force.

After failing to convince her father that marriage to Rory would be a terrible mistake, Arabela had tried to speak with her mother. With her typical blank mask in place, her mother merely said, "Do as your father tells you."

Arabela had tried, but the more she was near Rory, the less she could. Not when she knew how disastrous Rory would be as king. While she'd led a sheltered life, that didn't mean she was unaware of the political environment. Her father entertained often, and Arabela listened carefully to the conversations.

She'd heard the concerns other noblemen shared of angering the English and causing Edward, England's king who was known as Longshanks, to march on Scotland once again. Her father had only grown more determined when faced with opposition for his plan to make a Scotsman king. Some agreed with doing so, but the way he intended to do it caused concern. Several of her father's peers believed his actions—placing someone of his own choosing on the throne—would bring Edward's wrath upon them all.

Her role in his plans was small but pivotal as her marriage to Rory would unite him and her father. Her life's purpose was to serve as a pawn, to be used and traded, much like a horse. Why couldn't she accept her fate like her mother, Rhona?

Arabela leaned back for a glimpse of her, unsurprised to find her expression empty. Was that Arabela's destiny as well? To allow her mind to go elsewhere in order to bear her present circumstances? Her mother had mastered that for as long as Arabela could remember, only returning when forced.

"Our guests are cheering," Rory whispered in her ear. "Let us give them what they want."

Only then did she hear the calls and the rhythmic pounding of cups on the tables, the pace increasing as the roar grew louder. Before she could protest, Rory stood then grasped her arm to force her to rise. Her cheeks heated with embarrassment as he placed his hands on her hips and jerked her against him. The feel of his manhood pressed against her brought forth a vivid image of what their wedding night would be like.

Bile rose in her throat, making it impossible to speak. The idea of this man atop her—doing the things her maidservant, Edith, had shared—made her ill.

Rory grinned as he studied her. She wondered if he enjoyed her fear. He certainly took pleasure in it. He bent to kiss her and wrapped his arms around her so tightly that her entire length pressed against him. When he thrust his tongue inside her mouth, she nearly gagged. He tasted as badly as he smelled.

The crowd cheered at his bold act. She held a faint hope her father would stop this public display. But nay. He clapped along with everyone else. Her mother had yet to show any interest in her happiness or lack thereof about the wedding, so Arabela knew she'd do nothing.

What choice did she have but to stop Rory of her own accord? As his tongue swirled in her mouth, she bit down, catching him off guard. He jerked back to glare at her, though she supposed their guests thought he gazed lovingly into her eyes based on the shouts.

"You little bitch," he ground out.

"Next time, ask permission," she whispered.

"I won't have to once we marry. I'll take any part of you I want. Whenever I want. Wherever I want." The threat sent shivers sliding icily down her spine. He released her and grabbed her arm just above her wrist, squeezing painfully as he turned her to face those in the great hall. "My bride and I are most anxious for the morrow," he shouted to be heard over the din.

The guests laughed and called out bawdy encouragement, causing Arabela's cheeks to heat even more. She tugged on her arm but to no avail. Rory only squeezed harder, the pain making her forget her embarrassment. Not when she worried he might break it. "Release me."

"Not until you kiss me." He continued to smile, acting as if nothing untoward was happening.

"I'd rather die."

"That can be arranged. But not until after we say our vows, and you give me an heir." His fingers bit into her flesh, and her arm ached down to the bone. "Now kiss me before I show you the back of my hand."

Panic coiled deep within her, for she had no doubt he would. He'd already demonstrated his ability to fool everyone. She was certain he could turn striking her into her fault.

With little choice, she lifted onto her toes to do as he bid, pressing a brief kiss on his lips.

The guests jeered their displeasure at her paltry effort.

"Come now," he said loudly. "Don't be shy. You can do better than that."

Hate burned within her for him humiliating her like this. She felt powerless. Helpless. And worse—frightened. Her arm ached from his brutal fingers.

"Release me so I might kiss you properly." She spoke clearly with the hope their audience would hear and encourage him to comply.

Cautious interest lit his gaze, and he did as she requested. "If you bite me again, you'll pay," he whispered.

This interlude with Rory confirmed her plans, making her more determined to proceed with them. She need only make it through the remainder of the evening.

After pressing her nails into the palm of her hand to brace herself, she wrapped her arms around Rory's neck then raised up once more to kiss him soundly but with lips firmly closed.

Were all kisses so unpleasant? Wet, sloppy, and something she couldn't wait to end? Mayhap a convent *was* the right place for her.

The guests pounded their cups once again, deeming her attempt worthy. She eased back only to be held tight by Rory.

"I look forward to the morrow more than you know."

She smiled, this one nearly genuine. "As do I."

Because if all went well, she'd be gone.

~

Sir Chanse de Bremont stared at the holding just visible above the castle wall in the fading twilight. Grim determination swept over him at the task ahead.

"I'd wager you never thought to return here," Sir Matthew Longley said as he drew his horse to a halt beside Chanse's.

"True." He glanced at Matthew, brow raised. "Nor you, I'd guess."

Matthew scowled in response. "My departure was unexpected, so I have a few things here I'd like to collect."

Chanse's gaze shifted back to the holding a short distance away. Lord James Graham would not be pleased to know of his presence. But what of his daughter? "I have but one thing I intend to take. Lady Arabela."

"Graham might have something to say about that."

"I won't be asking his permission."

"Let us hope you're successful, or we might find ourselves sitting in the dungeon." Matthew shuddered. "As the previous captain of his lordship's garrison, I recommend we avoid that."

"Point noted. Avoid the dungeon."

Matthew frowned at Chanse's joking tone. "Mayhap I should clarify. We should avoid *capture*."

"I shall endeavor to do so."

"Chanse—"

Chanse held up a hand, palm out. "I'm well aware of what's at stake—our lives. Don't think I take that lightly. My mother would never forgive me if I were to die this far from home." He waited to see if the knight grasped his attempt at humor. Matthew was far too serious for his own good.

His friend frowned, obviously sifting through the faulty logic of Chanse's statement. "But—"

"I jest. Trust that I will take great care." His mother would follow him to the grave if he lost his life. She'd made that perfectly clear before he and his brother, Braden, had left England to follow their cousin to Scotland. "Now then, how do you suggest we enter?"

They'd avoided the road since mid-day to help prevent discovery. Approaching from the south gave them the added benefit of being able to use the cover of the crags and woods to hide their approach. To reach the parapet wall unnoticed, they needed both darkness and luck as the holding sat on a low rise with nothing to hide them.

Matthew studied his former home for a long moment. "I'm still not certain of the wisdom of this quest, but I'll show you the hidden steps once night falls."

"You mean *if* night falls." Chanse shook his head. "Darkness is elusive in this country during the summer months."

Matthew chuckled as he looked about the countryside. "Normally, 'tis a good thing but not for our purpose. You have to admit how beautiful this land is."

"You've mentioned that each of the last two days since we rode east from Berwick." The man had more pride in Scotland than his fair share.

Matthew lifted a casual shoulder. "I only speak the truth." Pride in one's homeland was understandable, but Matthew's love of his country bordered on obsession in Chanse's opinion.

"You haven't yet ventured to my home," Chanse said. "There lies beauty." He missed it and his family though he'd had a short visit earlier in the summer when he'd escorted his cousin, Garrick, and his new bride home.

In the spring, he and Braden had followed Garrick to Berwick, a bustling market city just north of the Scottish border. Garrick held the mission of discovering who was behind the unrest in the city and putting an end to it. King Edward himself had marched on the city over two years prior to make an example of the residents, a lesson the country would never forget. Thousands, including men, women, and children, had been killed when the English king had made his rage known because of Scotland's secret alliance with France, an act he considered a betrayal.

Garrick, Braden, and Chanse had pursued information they'd discovered that hinted at who continued to risk the wrath of the king. Rumors of the Sentinels of Scotland had led them to Lord James Graham, the man behind the group which intended to place a man of their choosing on the Scottish throne. The group's hatred of the English meant their choice would share the same trait. King Edward refused to allow such a thing to occur.

Regardless of who worked with Graham, the lord's latest plan had to be halted or more innocent people would die.

"Looks as if they're preparing for a celebration," Matthew said with a nod toward the outer bailey.

From the rise on which they'd halted, rows of colorful tents were visible. The scene wasn't so different from Chanse's previous visit. On that occasion, he hadn't been invited either but had managed to enter through the front gate. This time, doing so wasn't an option.

Chanse smiled grimly. "Sorry to disappoint them."

"Graham's anger is nothing with which to trifle." Matthew's tone held a hint of warning.

"I'm still a bit angry myself." Chanse had nearly lost Braden and his wife because of Graham. Vengeance was in Chanse's blood, something that ran deep in the generations that came before him. Not that seeking it was his purpose here.

Matthew nodded. He'd witnessed the event to which Chanse referred. "You're not a 'turn the other cheek' kind of man."

"Remind me to tell you of my mother some time. My uncle as well." Both had sought vengeance as had his grandfather. The result might not have been the one they expected, but justice had been served in a fashion with fate placing its own twist on the outcome.

"Graham went too far," Matthew said. "I couldn't serve a lord who acted without honor."

"And he does so again." Chanse reined in his anger, reminding himself that his purpose was to stop the upcoming wedding, not exact revenge.

"Do you suppose Lady Arabela will be pleased to see you?" Matthew asked, his tone doubtful.

Chanse glanced at him in surprise. "You can't believe she wants to marry that brute of a man."

"Sir Rory Buchanan is far from an ideal husband. But 'tis said he has the blood of kings running in his veins. The lady would make a fine queen, as she cares deeply about this country."

"Not with her father's hand guiding her on one side and Sir Rory's on the other." An image of the beautiful lady with a heart-shaped face filled his mind. She'd ignored him on his previous visit despite his attempts to win her over. Though he couldn't say he cared for her cool, haughty demeanor, she'd entered his thoughts unbidden more times than he could count. What might it take to warm that coolness?

"Your charm is known far and wide, but we shall see what the lady's reaction is to your plan." Matthew grinned. "Should make for an entertaining conversation."

Charming others had always come easily to Chanse. He might have developed the skill at a young age in order to draw attention away from his brother and onto himself but doing so had forced him to hone his ability. Anything to aid Braden in keeping his secret. Using humor to distract people had also proven helpful. If a situation or conversation grew overly serious, he calmed it with a light-hearted remark. Doing so had the added benefit of keeping others at arm's length.

While Lady Arabela hadn't succumbed to his charms during his previous visit, that had been his own fault. She'd thrown him off balance with her cautious, questioning looks. But when faced with marrying someone of Sir Rory Buchanan's reputation, he had to believe she'd be thrilled with the opportunity to escape.

"Have no doubt," Chanse said, "the lady will be pleased to see me. Overjoyed, in fact. I'd be willing to wager on it."

Matthew nearly chortled in response, placing a hand over his mouth to remain quiet. They were a fair distance from the holding, but sounds carried far in the quiet of twilight. "Overjoyed, eh? I'll take that wager. How unfortunate Braden isn't here to join in this one."

Hardly a day passed without Chanse and Braden wagering on something when they were together. His brother had wanted to come, but Chanse insisted he remain in Berwick with his new bride, Lady Ilisa. They'd been through enough. It was Chanse's turn to lead this mission.

Besides, how difficult could it be to enter the lord's keep and sneak out with Lady Arabela? He couldn't believe that she was happy about the upcoming wedding. Still, she was a dutiful daughter who did her father's bidding. No doubt she was ignorant of his true plans.

She'd be pleased to see him. Surprised, mayhap. But pleased. Especially once he added a charming spin to his plan to rescue her.

"Let us move a little closer so we're ready when night falls." Chanse kneed his steed forward.

"The steps in the castle wall are well hidden from the outside, but I think I can locate them even in the dark."

"Excellent. We'll leave the horses in the crags just ahead and venture the rest of the way on foot."

"I hope this goes as smoothly as you think it will. Once we gain entrance, I'll gather my belongings and meet you in the tower."

"Aye." But Chanse's thoughts were already on the lady who was no doubt preparing for her wedding at this very moment. Was she distraught? Resigned? Frightened? Wishing for a way to escape?

He smiled, looking forward to seeing her expression when she realized he'd come to her rescue.

CHAPTER 2

Arabela all but flew up the uneven tower steps to her bedchamber, the sound of voices and laughter from the great hall chasing her. She cradled her aching arm, and her heart pounded with worry. The evening meal had been a nightmare. That terrible kiss with Rory. Her father's excitement. Her mother's lack of concern.

She had no one to turn to. No one to aid her but herself.

Escaping wouldn't be easy, but as the last several days had shown, neither would being married to Rory.

Arabela chose escape.

She entered her bedchamber at the top of the tower and closed the door, shutting out the noise of the continuing celebration. Surely, they'd seek their beds soon in preparation for the feast on the morrow. The quiet night would provide the chance she needed to leave.

Arabela pulled the bag from under her bed and checked the contents again. She'd packed little as she would have to carry the bag on her journey. Extra weight would only slow her course.

What did one take when leaving their home forever?

Her chest tightened at the thought. Life here wasn't easy, but the idea of departing filled her with fear. Her father would never forgive her for what she did this night. Returning home wouldn't be an option. Unless, of course, he dragged her back. She shuddered at the thought.

Her leaving would be unacceptable to both him and Rory. She'd been a dutiful daughter most of her life, but deep inside her heart was a rebel. Each harsh word and unreasonable demand her father uttered had built defiance within her, layer upon layer, much like the wall that surrounded their holding, until the weight of keeping it hidden felt as if it would crush her.

Watching her mother withdraw further with each year that passed had given Arabela the courage to protest her upcoming wedding. The fog that held her mother in its grip seldom lifted. Arabela wondered if Effie, the village healer, gave her an herbal remedy of some sort to numb her.

Arabela didn't want to live like that. Couldn't. Wouldn't.

Her father had refused to listen to her objections, becoming more enraged each time she raised the topic. His response left her no choice.

Though she'd never ventured farther than she could see from her tower window, she intended to journey southeast toward the border, perhaps to Berwick or Dunbar. Edinburgh was too close. But a bustling city of some size might allow her to remain hidden among the residents. She could find work as she wasn't without some skills. Mayhap a baker or an alemaker could use her. She'd prefer to work in a stable with horses, but the idea of posing as a boy was daunting. A convent was another option as well. Though she couldn't say she had a calling, she would be pleased to spend her life helping others, and such a place might offer protection.

She'd taken dried meat, bread, and cheese from the kitchen earlier in the day. With so many guests at their holding for the festivities, food was plentiful. No one had noticed her passing through the busy kitchen and acquiring a few things.

The sound of her chamber door opening had Arabela quickly stuffing the bag back under her bed.

"Whatever are ye doin', milady?" Edith, her maidservant, asked. She strode forward and lifted the bed linens to reveal the bag. "Och, ye're not still goin' on about leavin', are ye?"

"Aye, I am." Arabela's heart pounded as she faced the woman who'd been more of a mother to her than her own. "Will you come with me?"

While 'twas selfish of her to ask, if Edith remained behind, her father might very well take out his anger on the older woman.

"Don't go, milady. I beg of ye." Edith clasped her hands before her, knuckles white. "Ye can't venture that far on yer own. 'Tis too dangerous."

"'Tis too dangerous to remain. Once Rory is king and I give him an heir, he'll have little use for me."

"That's not true. Yer sire won't allow anything to happen to ye. Sir Rory won't truly hurt ye. He only makes empty threats."

Arabela shoved up her sleeve to reveal the red marks on her arm. "Not so empty."

"Och!" Edith reached out a tentative finger to gently touch the darkening bruises, her brow wrinkled with concern. "How dare he touch ye like that?"

"I can't stay here. Not only will our marriage put me in danger but all of Scotland as well. Father knows his choice of Rory will anger England. King Edward wants someone he can control or who will at least serve as an ally. If England declares war on Scotland, how many innocent people will die?"

"But to leave all ye know? Think of the danger ye'll face."

Arabela's gaze dropped to her arm. "I'll face that no matter what I choose. At least going will be *my* choice."

Edith sighed, her brown eyes full of worry when Arabela looked up. "Life isn't always fair."

"Nay." Arabela bit her lip to keep from arguing that it never was. She took the maidservant's hand in hers. "I fear my leaving places you in danger but more than that, I would miss you far too much if you remained behind. Will you come?"

The woman's hesitation caused Arabela's breath to catch.

Then, with a single decisive nod, Edith squeezed her hand briefly.

She released it to take the woven blanket from the end of Arabela's bed. "It'll be cold at night. We'll need as many blankets as we can carry."

A lump formed in Arabela's throat as she watched the maidservant fold the blanket and tuck it inside the bag. At least she wouldn't have to say goodbye to Edith. "I have some food already."

"I'll fetch a few more things and pack me own bag as well," Edith said.

"Thank you. I don't know what I'd do without you."

Despite the concern that lingered in the older woman's eyes, Edith smiled. "Ye won't have to find out. I'll prepare."

"Excellent. I'd like to depart near midnight if those staying in the great hall are asleep by then."

"With luck, they will be. We'll take great care not to disturb them."

The idea of being caught before they'd even left the keep sent a wave of fear washing through Arabela. But not trying wasn't an option. "Aye," she agreed. "We'll be as quiet as mice."

Edith managed a smile then was gone, and Arabela was alone with her thoughts once again.

Her maidservant's anxiousness forced Arabela to think twice about the details of her plan. Though she'd come up with a dozen different ideas of how she might take her horse, she'd discarded each one. Going through the heavily guarded portcullis would be impossible. Her father had ordered twice the normal men to watch the entrance, partly for his guests' safety and partly to impress them with the number of soldiers he had in his command.

She moved to the narrow window to look out. If only Sir Matthew, the former captain of the garrison, had remained, she might've gained his aid to escape. He alone seemed to sympathize with her position. But nay. He'd chosen to leave with Sir Hugh and Sir Chanse, both who had been guests during the tournament her father had held two months past to celebrate her birthday.

Matthew's departure had been unexpected and concerning, especially when her father refused to tell her of the details. Why hadn't he bothered to bid her goodbye? The unexpectedness of it almost made her wonder if his departure had been unplanned.

She'd liked Sir Hugh and his wife, Lady Cairstine, and often thought of them. The lady had been the closest thing to a friend she'd had in a long while despite their brief acquaintance. When Lady Cairstine had fallen off the stairs outside Arabela's bedchamber to the floor below, Arabela had been horrified.

But the lady's miraculous recovery had been nearly as shocking as her fall. Though Lady Cairstine had claimed Effie, the village healer, had aided her, Arabela had a difficult time believing that. She'd known Effie for many years and while she was a skilled healer, she hadn't managed to produce any miracles prior to that.

Shrugging aside the questions to which she'd never have answers, Arabela studied the horizon visible in the fading twilight from her tower window. This was the last night she'd have this particular view. The realization was both heady and frightening.

Her gaze swung in the opposite direction to where she knew the steps were that led over the parapet wall. They were her best hope of escape.

She and Edith needed to be certain not to provide any evidence of their passing that could be tracked. A direct path might see them farther away more quickly, but she didn't want it obvious as to where they were going. In an effort to place a false trail, she'd asked the new steward how long it took to ride to Edinburgh. With luck, he'd remember her question when her absence was discovered and mention it to her father.

A flicker of hope filled her heart. Mayhap escape was possible. Difficult, aye. But possible. The idea of living a life of her choosing brought a slow smile to her lips. With skill and luck, she might be doing more smiling in the near future.

The idea of happiness was merely a dream but never had she held more hope than now. She closed her eyes, holding tight to the wavering feeling, well aware she'd need the sensation to keep her going in the days to come.

Chanse topped the curtain wall, pleased once again that Matthew had accompanied him. Though he'd known the general location of the steps from inside the holding, finding them in the dark from this side had been no easy task. Rather than actual steps, stones were positioned as footholds at irregular intervals, some small, others more noticeable.

Navigating them in the dark had been difficult.

Whether Lady Arabela was capable of climbing down them remained to be seen. Between he and Matthew surely they could manage to help her.

They stayed low as they hurried across the walkway along the top of the wall then moved slowly down the steps that led to the inner bailey. They paused when they reached the ground. All was quiet inside the holding from this position.

The path they followed skirted the small village that sat in the bailey. The blacksmith's forge had been banked for the night, the bellows silent. The baker, the potter, and the other shops had closed shutters as well. Though many lived in the rear of their shops, they'd already sought their beds for the night. Even the chickens had settled in their nests until morn.

Matthew paused ahead of him and leaned close. "I'm going to the garrison while you seek the lady." He pointed toward the keep, the outline of the three-story building still visible against the night sky. "I'll meet you in the tower."

"Take care," Chanse whispered. "I don't want to have to come and save you."

Matthew grinned. "I was going to say the same to you."

Chanse returned his smile. "I'll see you shortly."

Matthew faded slowly into the night.

Lady Arabela's chamber was in the top of the tower of the keep, a detail Chanse knew from his previous visit. The guests that had already arrived for the wedding were both helpful and a curse.

Helpful as 'twas impossible to lock everything tight for the night, and a curse as there were that many more eyes watching.

He stayed low in case some restless soul wasn't yet asleep and kept to the darkest part of the path, pausing every so often to listen.

He planned to enter through the kitchen, a separate building attached to the back of the keep and hoped the door that led to the great hall would be unlocked. From what little he could see, the kitchen used to be a completely separate building in case of fire, but at some point, it had been expanded and was now connected with a passage to the keep. No doubt Lord Graham preferred his food to arrive in the great hall still warm.

The scuff of a boot on the path just ahead halted Chanse's progress. He bent low as a man emerged around the rear of the kitchen, yawning as he staggered along. He took several more steps then stopped, too close for comfort.

Chanse stiffened, prepared to silence him by whatever means necessary, when the sound of him pissing filled the quiet night. As it continued, Chanse could only shake his head, surmising the man had much to drink earlier. Finally, the sound eased as the man gave a little shudder, adjusted his clothing and then headed toward the stables.

Chanse waited several moments before continuing toward the kitchen, taking care to avoid the puddle and hoping everyone else slept. He tested the door, relieved to find it unlatched. Pausing inside to sweep his gaze around the room, a mix of aromas struck him. Roasted meats, freshly baked bread, and the tang of sweat lingered in the air. Luckily, the room was empty. The coals in the hearth glowed, giving off enough light that he could see his way past the work tables to the door that led to the keep.

He opened it cautiously and listened. The passageway was pitch black, so he waited, hoping his eyes would adjust. A faint light coming from the entrance to the great hall became apparent, and he closed the door behind him and moved toward the light. The sound of snores, some faint, others much louder, rent the quiet of the night. He moved as far away from the entrance to the hall as possible and walked past it. He strode forward with an even pace that suggested a purpose, hoping that if someone saw him, they'd think he belonged there.

When he reached the tower steps, he couldn't help but study the floor before looking up the curving stairs. The thought of Ilisa, known as Lady Cairstine while she'd visited here, being shoved from those steps caused anger to build. Thank goodness she'd recovered.

He walked slowly up, not wanting to falter on the uneven steps, which were purposely built that way to slow an invader such as him. The door on the next level most likely led to Lord Graham's chamber. Though the idea of simply doing away with the man who intended harm to so many was tempting, murdering him in his sleep would be the act of a coward. Chanse was no coward. And doing such a ghastly deed the night before the lord's daughter's wedding would create sympathy amongst the people of Scotland. That wouldn't serve Chanse's purpose. Far from it.

He continued upward, pausing to listen a few times when noises from the great hall drew his notice. At last he reached the door at the top of the tower.

Would the lady be sleeping? Waking her without frightening her half to death would be no easy task. But he was certain she'd be pleased to see him, even more so once she understood his purpose.

He opened the door, his gaze catching on the form under the bed linens lit by a flickering candle on a low table and started forward. A sharp prick in the back of his neck halted him.

"Who are you?" a feminine voice whispered harshly.

Startled, he began to turn only to feel the press of a knife more firmly. He halted, still frowning at the bed. "A friend of the lady's."

"What kind of friend enters a bedchamber unannounced in the dead of night?"

Chanse knew who stood behind him. He stepped away from the blade, holding his hands away from his sides, palms out, to show he meant no harm. "One who comes to rescue the lady."

Silence greeted his words, and he took that as permission to face her, a smile on his face. He dipped his head in place of a bow so that he might keep her—and her knife—in his sight.

Lady Arabela Graham held the knife as though she knew how to wield it, making no effort to lower it though he knew she recognized him. Nor did she answer his smile.

Her heart-shaped face was even more beautiful than he'd remembered. And he remembered her clearly. Brown eyes framed by gently arched brows a shade darker than her hair. High cheekbones and a pointed chin. Thick, brown hair loosely plaited to fall over her shoulder tied with a single white ribbon. A cool, haughty expression still in place. "I am not in need of rescue. Leave."

His thoughts slowed, confused at the differing clues greeting him. The shape of a body under the covers. A packed bag on the floor near the foot of the bed. The lady dressed in attire better suited to a peasant than a bride-to-be. An *angry* lady who appeared far from pleased to see him.

Did she not wish to be rescued? He couldn't fathom that possibility. While he might not know her well, he knew enough to doubt that she had any desire to be queen. Then why would she not welcome him?

"You are pleased to marry Sir Rory on the morrow?" he asked.

"That is none of your affair. Now go." She waved the knife toward the door as though to encourage his departure.

"Put down the knife." The blasted thing was beginning to annoy him.

Her full lips firmed, her brow furrowed as she raised the knife higher in defiance.

With a quick move, he grabbed her wrist with one hand and took the knife with the other. "Do not threaten the one who has come to save you."

"I am not in need of saving," she protested, eyes wide as though she was alarmed by how easily he'd disarmed her.

"Would you truly have stabbed me?"

She lifted one shoulder casually as though undecided. The gesture both frustrated and intrigued him.

Loosening his hold on her wrist, he ran the circle of his fingers gently along her skin, noting her shiver at his touch. What could be the reason for that? Fear? Somehow that didn't seem to fit. Then what?

He studied her a moment longer then looked back over his shoulder at the bag and the lump under the covers. Damn if it didn't appear as if she were leaving. "Why don't you explain why you aren't in need of rescue?"

CHAPTER 3

Arabela stared at the handsome knight, unable to make sense of why he stood in her bedchamber on the eve of her wedding, making an outlandish offer to rescue her. Regardless, she certainly didn't need Sir Chanse to save her. Going with him would trade one set of problems for another. She wanted to escape from being used by a man—any man—no matter how attractive he was. The men she knew did what benefited them. She had no reason to suspect this one was any different. Therefore, his purpose wasn't to aid her.

"What do you *truly* want?" she whispered, tugging her wrist free from his unsettling grip.

"How do you mean?" His expression went carefully blank.

"I don't believe for a moment that you're standing here out of the goodness of your heart or some misguided sense of chivalry." She swallowed hard. If only either of those were true. The idea of someone coming to help her when only moments ago she'd felt so alone was far too appealing. Especially when rescue came with a powerfully built man whose smile could charm bees to give up their honey.

She might not know Sir Chanse well, but she knew enough to believe he didn't act without purpose. During his brief stay at her home to celebrate her birthday, he'd proven himself excellent in all forms of combat and shown his competitiveness. He'd won the favor of every woman at whom he looked, with the possible exception of her and her mother. Though at least he'd tried to charm her mother. He'd all but ignored her she remembered with a touch of resentment. But all of that had been done for a specific reason because he'd done it so purposefully. She just hadn't been privy as to his motive.

Drawing a breath to garner her will to resist her ridiculous attraction to the man, she held out a hand. "Return my knife and explain why you're here."

Hesitation flickered in his eyes as though he weighed his options. She waited, curious as to what spin he might put on his answer. Somehow, she suspected he rarely provided a fully truthful one. That charm of his served a purpose, she was certain of it.

His brow rose. "Do you promise not to stab me?"

"Nay."

The corner of his mouth lifted, causing an odd little dip in her stomach. "I am not here to harm you, my lady." He handed it back to her, handle first, despite her response. "I trust you will not harm me either."

"You still haven't answered my question," she said as she slid the blade back into the braided leather girdle that rode low on her hips.

"I already stated my purpose." He walked over to her bag, glanced at the contents, then fastened the closures. "I don't think you wish to marry Sir Rory. His reputation precedes him."

He had that correct but acknowledging it would surely put her at a disadvantage. "Why would you care whom I marry?"

"Let us have this conversation after we see you safely away. I have a feeling our discussion might take time to work through, and we have none at the moment." He hefted the bag under one arm, keeping his sword hand free. "After you, my lady." He gestured toward the door.

"I'm not leaving with you." She reached for her bag, but he held it firmly.

"Then with whom?"

Before she could respond, the door opened. Edith entered wearing her cloak, carrying a small bag as well. She gasped as she caught sight of the big knight. "Milady?"

"No need for concern," Arabela advised. "He's just leaving."

"Your maidservant is coming too?" His gaze flashed between them.

"He's escorting us?" Edith asked, her hopeful expression clearly stating her opinion. "How wonderful."

"Aye." "Nay." They spoke at the same time.

Arabela glared at him. "We're not accompanying you." How many times did she have to say it before he listened?

"This conversation is pointless." Chanse took Edith's bag as well. "We can discuss the details after we've made it out of the holding."

Edith looked at Arabela with a brow raised. "That sounds like a sensible plan, don't ye think?"

Arabela wanted to stomp her foot in frustration. Agreeing with him would surely give the knight the upper hand. Why did allowing Sir Chanse to have any advantage seem like a terrible idea?

"Very well. We will accompany you as far as the wall, but then we shall go our separate ways." She didn't budge, wanting his agreement before she took a step.

"We shall discuss it once we've safely escaped."

She frowned, aware he hadn't agreed.

"Follow me," he whispered as he opened the door again. "No speaking until we've made it outside."

"I know the way better than you," Arabela argued. Heaven knew where he'd lead them in the dark.

He turned to study her. "And if someone in the great hall wakes, will you stab him with your knife before he sounds the alarm?"

She scowled in response, the idea of stabbing anyone filling her with unease. Harming another to gain her escape was not part of her plan. "You'll be directly behind me, I assume. I'll leave that honor to you."

Before he could argue, she stepped onto the landing and glided down the steps. Her speed seemed to surprise him as he hurried to catch up. Edith was certainly older, but she'd climbed the stairs more often than Arabela and easily kept pace.

Arabela slowed as she neared the bottom of the stairs not far from the great hall. The coals of the fire still burned, casting a golden glow over the rows of pallets and slumbering people. Snores were the only sound she noted.

After a glance over her shoulder to make certain the knight and Edith were behind her, she walked quickly past the great hall entrance and down the passageway toward the kitchen. Though tempted by the proximity of the main door, taking that exit would lead down the steps into the inner bailey where there was a greater chance of being seen.

The faint light from the great hall faded, leaving her in nearly complete darkness. Her heart pounded as she held one hand before her and trailed the other along the stone wall to make certain she didn't lose her way.

Except her outstretched hand touched something that shouldn't be there.

She gasped and drew back in alarm. Sir Chanse bumped into her, stopping as well, completely silent.

A hand touched her arm then her shoulder.

"Chanse?" The whisper was so low she wasn't certain she truly heard it.

"Matthew?" Chanse asked from behind her, equally quiet.

Uncertain what was happening, Arabela remained still.

"Aye. All is well?" the man asked.

Matthew? The former captain of the garrison? Her heart thundered in her throat. She couldn't wrap her thoughts around why he was here. Nor why he was with Sir Chanse.

"Aye."

The hand on her shoulder lifted, and he stepped away. She could only assume he turned toward the kitchen. Chanse nudged her from behind. She continued her path in the dark, hand outstretched before her so she didn't run into Matthew, her thoughts scrambling for purchase.

They soon reached the empty kitchen where the coals in the hearth cast a faint light.

"Sir Matthew?" she asked, staring at the man she considered a friend of sorts. Or at least she had before his abrupt departure.

"'Tis good to see you, my lady." He must've seen the question in her eyes, for he added, "All will be explained once we're on our way."

He turned, revealing a bag slung over his shoulder, and led the way out the kitchen door. He paused to search the inner bailey before at last stepping into the night.

Uncertainty filled her. Why were these two men together? Why had they come? Not for a moment did she believe it had been to rescue her. What then?

Matthew's presence shifted her thinking, making her question whether she and Edith should make their own way or accompany the men. Her mind spun as she followed him toward the wall where the steps were located. Walking between the two knights with Edith provided her with a feeling of protection, something she hadn't realized how much she appreciated until now.

At the very least, she was willing to listen to the reason the two were here.

She'd known this evening would be unsettling, but the cause for that was far different than she'd anticipated.

Matthew walked with purpose as if he still belonged in the holding. A glance behind her showed Edith and Sir Chanse following closely. Matthew climbed the steps first, gesturing for her to wait until he checked the narrow walkway along the wall. Several moments passed before he waved them forward, his gesture barely visible in the dark.

"Stay down, my lady," he advised as she reached the top. He turned back to help Edith.

A glance farther along the wall in the direction of the portcullis revealed the hint of shadows as well as the murmur of voices. Her heart pounded at the sight. While the guards rarely ventured to this part of the wall, that didn't mean they wouldn't do so this evening.

She crawled to the outer edge and looked down. The wall was well over the height of three of her. A fall could cause serious injury. Locating the seemingly random stones that served as steps on the outer wall at night when everything appeared completely different was more difficult than she'd expected.

She searched along the wall for a stone that jutted out. But the one she found didn't feel right. Why did it seem so much smaller than before?

"Allow me, my lady," Sir Chanse whispered.

"How would you know where they are?" she asked, both ridiculously breathless and annoyed by his offer at the same time.

"I don't," he admitted. "But I believe I have a longer reach than you."

Scowling, she shifted out of the way but continued to run her hand along the wall, hoping she'd be the one to find the correct path. This was her home after all, and she'd been up and down the steps more times than she hoped her father realized. She glanced back at where the steps on the inside stopped then closed her eyes and reached, trying to use her memory rather than logic. Her hand closed over the proper stone.

"Here it is," she announced in a whisper, pleased with herself for finding it before the arrogant knight as Edith and Matthew joined her.

"Good work." Chanse gave a single nod before gently tossing the bags to the ground then lowering himself over the wall.

"I should go first." Though Arabela wasn't certain why she felt the need to argue, she did. The situation was spiraling out of her control, and she didn't like that. If she didn't take it back now, she feared she wouldn't be able to.

Except Chanse didn't bother to respond. He merely glared at her, although it was difficult to tell in the dim light. "You will not risk your pretty little neck attempting this."

"But I've—"

His head disappeared over the edge, effectively cutting off her protest.

Arabela nearly growled as she followed him over the edge,

wondering if this sort of behavior was what she should expect if she agreed to accompany him. She chose to ignore the voice in her head that questioned whether she truly had a choice.

∼

CHANSE SWUNG his foot back and forth, hoping to find the next stone without the lady's aid. It took several attempts, but he located it at last. The next one was easier to find. He looked up to see the outline of Lady Arabela's slim form above him. "Can you manage it?"

"Aye."

He knew she'd do so no matter the danger. The woman was more stubborn than he'd anticipated. Convincing her of the wisdom of traveling together wouldn't be easy. Better to continue moving and hope she complied.

Her foot lowered, missing the first step. He reached out and took hold of her ankle to place it on the stone, admonishing himself for noticing how shapely it felt.

He lowered another step then quickly realized she knew the location of the next stone. She whispered something and soon another form joined them on the wall. When she reached up, he guessed she was placing her maidservant's foot onto the first step.

After waiting only a few brief moments, she lowered again so he did the same. Within a short time, they were all at the base of the wall.

"We will walk slowly two at a time to the crags," Chanse ordered, hoping that would help keep the guards from noticing them.

Matthew nodded, tucked one of the bags under an arm, while Chanse did the same, then offered his other arm to Edith. Chanse extended his arm to Arabela, certain she wouldn't take it.

She didn't, though her expression was hidden. Mayhap that was for the best. He could imagine her glare well enough without light to see it.

They walked together, pausing several times to allow Chanse to listen for sounds of possible pursuit. Thus far, he heard nothing, much to his relief. He knew from experience that it was often movement that would catch a guard's eye, especially in the dark. Matthew and Edith followed slowly.

Chanse watched with approval as Matthew turned back to brush their footprints from the ground to hide their progress where the foliage was sparse. Come morn, the less the guards had to use to track them, the better.

At last they made it to the horses they'd hidden from view among the crags. Chanse hadn't anticipated the maidservant's presence. In truth, he hadn't thought much further than gaining entrance to Lady Arabela's bedchamber.

Normally, that lack of forethought aided him. Thinking and planning only led to concerns as a lengthy list of reasons a mission might fail arose. He preferred acting with the belief a path would reveal itself as he proceeded. He could only hope that proven method wouldn't fail him in this quest.

"Two?" the lady asked, her voice a whisper. "You only have two horses?"

He scowled, not appreciating her pointing out the fault in his logic. "We couldn't travel with four horses."

"Why not?"

Why not indeed? He had no answer. He raised a brow at Matthew, wondering why he hadn't voiced the idea.

Matthew lifted a shoulder, suggesting he hadn't considered it either.

"The more horses we have, the greater trace we leave to be tracked." That reason sounded logical even to his ears.

"Humph."

He had no idea what her response meant. Did she believe him? Did she intend to accompany them without an argument?

"Matthew, what are you doing here?" Arabela moved to stand before the knight as he readied his horse.

"Rescuing you, my lady."

Chanse turned away for a moment to cover his smile. When he looked back, it was to find Arabela with her hands on her hips, glaring between them.

"I don't believe either of you," she said, still whispering.

"We can discuss the details when we're safely away from here." Chanse didn't believe for a moment that their success at leaving the holding meant they were safe. The journey had only begun.

"Nay." Arabela stepped to Chanse's horse where he'd set her bag behind the saddle so that he could tie it securely. She pulled it down and held it tight. "I'm not leaving with the pair of you. I don't know what you're up to, and I refuse to be a pawn in whatever game you play."

"But, milady..." Edith began, clearly not in agreement with her mistress.

Chanse's ire rose. The woman's stubbornness was ridiculous. They'd be lucky if they avoided capture by first light, and she was wasting valuable time. "We're here to help. We seek the same goal as you. Why wouldn't we leave together?"

"Because neither of you is being honest, and I'm tired of being used. From this point forward, I'm forging my own path." She glanced at Edith, but the maidservant remained silent. "You're welcome to travel with them if you prefer."

Arabela turned away and took several steps.

Something inside Chanse snapped. Did she think it had been easy to enter her father's holding and the keep? That he was doing this for some selfish purpose? Nay. Stopping the wedding was for the good of her country. Yet he couldn't bring himself to admit to her that he was more concerned with halting the wedding than aiding her. Surely that was obvious.

He strode forward, tugged the bag from her hand even as he turned her to face him. Then he bent low and lifted her over his shoulder.

"What are you doing?" The fright in her voice had guilt rolling through him.

"Hush, my lady," he warned. "You'll raise the alarm before we're away."

"Put me down at once." Her stiff form shifted as she pummeled him in the back. He couldn't help but note she kept her voice barely above a whisper. She might not want to go with him, but she didn't wish to draw the guard's notice either.

"I'm placing you on the horse, and we're leaving." He tossed the bag to Matthew, ignored Edith's wide eyes, and set Arabela on his steed. He leaped up behind her before she had a chance to move and reached around her to take the reins, keeping her in the circle of his arms.

"Release me," she demanded, voice trembling with anger.

"Nay."

"This is outrageous. You promised I could leave of my own accord."

"I made no promises." He kneed his horse, every instinct within him pressing him to hurry.

"So I'm to be your captive?" She looked over her shoulder at him, disbelief visible in the taut lines of her face.

Captive? He hated to think it had come to that, but the result was the same—halt the wedding. Nothing else mattered. "Call it what you wish, but we're leaving together."

CHAPTER 4

Arabela's thoughts spun as they rode through the crags then into the woods where the darkness deepened. She couldn't believe Sir Chanse had the audacity to toss her over his shoulder like a sack of oats. How had the knight changed from rescuing her to becoming her captor? Her mind—or mayhap her emotions—couldn't keep pace with the shift.

The circle of his arms felt confining and restrictive, an unwelcome barrier between her and freedom. The idea of sliding off the horse and running tempted her. But would any purpose be served in attempting to escape now when he could so easily catch her? She could threaten him with her knife again, but to be effective, she'd have to catch him off guard, something that was impossible when she rode before him. Surely a more opportune time would present itself.

If only she could see Matthew, she'd know what he thought of this. Yet he hadn't protested once. She feared that meant he sided with Sir Chanse.

The tangle of her thoughts made logical decisions impossible. The events of the past few days were too much. Worry, sleepless nights, and even fear had taken their toll and suddenly caught up with her.

Not only was she leaving her home and everything familiar, she was also doing so in the company of a man she hardly knew. A man who couldn't be bothered to provide an honest answer. A man she wasn't even certain she liked, let alone trusted.

Sir Chanse allowed the horse to pick its path along the dark hillside. The rough terrain caused her to bump against his powerful body continually, a sensation she didn't appreciate as it reminded her of her predicament. And of him.

While her current perch was preferable to remaining in her chamber awaiting her wedding day, her concerns hadn't lessened. She'd merely traded one threat for another. If only she'd left earlier, she might be making her own way at this very moment. Yet as she glanced around the woods, so unfamiliar and foreboding in the dark, she wondered if she'd have been brave enough to trek through them toward freedom.

"Have you decided?" The deep, quiet voice from behind her cast shivers along her spine, interrupting her thoughts.

"Decided what?"

"Whether to attempt an escape."

Her breath caught at the accuracy of his remark. Was he somehow privy to her thoughts?

"'Tisn't so difficult to hazard a guess as to what must be going through your mind," he continued.

"Oh?" She refused to give him the satisfaction of admitting he was right. The man was far too arrogant already in a completely different way than her father or Rory. Somehow his confidence was appealing.

"I can only imagine your concern at facing marriage to a man such as Sir Rory."

"Humph." Her limited word choice reflected her sluggish thoughts. Should she blame it on the situation or the man who held her? Her awareness of him—something she'd noted from the moment they'd met—puzzled her. But his mention of Rory made her rub her sore arm. She'd have to endure much worse if she was forced to marry the man.

"You must believe me when I say we have the same goal—to keep you from marrying Sir Rory."

"That much I believe. 'Tis the reason behind your goal that concerns me."

Several moments of silence passed before he responded. "Does it matter overmuch? The result is the same—halting the wedding. And saving you."

The latter had nearly been added as an afterthought. But was he right? Did the reason matter? In some respects, he had a valid point. The result *was* of grave concern to her. But the reason mattered as well. At least to her, it did.

Before she did anything drastic, she wanted to speak with Matthew in private. Understanding why he'd left and even more, why he'd returned would help determine her next step. But that might have to wait until they halted.

Though she hadn't answered his question, she decided she wasn't going to. Not yet anyway. He could wait until she had an answer with which she was comfortable.

THE NIGHT PASSED SLOWLY—FAR too slowly— for Chanse's liking. He'd spent his fair share of sleepless nights in uncomfortable places and positions, but this one proved challenging even for him.

Because of Lady Arabela.

His guilt mounted with each step as her stiff form continually bumped against him. He'd been certain she'd be pleased to accompany them. Hell, he'd even wagered with Matthew on it. Instead, he'd taken her captive. Treating women with respect was something he'd learned from an early age. What would his mother say if she heard of this? Or rather, when. Secrets were impossible to keep in his family.

They bypassed the road and wound through woods and over hills with the hope of avoiding discovery. Their pace was measured because of the darkness, leaving Chanse too much time to think. Bringing her against her will had never been part of his plan. He'd been so certain she'd be pleased to accompany him. Pleased to escape a terrible fate.

Was it his fault she'd acted so unreasonably? What choice had she left him? However, the rigidness of her body shouted that he was in the wrong. He nearly growled in frustration but held back, unwilling for her to know of his doubt.

Somehow, he'd have to convince her of the wisdom of this journey over the coming days, a difficult task when she seemed resistant to his charm.

When the night grew too dark to continue safely, he called a halt. No purpose would be served in risking injury to the horses or losing their way.

"Do you promise not to leave?" he asked Arabela as he assisted her to the ground.

Silence was his only answer. He was certain a glare accompanied it but 'twas too dark to tell.

"We'll rest a short while until there's enough light to continue," he told Matthew.

"I'll take the first watch," Matthew offered.

"Wake me when you tire." But Chanse knew he wouldn't sleep. Not when he worried what Arabela would do.

He set Arabela's bag on the ground for her to rest her head and spread a blanket before it with another to place over her. She and Edith lay next to each other, neither of them speaking a word.

After dismissing the idea of tying a rope between the lady and him, he settled into position within an arm's reach of her, expecting her to attempt escape. Matthew would certainly hear her, but Chanse considered this his problem. His friend most likely thought him crazed for treating Arabela as he had.

The idea only worsened his guilt.

He must've dozed briefly for he woke to Matthew's hand on his shoulder. He rose and traded places with him to keep watch. Arabela and her maidservant were still and quiet, but he doubted whether they slept either.

When a hint of dawn dimmed the stars and lightened the sky, he woke Matthew. "Time to leave."

As he and Matthew moved toward the horses, Arabela sat up, her maidservant stirring beside her. Their night had been brief with only a few hours of rest, but they both rose, shivering in the cool air.

Matthew nudged Chanse with his elbow. "It seems I won the wager."

Chanse frowned, uncertain to which one he referred.

Matthew's smirk suggested he took great pleasure in reminding him. "The one about the lady being 'overjoyed' to see you."

"Aye, that you did." Chanse shook his head at just how wrong he'd been about that.

They went about preparing the horses. The lady watched Matthew closely as she folded their blankets.

She surely wished to speak with him. Chanse understood that. Matthew had spent several years in Lord Graham's garrison before reaching the position of captain. It was only natural that she seek a familiar face. That didn't mean he liked it. He chose not to focus on the reason.

Chanse regretted not doing more to win her over during the tournament. Doing so would've made this journey easier. But her cool demeanor had suggested she was firmly supportive of her father and therefore his plans.

Something about her unsettled Chanse. If he determined the cause of the feeling, mayhap he could put an end to it. Meanwhile, he intended to do his best to ignore her, despite the fact that she rode in the circle of his arms. His priority was to get them as far away as possible while avoiding detection. The lady's happiness had to be secondary.

As the last thought flowed through his mind, his mother's voice berated him. He clenched his jaw, but her reminders of how a true knight behaved had been taught to Braden and him since they were old enough to understand. His father had been in full agreement with her values. Partly because he swore that she based her ideals on him. Chanse smiled at the memories of his parents teasing each other on the subject.

He must've made a sound as Arabela glanced at him.

"What do you find so entertaining?" she asked.

"Nothing," he said with a shake of his head. But when she pursed her lips, he had the distinct idea he'd hurt her feelings by not sharing. That wouldn't aid the situation. "I was thinking of my mother and father."

A frown marred her brow as if she couldn't understand why that would make him smile. He couldn't blame her. He'd met her parents and found little about them to make him smile either.

"They tease each other relentlessly," he added.

"Truly?" Disbelief laced her tone even as she shivered.

"Aye. 'Tis highly entertaining most of the time." He couldn't resist adjusting her cloak to protect her against the crisp air.

Arabela shook her head as though unable to imagine it. "Was their marriage arranged?"

"Nay. But they met under...difficult circumstances." Now that he thought on it, those circumstances weren't so different from his and Arabela's. His father had been following an order whereas Chanse had taken it upon himself to take this action, though he had no doubt stopping the wedding was the right thing to do.

Chanse hoped those in England who'd requested the unrest in Berwick to be watched would approve. To him, it seemed the only solution to a difficult problem. Drastic, mayhap, but if England declared war on Scotland again, that would be far worse. War should be a last resort in his opinion.

"What sort of circumstances?" she asked, following him as he moved to his horse.

"My father was tasked with escorting my mother to her guardian when her mother was killed, but she didn't want to go."

"That sounds oddly familiar." Her sarcastic tone took him by surprise. He'd started to think the woman didn't have a sense of humor. "How did they set aside their differences?"

He scowled, reluctant to share more for fear it might give her ideas. "My father came to see the wisdom of my mother's opinion on the drawbacks of her new guardian but not until after he delivered her to him."

"Wasn't that too late?"

"Nearly. 'Twas much more difficult to free her." He tightened the cinch on the saddle then tied Arabela's bag to the back of it.

"So it would've been simpler if he would've listened to her from the start," she suggested with a brow raised in question.

Chanse knew exactly where Arabela was going with the conversation, and he didn't care for it. "I hardly think you can compare our situation to theirs." Never mind that he'd done so.

"He escorted her somewhere even though she didn't want to go and realized too late that she was right, and he was wrong. I fail to see the difference."

"You and I want the same result. We merely have different opinions on how to achieve it." He motioned toward his horse, anxious to leave. They were wasting time with this discussion.

"If you'd care to be forthcoming as to why and share where we're going, I might reconsider." She glanced again at Matthew only to see him assist Edith onto the horse.

Chanse mulled over her request as he lifted her into the saddle. In truth, he wasn't certain where they would go. Most likely toward Berwick though he was willing to change the destination if they were pursued. But telling her that or anything more could endanger the mission he, Braden, and Garrick had been working on for months. He had to assume her loyalty lay with her father, not two knights who'd tried to save her when she insisted she didn't need saving.

Nay. Telling her anything held too much risk.

"You'll have to trust me for the moment," he said, his gaze holding hers. "I want what's best for you."

"Those words are quite similar to what my father said when he told me of the betrothal." She raised a brow. "Who am I to believe?"

Though he told himself her opinion didn't matter, he couldn't resist adding, "Time will reveal that answer soon enough."

He wished the light were better, so he could see her eyes. But she faced forward once again. He settled behind her and reached to take the reins. The length of her loosely plaited hair fell down her back, teasing him. He wanted to touch the dark mass to see if 'twas as soft as it looked. A sweet scent teased his nose, and he bent his head to better catch it.

Lavender? Nay. Something more. A floral scent with a hint of spice. He bent closer to sniff it once more, but the identity of it remained elusive. He didn't care for puzzles, and he certainly didn't need another reason to be intrigued by the lady.

His focus needed to remain on their safety during this journey. He had to keep his wits about him, so any pursuers didn't come upon them unexpectedly. Determining ways to lose any who tracked them was his priority. Not the lady before him.

~

"Where is Arabela?" Lord James Graham asked his wife as they entered the great hall to break their fast.

The odor of stale sweat lingered in the air, no doubt a result of the many people who'd slept there the previous night. The pallets had been stowed, and the preparations were underway for the wedding feast to be held after the vows were said. Hopefully, the smoke of the fire and the scent of roasting meat that already turned on a spit in the huge hearth would soon cover the stench.

"I didn't see her at mass," he added, though she didn't always attend of late.

"Arabela?" Rhona asked as if she needed a moment to clarify of whom he spoke.

"Aye, our daughter," he said with teeth clenched.

Her lack of concern over anything made him want to strike her with the back of his hand to see if that garnered a reaction. While at times it pleased him to witness less of the hysterics she'd been prone to when they first married, he was growing weary of her vacant stares.

"I don't believe I've seen her. No doubt she's in the stables. Shall I have a servant fetch her?"

"Have one look in her chamber first. Mayhap she overslept." That would be unusual, but as a soon-to-be bride, she might've suffered a sleepless night before the wedding. She'd made her dislike of Rory clear, but that didn't concern him.

Rhona stepped away to do his bidding.

James knew the knight was coarse in both disposition and appearance. But his ties to Donald, a great Scottish king, would thrill the people of Scotland and unite the country. Those ties were questionable at best, but they were enough to allow James to make the claim that Rory was destined to sit on the throne. With Arabela by his side of course, and James directly behind them both.

He smiled with satisfaction at the thought of steering the direction of his country. He intended to guide it as far away from England as he could manage. The damned English had too tight of a hold on Scotland, choking the very life from them. Removing their people and influence from the country remained his priority.

As he took his seat at the head table, a servant rushed to place bread, cheese, and ale before him. All of the servants knew of his preference that they hurry to do his bidding, especially when guests were present.

"The new steward is searching for her," Rhona said as she took her place beside him.

He reached for her hand on the table, squeezing it tightly to make certain he held her full attention. "Be sure your thoughts are clear for the festivities."

"I don't know what you mean." She tried to pull away her hand, but he held tight, wanting her agreement. After losing the tug of war, she finally met his gaze. A hint of anger lingered in the depths of her eyes.

"I have no doubt my meaning will come to you if you give it some thought." He released her hand after one final squeeze. "Once the vows have been said and the feast is underway, you may dull your senses with whatever you wish."

She opened her mouth to deny it, but he waved dismissively.

"Do not bother to lie to me," he whispered. "I am no fool."

"Nor am I," she answered heatedly.

That heat was enough to stir his senses, exciting him in ways he hadn't felt for some time. He studied the spark in her eyes, considering what he wanted to do with her.

"My lord?" The hesitant voice of a servant interrupted him.

"Aye?"

"I-I'm afraid Lady Arabela is g-gone."

"Gone?" James repeated the term unable to comprehend what the blasted man could possibly mean.

"She's nowhere to be found. Her maidservant is missing as well."

Anger ripped through him like fire. He jerked to his feet. "Find her. Forthwith." He turned to glare at Rhona whose eyes were wide with surprise. "You had better look for her as well. I will not have this day turned into a nightmare because that silly girl decided to do something stupid."

Those in the great hall stared as though uncertain what to do.

"Find her!" he yelled, his voice echoing through the keep.

CHAPTER 5

As daylight filtered through the trees and slowly warmed the air, Arabela considered how best to question Matthew the next time they stopped to rest. The challenge would be to do so without Chanse listening to every word. 'Twas imperative she learned why Matthew left and why he'd returned—with Chanse.

She hadn't attempted an escape since they'd left but doing so remained a possibility. Striking out on her own was intimidating, and she wouldn't make that decision lightly. Her plans depended on Matthew's response to her questions. Surely, he'd speak more freely if Chanse were absent.

Just when she'd determined she couldn't bear another moment on the horse, they halted. The men allowed the animals to graze and saw that they had water. As the two knights spoke quietly, they watched their surroundings and often paused to listen. Chanse had warned Arabela to speak softly and avoid making noise if possible. She might not be certain how far she wanted to travel with them, but she had no desire to be caught by her father or Rory's men.

Those at home must've realized by now that she was gone. Did they think she'd left of her own accord, or had they determined someone aided her? Or mayhap they thought someone had taken her.

Did her mother know she was gone? Did she care? She bit her lip at the pain the thought brought.

"How are ye farin', milady?" Edith asked as she stepped closer.

"Sore, as I'm certain you are."

The older lady managed a smile, which emphasized the wrinkles on her face. "How can it be so tirin' to sit on a horse?"

Arabela nodded in agreement. Tiredness tugged at her, but she needed to keep her wits about her. "I'd like to ride with Sir Matthew for a time if that's all right with you."

"Certainly. 'Tis good to have him with us."

"I can't help but wonder why he didn't return when he rode with my father to find Sir Hugh after the tournament. I want to ask him that, along with a few other questions."

"Ask who what?"

Arabela turned with a start to see Chanse directly behind them.

She didn't bother to hide her scowl. "You're interrupting a private conversation."

"There are no private conversations while we're on this journey. If you have questions for Matthew or me, then ask. We've no secrets between us."

Matthew joined them, his gaze holding steady on hers. "He speaks the truth, my lady. I'm certain you wish to know why I returned after all this time."

She nodded. "Aye, but I'd like to know even more why you left."

The knight's brow raised. "Your father didnae tell you?"

"Does that surprise you?" she countered. Her father rarely told her anything.

"I should've expected as much." He glanced at Chanse as though uncertain how to respond. Why did it matter what Chanse thought? "I rode with your father to bring back Sir Hugh shortly after he left the tournament. Your father was misinformed by Monroe, the steward, that Sir Hugh had...something he wanted."

Again Matthew's gaze flicked toward Chanse. Chanse gave a small shake of his head, leaving Arabela to wonder what he meant.

"The steward was mistaken," Matthew continued, "but refused to accept that. Monroe threatened Lady Cairstine, and Hugh killed him for it."

Arabela gasped in surprise. To think the large but gentle knight she'd come to like during their brief stay had killed the man who'd served as her father's steward for several years shocked her. She thought Monroe had left along with Matthew. She hadn't known he was dead. "Why would Monroe want to harm Lady Cairstine?"

Matthew shifted, making her wonder how much of his tale was true. Or rather, how much he'd left out. "I never liked the man much. His actions that day were terrible and illogical. Sir Hugh was justified in his deed."

She realized he hadn't exactly answered her question, but the information he'd revealed brought even more to mind. "How did my father react?"

"It took some convincing," Chanse offered, "but I believe he understood Sir Hugh's action in the end."

Arabela nodded, aware he'd been witness to the situation as well. But 'twas Matthew's words she wanted to hear, so she looked back at him. "Why didn't you return with my father?"

"The...meeting convinced me that my views no longer aligned with Lord Graham's. My years of service to him had been fulfilled, and I thought it best not to remain. I accompanied Sir Hugh and Chanse to Berwick and decided to stay there for a time."

His few words only made her more curious as to what had truly happened. She couldn't imagine what Monroe had thought Sir Hugh had that was worth so much risk. What part had her father played in it? He was so certain he knew what was best. But more than once she'd been working in the stables or lingered in the great hall and overheard conversations that reflected the pitfalls of his beliefs.

His secret meetings with the Earl of Rothton and others weren't so secret anymore, not since several had been held at the keep. And certainly not since her betrothal to Rory. Her father's boldness had drawn notice, and she tended to think he welcomed it. But did that have anything to do with what happened with Sir Hugh?

"Enough questions for now. We must be on our way again," Chanse said.

Arabela was only more confused with the additional information they'd provided. Before she knew it, Chanse had guided his horse close and lifted her onto the saddle. Though she'd prefer to ride with Matthew so that they could speak further, she was too tired to argue with Chanse.

Mayhap it would be best if she had time to consider what Matthew said. She'd had no regard for Monroe and hadn't been unhappy to see him go. The idea of Hugh killing him was shocking, but the knight's obvious love for his wife would've demanded he protect her at all costs. She respected that.

As she reached for the pommel of the saddle to adjust her seat, the sleeve of her kirtle fell back to reveal the darkening bruises on her arm from Rory's grip. Shame heated her cheeks, and as quickly as possible, she pulled her sleeve into place, hoping Chanse hadn't seen them.

He said nothing as he mounted the horse behind her, and they were on their way once again. She breathed a sigh of relief that he hadn't noticed. With luck, they'd fade before he caught sight of them. Why she felt ashamed, she didn't know. Rory's actions weren't her fault although she'd known what she said would anger him.

They'd ridden only a short distance before Chanse carefully eased back her sleeve. "What happened there?"

For a moment, she considered lying. Admitting the truth made her feel weak and helpless, and she was tired of feeling that way. But the bruises were easily identifiable as someone's hand. "Rory didn't care for how I was acting."

Chanse cursed under his breath. With a gentle finger, he traced the bruises. "I'm sorry some men are such ill-mannered pigs. He has no right to treat you in such a manner."

The tenderness of his words freed something deep within her, lessening her shame. Still, she couldn't help but pull her sleeve down again to cover the marks. "'Tisn't your fault."

"Nor is it yours."

She squeezed her eyes shut at the sudden rush of tears. His reminder was something she already knew but hearing it from him meant so much more. The man was an interesting mix of contrasts. Tough yet tender. Charming but unyielding. And stubborn.

She had yet to decide the most important question of all—did she trust him?

~

By midday, Chanse knew they were being followed. While he didn't see or hear anyone, he sensed it. Logic pointed toward that conclusion as well. Graham wouldn't allow his daughter to escape the marriage without putting up a fight. Sir Rory wouldn't either.

They paused to rest the horses, and Chanse approached Matthew, making certain the women wouldn't overhear.

"I think we're being pursued," Chanse said as the knight ran his hands over his horse's legs and checked its hooves.

"I feel it as well." Matthew straightened and held Chanse's gaze. "I hoped to gain more ground before they realized which direction we took."

"As did I. Increasing our pace is not an option when we're carrying two on each horse." Chanse studied the countryside, searching for something that could help to hide their passing. "We've kept away from the road, which has aided us. If we ride in a stream for a time that might throw them off our trail. Do you know if one is near?"

"We rarely came through the woods this far from the holding. But if memory serves me, a stream of sorts is in the valley over the next ridge."

Chanse glanced at Arabela. Thus far, she seemed to be enduring the journey well. But they'd only just begun. "Let us not linger here overlong. We need to be on our way shortly."

"Aye." Matthew returned to seeing to his horse.

Chanse moved to where Arabela stood with her maidservant. "We'll be moving again soon."

"But we just halted," Arabela protested. "The horses need more of a rest than this."

"We'll allow them additional time once night falls." He appreciated that her concern was for the horses rather than herself. Few others would share the same worry. Their stop for the night would be brief as well and only during the darkest hours, but he decided those details could wait. "Walk for a time to ease any aches."

While it would improve all of their spirits to have a hot meal and a fire when darkness came, that wouldn't be possible until he knew they'd escaped their pursuers. *If* they escaped them.

He saw to his horse, murmuring a few encouraging words to the steed that had seen him through many journeys. Braden always insisted Chanse speak to his horse. His brother had a soft spot for animals, especially horses, but Chanse sometimes wondered if Braden wanted him to talk to the steed so Braden would have something to tease him about.

"What do you say when you speak to him?"

Chanse stilled at Arabela's question, wishing she hadn't witnessed it. "A mix of encouragement and gratitude." He turned to look at her, certain she'd think him crazed.

Instead, she nodded with approval as she moved to the horse's head and rubbed the spot just above his eyes. "What's his name?"

"Alastor."

"Isn't that Greek?"

"Aye," he said, impressed that she knew.

"What does it mean?" she asked as she shifted to run her hand along his neck.

"Avenging spirit." The gray courser was both fast and strong and had served him well over the years.

"Do you have a destrier as well?"

"Aye." He'd left his larger war horse with his father. But he didn't want to discuss where that was. The lady would be even less likely to agree to accompany him if she knew he called England home. Many along the Borderlands sounded more English than Scottish. His ancestry would be apparent in the Highlands, but not here. The time had come to change the subject. "Do you know of any streams nearby?"

She shook her head. "I've never been this far from home."

Chanse was surprised. "I thought your father had a keep near Berwick."

"He does, but I've never been there. This is the farthest I've been."

While travel was limited for villagers, most nobility traveled between their holdings. Chanse had journeyed through much of England as well as to France and Poitou. The idea of not having a view other than what he could see from home was unpalatable. Seeing how others lived—and died—had changed his way of thinking and how he acted.

For a brief moment, he wished he could take Arabela to see all the amazing sights he had, to meet people who didn't speak the same language and eat food she'd never before tried. He loved home and family more than anything but going away made coming home all the sweeter. How could one truly appreciate what one had until seeing how others lived?

He gave himself a mental shake. That was not his concern. He'd be doing well if he kept them from being caught. Showing Arabela what she'd missed in life was not part of his plan.

"Mayhap you'll have the chance to see more someday soon." Chanse gestured toward his horse. "Let us go."

He helped her up again though he was certain she could mount without aid. She seemed very comfortable around his steed even if she was sore from so much time on horseback.

Matthew led the way over the ridge, winding through the trees rather than taking a straight path. With two people on each horse, a meandering course remained their best defense.

"Where did you intend to go if you've never ventured from home?" Chanse asked. The thought of Arabela coming this far on foot with only her maidservant when she had no experience traveling made him wonder about her plan to escape.

"I planned to follow the road but keep enough distance from it to escape notice."

That wouldn't have been a bad idea except that long parts of the road had no cover nearby. With nothing to hide her, she would've been caught easily.

But mentioning that would serve no purpose. He appreciated the idea that she was brave enough to consider leaving all that was familiar and take a dangerous journey. Foolhardy, perhaps, but brave.

Chanse waved Matthew ahead and rode a short distance to the highest point of the ridge that provided a view of the valley they'd just passed through. To his dismay, three men rode into sight in the far distance, their slow progress suggesting they scoured the ground for tracks.

"Damn," Chanse muttered. Though he'd expected it, seeing proof was another matter.

"They're following us?" Arabela sounded breathless at the thought.

"Aye."

"What are we going to do?" She glanced back at him, eyes wide.

"Make certain they don't find us."

He kept to the trees and started down the other side of the ridge, guiding his horse away from Matthew's. Those who tracked them would hopefully be slowed while they determined which horse to follow.

They rode along the hillside for a short distance before turning toward the narrow valley once again. Though he listened, he didn't hear the sound of running water. Had Matthew been wrong? But his horse perked up and increased the pace slightly. That might very well mean water wasn't far.

Soon enough, a stream came into view. It looked wide enough to serve his purpose and not so swift or deep as to make it difficult to cross.

Matthew slowed his horse and turned to look at Chanse from a stone's throw away. Chanse didn't want to risk calling out an explanation to him so signaled for him to ride in the water upstream. The other man frowned but gave a reluctant nod.

Rather than follow Matthew, Chanse rode into the stream and

crossed to the other side a short distance downstream. He continued up the bank and into the trees.

"Where are we going?" Arabela glanced at him then at where they'd left Matthew and Edith, her concern apparent.

"Not far. But this will confuse those following us."

The tightness in her body eased. Did she think he'd intended to part ways with Matthew and her maidservant? She didn't relax completely until they made their way back to the stream then up to meet Matthew. Walking the horses in the water held risk but was worth confusing their pursuers.

"Our progress is slow with only two horses," she remarked. "I tried to determine a way to leave with mine but couldn't think of how to manage it without arousing suspicion."

"That was probably for the best."

Did she realize how slow her journey would've been on foot? She would've tired before she made it out of sight of her holding. That spoke of how determined she was to avoid marrying Sir Rory. Her courage was commendable. His respect for her went up a notch.

Mayhap he'd misjudged her on his previous visit.

They continued riding upstream for a long distance. Then he and Matthew rode along the bank in two different places on opposite sides of the stream. Chanse dismounted and brushed his horse's tracks from the bank while they waited for Matthew and Edith to join them.

The day was a fine one with the vivid blue sky overhead and mild temperatures. While that helped them make good time as opposed to traveling in poor conditions, it also aided any who followed.

"How do you know we're riding in the proper direction?" Arabela asked as she glanced around at the changing landscape.

"I know we're moving in an easterly direction. For now, that is enough."

"But how do you know?"

Her question nearly made him smile. "If I weren't, the sun wouldn't be where 'tis now." He glanced over his shoulder at it. "The sun and stars have guided me through many countries. You're never truly lost if you can see them."

"I should like to learn to navigate by them as well. Would you teach me?"

A rush of surprise filled him. He might not be able to show her the things he'd seen, but he could do this. And mayhap when she needed to use what she learned, she'd think kindly of him. "I'd be pleased to do so."

~

ARABELA ENJOYED the afternoon more than she'd expected. Certainly, it was uncomfortable and tiring, but she preferred to count her blessings. The biggest one was that rather than being married and attending her wedding feast with the worry and fear of what the night would bring let alone the future, she was riding through land she'd never before seen in the company of a kind and handsome knight. The worry of being caught lingered but better that than the worry of what demands Rory would make upon her.

The terrain was changing the farther they traveled. The forest was denser than near her home, partly because no one had chopped down the trees to build structures in this area. Rather than fields of crops with a distant view of hills and crags, she was *on* those hills and crags. She had her first taste of freedom, and she loved it.

She had to admit 'twas somewhat of a relief to leave the worry of their path and whether they were being pursued to Chanse. Escaping on her own would've been more difficult than she'd realized.

Chanse's patience as he taught her how to determine their direction was unexpected. In fact, he was far more charming when he wasn't trying to be. That was unsettling. His even mood and gentle teasing were unusual compared to other men she knew. The flash of his smile greeted her often when she looked back at him.

Unsettling, indeed.

It didn't take her long to realize the feel of his body against hers as they rode along was something to which she'd never grow accustomed.

As he explained the location of the sun in comparison to which way she faced, she frequently turned to look at him. The line of his jaw, the power of his arms, and the breadth of his chest fascinated her. Thank heaven she rode in front of him else she feared she'd do nothing other than stare.

Matthew was fit as well with broad shoulders and a handsome face. He had to be near the same age as Chanse but looking at him didn't make her heart beat faster. Was that simply because she wasn't in such close proximity to him? Somehow, she didn't think so.

Learning to tell what direction they traveled seemed like a wise notion. She had yet to decide if she wanted to continue with Chanse and Matthew, which made it even more important to know where she was going. Setting off on her own on foot when she could ride with them seemed a foolhardy idea. But all that could change. She wouldn't know what to do until Chanse advised her of his plans.

No matter how charming he was, she refused to be used by him or any man. That was why she'd left home.

But for now, this journey served her purpose. She was moving away from Rory and his threats and her father and his plans. Mayhap not the way she'd planned, but that was often how life unfolded, wasn't it?

They rested briefly again then forged ahead. Chanse and Matthew were constantly listening and watching. Arabela kept her eye on the horse as she knew it would know of another horse's presence long before she did.

As the sun sank, her weariness grew. The idea of sleeping was more appealing by the moment. Her hips ached. Her bottom felt numb. She caught herself sinking back against Chanse more often, only to straighten when she realized what she was doing.

"Rest if you need to," Chanse said. He placed a hand on her arm to encourage her to lean back.

"I'm fine," she insisted though if she wasn't careful, she feared she'd topple from the horse.

"We'll stop for a time when the night deepens, but we need to continue for as long as we can."

She nodded, too tired to argue. Escaping was the priority, not resting. But her body refused to listen.

The next thing she knew, they'd halted, and Chanse was easing her from the horse. She must've dozed off after all. Her legs protested when he set her on her feet, causing her to gasp at the pain.

"I've got you." Chanse lifted her to cradle her in his arms and strode toward a smooth area of the small clearing.

She wasn't so tired that she didn't notice the strength of his arms around her. He carried her as if she weighed nothing, the sensation causing unfamiliar flutters in her stomach. His arms remained around her after he'd once again put her on her feet to make certain she had her balance. His gentleness only created more flutters.

She and Edith spread a blanket on the ground and used their bag for a bolster. The small task was all she could manage before she sank to their makeshift bed.

Chanse and Matthew saw to the horses. Though Arabela felt guilty for not aiding in some way, she could hardly keep her eyes open. The hard ground wasn't the most comfortable, but anything was preferable to being on the horse.

With a sigh, she placed a hand over those continuing flutters and closed her eyes, appreciating the feeling of being safe.

～

EXHAUSTION HAD CAUGHT up with Chanse as well. Too many nights with little to no sleep and remaining on constant guard were wearing on him. The pressing feeling of pursuit had eased. He hoped that meant their efforts to lose the pursuers had paid off and wasn't a result of his tiredness.

"I'll take the first watch," Matthew offered.

"Are you certain?"

Matthew nodded.

Chanse appreciated his offer more than he could say. Surely a little sleep would aid him. "Wake me when you're ready to rest."

Chanse leaned against a tree a short distance from the women. The cool night and hard backrest weren't ideal, but that would keep him from resting too soundly.

He woke abruptly, uncertain what woke him or how long he'd slept. The night was still dark, too dark to make travel safe. A glance at Matthew showed him running a hand over his eyes. Chanse caught his notice and motioned for him to rest.

Matthew didn't argue. He lay down not far from the women and appeared to be asleep within moments.

Chanse rose and stretched before stepping close to the Arabela and her maidservant. Both looked as if they slept soundly. Arabela was exhausted, but not a word of complaint had passed her lips. He could only imagine the worry she'd experienced over the past few days while making plans to escape and then keeping the pace he'd set. No wonder she was tired.

The sound of a twig breaking nearby cracked the silence. He stilled, his breath frozen in his chest as he waited, carefully listening for more.

CHAPTER 6

Chanse's nerves stretched taut as he braced for another sound, prepared to attack. But no additional signs of someone approaching reached him.

He couldn't see much of the horses, but they remained quiet, suggesting that whoever was close hadn't arrived on horseback.

If Graham's men had found them, why would they attempt to advance with stealth? They'd ride boldly in to take advantage of the element of surprise.

Who then?

A scuff of a shoe not far from the horses reached him. With careful steps, he walked over to tap Matthew's foot with his. Then he continued toward the horses, knowing his friend would follow. His steed lifted his head at Chanse's presence then looked in the opposite direction.

Chanse ran his hand along the horse's side to thank him for the assistance. He bent low to walk under the horses' necks, staying close to hide his movements. He drew his knife from its sheath and waited for a sign to guide him.

A shadow shifted to his left, and he rushed toward it, the darkness forcing him to guess the exact location of his target. The form he tackled was not covered in mail, but that didn't mean he was any less of a threat. The man grunted from the impact as he hit the ground, Chanse on top of him.

"Who are you?" Chanse asked, holding his blade near the man's face so he could see the weapon despite the darkness.

The man shoved at him, trying to break free, his movements desperate.

Chanse tightened his hold to make it clear that wasn't possible. "Who are you?"

"Just a hungry man in search of food."

Chanse didn't believe him. He glanced about, certain the man wasn't alone.

A muffled yell sounded nearby.

"I believe I found his companion," Matthew said.

The fight went out of the man Chanse held.

"Why are you here?" Chanse asked.

"'Tis true," insisted the man Matthew held as the pair walked through the trees. "We haven't eaten in days. We're near to starvin'."

Chanse continued to watch the shadows to see if more men appeared, but he didn't hear or see anything.

"We have little food to spare," Arabela said from behind Chanse. "But we'll share what we can."

Chanse clenched his jaw, wishing she hadn't made the offer. That would likely only encourage the pair to continue following them.

"How many of you are there?" Matthew asked.

"Just Samuel and me."

Chanse shook his head with frustration as he released his hold on the man. They wouldn't say if there were more. He intended to stay on guard until the two were on their way and afterward for some time. 'Twas bad enough that Graham and Rory's men were in pursuit. They didn't need a couple of thieves following them as well.

Arabela returned to her bag and, with Edith's help, pulled out several things, the darkness hiding the identity of the items.

Chanse stepped forward to take what she held, not wanting her to go anywhere near the men for fear they'd try to grab her. Keeping her appearance hidden would be wise as he didn't want them to be able to describe her if they happened upon Graham's men. For once, the darkness of the night was in his favor. Her beauty was far too memorable. Even now, rumpled from sleep with pink cheeks, she was breathtaking.

"Stay back," he whispered to her.

Then he handed the food to the first man who now stood. His coarse woolen attire fit his claim, but Chanse watched the two closely. "This is all we can spare."

"Ye have our gratitude." The man reached for the cheese and bread with wariness then sidled toward his companion.

"If I see you again, it won't end well," Chanse warned. "Do I make myself clear?"

"Aye." The man enthusiastically nodded as though to convince Chanse of his agreement. "Ye won't be seein' us again." He glanced past Chanse's shoulder to where Arabela stood. "Thank ye, milady."

The fact that he'd addressed her as a lady was not a good sign. Her way of speaking and posture revealed a certain refinement. Not many ladies could be in the woods in this area. He'd have to hope whoever was following them didn't come upon these men.

"Go." Though tempted to draw his sword to make his threat clear, Chanse merely placed a hand on its hilt.

The man's gaze dropped to Chanse's hand then he turned toward his companion, gesturing for him to follow. The two hurried away, their movements quickly hidden by the night.

Chanse's unease continued despite their disappearance.

Matthew moved close. "Shall we be on our way? Dawn cannot be long in coming now."

Rest would be impossible after this, and they were all awake. By the time they readied the horses, they'd have enough light to travel.

Chanse nodded then turned to Arabela and Edith. "Speak quietly until we're well on our way."

The women nodded, Arabela's gaze lingering on where the men had last been seen.

With so few things, it didn't take long to gather their possessions and tie the bags to the saddles. They were soon riding through the woods once again.

"Do you suspect those men of something other than wanting food?" Arabela asked.

"If they were honest men, they wouldn't have approached our camp in the dark of night." Thoughts of what could've happened filled his mind and refused to let go. "I hate to think what you would've faced if those two had come upon you and Edith when alone in the middle of the night."

She nodded but said nothing. Did that mean she realized the danger if she were without escort? He wanted her to truly understand with the hope it convinced her not to attempt an escape.

Matthew and Edith rode just ahead of them. Chanse pulled back on the reins and leaned forward to better make his point to Arabela. "I don't mean to frighten you, but I hope you better understand the dangers of traveling alone. The thought of anything happening to you chills my blood."

She frowned as though surprised. "Truly?"

"Truly." He drew back a stray strand of hair from her cheek.

Warmth filled his chest as he held her gaze. The sensation surprised him. The realization of how far he might need to go to protect her from harm struck him. The odd thing was that he knew he'd do so without a second thought.

～

CHANSE'S WORDS ran through Arabela's mind with each step the horse took. The notion that this handsome knight would feel any concern over her surprised her. She knew she shouldn't make overmuch of it but couldn't deny how much it pleased her.

The idea of those men coming upon her and Edith while they slept was frightening. The outcome would've been far different than the one they'd experienced. In truth, she'd prefer to continue with Chanse and Matthew for the remainder of their journey. If only Chanse would tell her of his plans, including where he intended to take her.

Weariness dragged at her despite the brief rest she'd had. Now that the fear brought by the two strangers had worn off, she felt weary down to her bones. When she nearly slid from the saddle, Chanse drew her back against him and tightened his arms around her. Odd that what had felt like a prison, days ago, now felt reassuring.

"Sleep," he said, his deep voice a rumble in her ear.

As though both her mind and body had his permission, she dropped into a dreamless sleep, only waking when daylight came in full.

"Oh." She sat up, hoping she hadn't embarrassed herself while asleep against him. "I'm sorry to have slept so long."

"No need to apologize. I know you're tired."

"You must be as well." She glanced back, annoyed to see he looked in fine health as always.

"Indeed. There will be time for rest once we have you safe."

"And where would that be?" If he'd share their destination, she could surely press him to tell her what his plans were for her.

"We have options. The choice depends on our pursuers."

"Are we going to Berwick?" The idea had crossed her mind once she realized they were headed east. The city would be far enough from her home and busy enough to make finding her difficult. At least, that was her hope. Added to that was the advantage of it being a market where strangers were frequent, so her presence wouldn't be noticeable. Though her father had a holding not far from the city, he rarely ventured there as he said it was too close to the English border.

"Possibly."

"What do you intend once we reach our destination?"

A long moment of silence greeted her question. She'd hoped by now he'd be willing to tell her.

"You do realize I'll find out eventually," she added, wanting to convince him—needing him to trust her.

"Aye, you will. No purpose would be served in me telling you now, would it?"

"Of course, it would. You'd put my mind at ease for one thing."

"How so?" The casual note in his tone annoyed her. How could he not realize how important this was to her?

"We are speaking of my future."

He met her comment with silence. What did that mean? Did he hope to use her for days or weeks or months to come? The thought terrified her. She didn't want to be anyone's prisoner. Even if he was attractive and chivalric. That had been the very reason she didn't want to leave with him in the first place.

"I can't make promises as to what will come next," he said at last.

She waited, feeling utterly helpless. Going anywhere on her own after the night's visitors seemed impossible. But so did remaining his captive. Where did that leave her?

When he said nothing more, she looked back at him, her anger building. "I have a right to know."

"Aye, but I have no answer. Not yet."

She wanted to scream at him. To tell him that she wasn't a bundle of wool to be carted around until a value was established. She was a woman with dreams who wanted to fill a purpose of her choosing.

Then she closed her eyes and bit her lip. What was she thinking? She was a *woman*. Such things were not a possibility. She'd be lucky to avoid marriage to Sir Rory.

Living without the protection of a man meant facing danger every day. If she didn't want marriage, her only true option was to join a convent. Even that was questionable since she had no dowry to offer. Mayhap if she threw herself on the mercy of the prioress, she would be welcomed. Taking her vows might allow her some protection from being forced to take part in her father's grand plan.

She swallowed against the lump of hopelessness in her throat as tears threatened.

Should she have married Rory and hoped for the best? Mayhap she could've been blessed with children who might fulfill her longing for family. She couldn't help but rub her arm which still bore his marks. Would she have survived long enough to have a babe with him?

Her life was so unsettled that it was hard to know how to act or what to think. She felt adrift at sea, vulnerable to the mercy of the next wave that rocked her.

"Arabela," Chanse murmured.

She shook her head. She didn't want to talk. Not to him. He couldn't possibly understand how she felt. He had the freedom to come and go as he pleased. His choices were only limited by his wants and needs.

He touched her shoulder, but she shrugged off his hand. If he couldn't be honest with her, she didn't want to talk. Not when her feelings for the man were already confused enough. She couldn't risk coming to care for him in any way.

She swallowed hard, worrying that it was already too late.

~

LATE THAT AFTERNOON, Chanse drew his horse to a halt at the edge of the trees to better view the village in the valley below. Though small, it boasted an inn. Staying at one held risk but would also give them the chance to discover if anyone was searching for them in the area.

Arabela had been quiet and sullen since he'd refused to tell her of his plan. He couldn't bring himself to admit that he didn't exactly have one. She'd think him crazed. Nor did he trust her enough to tell her what little he did intend. He only trusted family. All others too often proved themselves unworthy.

If they could make it as far as Berwick, he'd be pleased. Braden and Ilisa remained there, and he could discuss the choices with his brother. Could they stay in the city for long? Probably not. Graham would eventually search there.

They might have to cross the border into England. But that idea held risks as well. If Graham discovered their whereabouts, he'd come after his daughter. That wouldn't sit well with King Edward.

In truth, Chanse didn't know where he could take Arabela that would keep them both safe. He could only take this mission one day at a time, adjusting his course as they went, much like a ship at sea, altering its sails to better capture the wind.

The doubt and guilt that plagued him eased at the thought. He had no reason to trust her and wasn't about to. Her hurt feelings were of little concern. Not when her life was at stake, as was his own.

He'd nearly convinced himself of that when she shifted in his arms, glancing over her shoulder at him but not truly looking at him. No doubt she wondered what they were doing here, staring at the village below, but she didn't ask. Apparently, she wasn't speaking to him.

He much preferred the conversations they'd shared earlier than the wall of silence that now stood between them. But he wasn't willing to give her what she wanted. That left them in silence.

Matthew drew his horse closer. "What are you thinking?"

"It might be a good time to find out if anyone has been searching in this area for us." He glanced at Matthew. "A hot meal and a soft bed would be welcome as well."

"Indeed." The knight glanced over his shoulder at Edith who rode behind him. "What say you, Edith?"

"'Twould be nice indeed." She glanced at Arabela, surely wondering at her silence.

"Lady Arabela, are you in agreement?" Matthew asked.

"I don't believe my opinion matters."

Chanse scoffed. *Women.* Why did they have to be so damned difficult? He realized he was asking her to trust him when he didn't trust her. Was that so much to ask? He rubbed his forehead, the ridiculous circle of his thoughts causing his head to ache. He must be more tired than he realized.

Matthew raised a brow, but Chanse only shook his head. He wasn't about to try to explain her response.

Chanse studied the village but saw nothing unusual. The inn didn't appear especially busy though several people passed in and out of its entrance as they watched. A large stable stood nearby to shelter horses, partially hidden by the corner of the inn. Both the inn and the stable looked to be in good repair.

The village itself consisted of several dozen structures, most lining the road that passed through its center. A haze of smoke lingered in the air and added a cozy look to the thatched roofs. Many of the cottages boasted tofts with vegetables planted in neat rows. Others had pens of animals nearby.

"Shall I see if anything untoward is happening?" Matthew asked.

"It wouldn't hurt," Chanse responded after a moment of consideration. "Leave Edith with us. They won't be looking for a man alone."

The maidservant slid off the horse before Matthew could offer assistance. "Stay safe," she said as she stepped away.

Matthew nodded, his gaze already on the village below. Rather than riding directly toward it, he stayed in the trees, disappearing for a time until he reached the road, then following it into the village.

Chanse wished he would've volunteered to venture into the village. Watching and waiting was far more difficult than being the one who took the risk of asking questions. Especially with a silent Arabela before him.

They lost sight of Matthew as he entered the village. A short time passed before they saw him riding to the inn and dismounting at the stable.

"We should stretch our legs while we wait," he told Arabela. He swung his leg over the horse and hopped to the ground, prepared to lift her from the horse. But much like Edith, she dismounted before he could assist her. She was even unhappier with him than he realized. "Stay close."

Arabela didn't bother to acknowledge his words as she walked toward Edith.

The day was a fine one with only a few clouds lingering in the sky, a gentle breeze bumping them along. He was grateful to have avoided rain thus far.

Chanse scratched under his horse's forelock, murmuring gratitude for the steed's efforts. Keeping an eye on the village, he ran his hands along the horse's chest and down its legs to check for any sores or tenderness.

Arabela and Edith walked through the trees. No doubt she was telling her maidservant what a cad he was. The idea annoyed him more than he cared to admit.

He considered acquiring another horse in the village, but did he dare trust Arabela to ride by herself? As angry as she was with him, she might try to leave. That was a worry he'd prefer to avoid. If he wanted to remove it, he needed to explain why he couldn't tell her anything. With a sigh, he studied the view below.

Four men rode into sight on the road, catching his notice. The speed at which they traveled suggested they rode with purpose. As they neared, and details of their appearance became clearer, his concern grew. They could easily be men-at-arms based on their attire. Graham's holding was some distance from here and was by no means the only holding in the area but still he worried. With luck, Matthew would notice them and take greater care.

A glance over his shoulder sent his heart pounding. He didn't see the two women anywhere. His gaze swept the trees, but still nothing. Cursing under his breath, he took the reins of his horse and led it into the trees. He paused to search several times as the woods were thick enough to make finding them a challenge.

"Arabela," he called but kept his voice quiet.

No response. Heart now hammering, he prepared to mount to search for them when the flare of a kirtle near a tree caught his eye, and both women came into view. They weren't running from him as he feared but walking in a large circle.

At that moment, Arabela glanced at him. Her chin lifted, suggesting a hint of rebellion in her demeanor. The fear and anger that had flooded him left as quickly as it had come. Damn if part of him didn't admire her refusal to give up. He'd venture a guess that such behavior would continue to be directed his way until he gave her a reason to trust him.

He hid his smile and did his best to keep his expression stern. The last thing he wanted was to encourage her to press the boundaries of safety simply to annoy him. Such behavior held too many risks.

With quick strides, he led the horse toward them. "Do not leave my sight. For all we know, your father's men might be watching even now."

Her chin rose higher. The movement caused his attention to drop to her mouth. The urge to kiss her nearly overwhelmed him. If Edith hadn't been standing next to her, he would've. The lady was far too tempting. He tore away his gaze, trying to remember what he'd been saying.

"We are being careful," she said. "We don't wish to be caught any more than you do."

Chanse knew her words to be true, but she had to take greater care. Somehow, he needed to find a way to make her understand that. "Let us watch for Matthew to make certain he doesn't fall to any harm."

They returned to the tree line to wait and watch.

"Did you see the group of men riding toward the village?" he asked Arabela.

"Nay."

He thought she might recognize them.

Time passed slowly. Chanse hadn't expected Matthew to be gone this long. Though tempted to ride to the inn to see what was happening, he didn't dare leave Arabela and Edith alone. He considered himself a patient man, but that trait was tested as they waited.

At last the four men left the inn and mounted their horses, continuing their journey east.

Arabela moved next to Chanse, her brow furrowed. "Those are Rory's men. I'm certain of it. Do you think Matthew is well?"

"If he doesn't join us soon, I'll ride down to make certain he's safe." That was the last thing he wanted to do, especially with those men in the area. Nor did he want to leave the women to do so.

They all breathed a sigh of relief when Matthew exited the inn and walked toward the stable. Soon he was riding down the road past them before turning up the hill toward the trees.

Chanse gestured for the women to follow him deeper into the woods and, within a short time, Matthew joined them.

"That was interesting," he said as he dismounted to stand beside them.

"Arabela says those were Rory's men," Chanse said.

"Aye. I overheard them. They're asking questions of all who were in the inn."

"Did anyone tell them anything of interest?"

Matthew grinned. "They learned that two women meeting the description they gave were seen far south of here. The men are meeting with others searching on the morrow and will share their news. According to them, that is the first information they've had since the women left."

Chanse shared his smile. "Excellent work."

Arabela didn't look reassured in the least. "How many men are searching for us?"

Matthew's grin faded. "From what I overheard, most of Sir Rory's men as well as Lord Graham's."

She turned away but not before Chanse noted the worry in her expression. Did she think they wouldn't bother searching for her? Did she not realize that without her, her father's plan would fail? He had no other daughter to take her place. Her disappearance ended Sir Rory's dream of being king as well. Neither would abandon their scheme without a fight.

He wanted to gather Arabela in his arms and reassure her that all would be well and somehow, they'd make it through this together.

But he remained in place, waiting to see how she reacted once Matthew's news settled into her mind.

After a few brief moments, she turned back to look at Chanse. "Does this change your plan?"

He glanced toward the inn, realizing the idea of staying there for a night held too much risk. The men might come back.

Matthew held up a hand as though to halt his reply. "I was able to purchase additional supplies." He patted his saddlebags. "I have a few things for our supper and learned of a good place to make camp for the night."

"Let us find the place. We'll have a hot meal this evening." That was the best Chanse could do though the disappointment that flitted across Arabela's expression caused guilt to fill him.

He gestured for her to come forward, but she didn't budge.

She folded her arms across her chest and glared at him. "I'm not going anywhere until you tell me where we're going and why."

The woman wasn't going to make this easy, was she? He'd be damned if he would admit how loose of a plan he had. He turned to Matthew. "Why don't you go ahead with Edith so that I might have a moment to speak with Lady Arabela?"

Matthew nodded as he glanced between them. "Of course." He assisted Edith to mount and looked back at Chanse. "Ride toward the cliffs we passed not long ago. We'll meet you there." He mouthed the words, "Good luck," before riding away.

Chanse walked to stand before Arabela, his frustration building. "I'm doing my best to see that we escape safely. Having you challenge me is of no help."

"If you'd answer even one of my questions, we wouldn't be having this conversation." She met his gaze, her dark eyes holding steady on his.

Damn if she didn't lift her chin.

Something inside him snapped. Frustration wasn't the only thing building within him. The attraction he thought he had tightly reined in released in a rush.

His gaze dropped to her mouth as he took hold of her upper arms and drew her against him.

Her small gasp of surprise didn't stop him.

He kissed her as all thought halted and desire took over. Her lips were soft and warm beneath his.

Her body stiffened for a moment before softening as though molding to him.

Rather than the outrage he'd expected, she placed her hands against his chest and ran a hand along the linen of his shirt, causing his heart to pound steadily.

He deepened the kiss to better taste her sweetness and drew her even closer into the circle of his arms. Though he knew he must smell of sweat and horses, she didn't push him away.

Too late, he realized his mistake. Kissing her had only complicated the matter further. He eased back, unable to resist running a finger along the softness of her cheek. And made the mistake of looking into her eyes only to see questions still lingered there—questions to which he had no answers.

"I regret that I cannot answer your questions. You are still my captive." He said the words gently to lessen the blow. Before she could respond, he bent and lifted her into his arms and carried her to the horse.

CHAPTER 7

Arabela hardly knew what to think as Chanse lifted her onto his steed. The range of her emotions shocked her. How could she feel attraction for the knight when he angered her so?

But she wouldn't lie to herself. That moment of passion had been a complete surprise. As had her desire to return the embrace. The difference between Chanse's kiss and Rory's was night and day. Describing them both as 'kisses' was like comparing heather with a thistle.

Chanse might be her captor, but he treated her more gently than the man she was supposed to marry. What sense did that make? Her world had truly been turned upside down.

Despite what he'd said, she didn't consider herself his captive. Not when she'd decided against leaving for the time being. She wasn't certain if she'd be able to escape him, but neither had she tried. For now, their goals aligned. Whether that would continue remained to be seen.

She studied his profile as he gathered the horse's reins and placed them over the pommel of the saddle before mounting behind her. As he settled into place, she'd never been more aware of his thighs pressed against hers or the circle of his strong arms as he reached for the reins.

What was it about him that caused this unexpected longing inside her? 'Twas almost as if she had a physical reaction over which she had no control. But it wasn't merely physical. Despite how frustrated she was, she respected him. She didn't believe he was doing this for his own personal gain, but instead, he did it for some greater purpose.

From what she knew, Chanse was a fierce knight but also a genuinely kind person unless crossed. He'd been respectful to her and Edith. He and Matthew had developed a deep friendship that was evident in their conversations. He even treated his horse well.

He was everything Rory was not.

However, none of that mattered if Chanse's goal no longer matched hers, whatever that goal might be. There was a fundamental difference in what they each wanted if she looked beyond the escape of her wedding. She wanted freedom and, while she didn't know what his intentions were, Chanse certainly hadn't journeyed all this way for that.

She refused to be used yet again. What if Chanse decided to trade her back to her father if some agreement were reached? The idea made her ill. She had to find a way to gain Chanse's trust. Once she knew his plan, she could determine how much of it she agreed with and then decide her own path.

"If you would but tell me what your intentions are," she began, unable to let it go.

"I cannot do so. Don't ask me again." His tone brooked no argument as he lifted the reins.

"As long as you understand that I have no intention of serving a purpose that doesn't benefit me." The statement sounded selfish but 'twas true. She looked back at him only to realize her mistake. All thought fell away at the intensity of his eyes as he stared at her. At the *heat* in his brown eyes.

The breath in her lungs left in a whoosh, and she forgot the reason behind her words.

She turned to face forward again, unable to look at him and *not* think of that kiss. Surely, *he* was thinking of it.

More than anything, she wanted to know if he'd do it again.

Her cheeks heated at the thought and when they came upon where Matthew and Edith waited, she could feel the weight of their stares. No doubt her pink cheeks made them wonder what had occurred.

She said nothing as Chanse and Matthew discussed their destination. One of the men working at the inn's stable had mentioned the location of a cave when Matthew asked about a place to stay other than the inn that would offer some protection.

The unforgiving rock face they were near seemed an unlikely shelter to Arabela, but they followed it for some distance until at last reaching a cave of sorts.

"This should work well," Matthew said as he studied the hollow in the cliff. "We might manage a fire this evening."

"Perfect," Chanse agreed. "'Tis early yet, but the horses deserve additional rest, as do we all." He dismounted and reached for Arabela.

She told herself to slip off without his aid, but her body didn't listen. Instead, she waited until he placed his hands on her waist, then she rested her hands on his broad shoulders, noting the corded muscles there.

Her stomach fluttered, and her gaze dropped to his lips as he effortlessly lifted her from the steed. How easy it would be to wrap her arms around his neck and sink into him. To rely on him to protect her. If only so much didn't stand between them.

But it did, she reminded herself as he set her down. When he didn't release her, she looked at him once again.

"Do not think to leave, Arabela. 'Tis far too dangerous."

"I have yet to decide what holds more danger. You or the road."

His nostrils flared, and she wondered if he, too, fought the attraction between them. Or was it anger that caused his reaction? He bent his head, causing the flutters to begin anew. "I would not see you hurt," he whispered in her ear. "Don't go."

The feel of his breath sent shivers along her flesh and caused her entire body to tighten. Did he realize what he did to her? Did she cause a similar reaction in him?

She eased back so that she might see his face then reached up to touch the surprisingly soft hair just behind his ear. The dark centers of his eyes widened at her touch.

Mayhap he wasn't immune to her either. The thought made her smile.

"What has you so pleased?" he whispered, his hands still holding her waist.

She shook her head. "If you can keep secrets, so can I."

The corner of his mouth quirked upward. "As long as they don't place you in danger."

She didn't respond as she had yet to determine whether that was true.

He released her and saw to his horse while she and Edith gathered firewood. He watched them closely as they moved about.

The thought of a fire and a hot meal improved her spirits. She might not know what was going to happen on the morrow, but captive or not, this evening promised to be a good one.

She returned to the cave with an armload of wood to find Chanse had lit the fire and was placing an odd-looking spit above it. "Whatever is that?"

"'Tis used to either roast meat or hold a pot over the fire." He gestured toward the small kettle nearby with a hook on the handle.

Next to it were several woven pouches. "And those?" she asked as she set down the wood.

"Dried herbs to season the food."

Her mouth watered at the thought. After so many meals of bread, cheese, and dried meat, soup sounded heavenly. The weave of the pouches intrigued her, and she couldn't resist touching them. To her surprise, the weave spread as she lifted a pouch. "I've never seen the like of this."

"'Tis made with a special loom," Chanse said. "My mother, aunt, and cousin are some of the few who know how to do it, but I don't remember what they call it. They make all sizes of bags, and they stretch to fit what is put in them."

"How interesting." She wished she could see how it was done. Then the scent of herbs caught her notice. "I'm surprised you carry things to cook with you."

"We spend much time on the road and finding ways to bring comfort makes it easier to bear." He reached into one of his saddlebags on the ground nearby and retrieved four small wooden bowls that stacked inside each other.

Her stomach grumbled at the idea of a bowl of steaming soup, and she placed her hand over it at the embarrassing sound. How might it respond when the meal was ready?

Chanse chuckled, his gaze meeting hers. "Mine is doing that as well."

She much preferred this version of the knight to the stern one who refused to answer questions.

Matthew rolled a large log toward the fire for them to sit on while they watched Chanse continue his preparations.

"'Tis highly entertaining to think a knight with his skills can cook," Matthew told her and Edith. "But he's a talented one, and I appreciate his abilities."

Chanse scoffed. "Any who made an effort would be considered talented after eating dried bread and old cheese for days on end. Or worse, those tasteless oatcakes of which you're so fond."

Matthew laughed then rose to take the pot. "Shall I find some water?"

"Aye."

"Can I help with something?" Edith asked. "I can't say that I care to sit idle."

"You might search for some edible roots," Chanse said. "Sometimes onions grow along the meadows. Berries might be ripe as well."

"I'll come along to help," Arabela said.

"Mind that neither of you goes far," Chanse said. "Stay within sight of camp."

Arabela wondered if he requested that out of concern for their safety or fear of them taking the opportunity to leave. Probably both. However, the idea of leaving before the meal was ready held no appeal. Her stomach wouldn't stand for it.

Edith had some knowledge of plants and found a few things she thought could be added to the soup. Arabela found a bush with blackberries and picked as many ripe ones as she could find, holding them in her kirtle to carry them back to the fire.

"Berries?" Chanse asked with a grin.

She was ridiculously pleased with his enthusiastic reaction.

He examined the roots Edith brought, discarded a few, and cleaned the rest with the water Matthew brought then roughly chopped them.

The supplies Matthew purchased from the inn included venison, onions, and turnips. Chanse soon had a stew simmering over the fire. Matthew had also bought freshly baked bread that smelled heavenly.

While the stew cooked, Matthew shared what Rory's men said.

"They told everyone they're searching for two women but refused to give any additional details. Sir Rory would not want the knowledge that his bride-to-be would rather run than marry him spread across the country."

Though Matthew's words were lighthearted, they reminded Arabela of the seriousness of the situation. 'Twas one thing to escape home and a completely different thing to remain hidden. The days and weeks and months ahead suddenly felt like a blanket smothering her. How could she possibly manage to stay out of sight for any length of time? What kind of life would she have when she was in constant fear of being discovered?

She jerked upright from the log, muttered a few words of excuse, and stepped away. Drawing deep breaths to slow her suddenly pounding heart, she walked into the trees and away from the watchful eyes of the others. To her relief, she heard them continue talking. With luck, no one realized her moment of panic.

She leaned against a tree and continued to gulp in air, unable to catch her breath. The idea of remaining on the run, never feeling truly safe, always on alert was nearly more than she could bear.

"Is all well, Arabela?" The quiet concern in Chanse's voice brought tears to her eyes. He'd appeared at her side without her even realizing it. So much for her ability to remain alert.

"I—" She stopped unable to speak past the lump in her throat. Before she could try again, strong arms wrapped her tight.

"What?" he prompted. His hand brushed her hair soothingly as he held her.

"'Tis far from over, nor will it be any time soon." She gave in to the urge to rest her head against the comfort of his shoulder. "The realization is overwhelming."

"You need only take it one day at a time."

To think of the numerous people involved, from those who searched for her to those from whom she'd need help to continue her escape—all for her. Suddenly her wish to leave seemed even more selfish. Her presence could place anyone she was near in danger. Panic surged through her anew.

What had she done?

She leaned back to look into Chanse's eyes. "I fear I made a terrible mistake."

~

CHANSE STIFFENED AT HER WORDS, not caring for the worry in her expression. "How so?"

"You should take me back. I should never have left." Arabela's eyes filled with tears.

His chest tightened at the mix of fear and panic in her voice. "I think you might have forgotten why you ran away."

"This is too much. I should've married Rory and avoided all this. As Rory's wife, I might've been able to do something." She shifted in his arms, her eyes darting back and forth, revealing her racing thoughts. "Those men surely aren't the only ones searching for me. My father's will be as well. They won't stop until they find me."

He hesitated, uncertain what he could say to reassure her. "Think of those who would be in danger if your wedding had taken place."

"But—"

"Arabela." He said her name firmly, wanting to reach through her panic to gain her attention. "Think." Though she continued to try to move away, he held tight. "Breathe."

She drew a long shuddering breath. Then another.

He took that as permission to gentle his hold. "I know how difficult this is. Truly. But you must keep the result in mind. Stay strong. You—that is to say, *we*—did the right thing by leaving."

Would reminding her that she had little choice in the matter ease her fears? Her willingness to leave her home with them had made his mission easier, but he would've taken her regardless. She was the key to stopping the wedding. For his plan to succeed, Graham needed Arabela.

She reached up as if to place a trembling hand on her mouth only to have her sleeve fall back, revealing the still fading bruises. Her gaze caught on the marks, and the tension in her body eased.

"Giving the rest of your life to your father's and Rory's plan would harm not only you." Chanse ran gentle fingers over the bruises, the sight of them angering him though he did his best to hide it. "But the people of this country as well. And for what purpose?"

She lowered her arm and looked at him. "To unite Scotland?" Since she posed it as a question, he knew she didn't believe it.

"Do you truly think that's what would happen?"

"Nay, but I could be wrong."

"I don't think you are."

"The idea of remaining in hiding for months is overwhelming."

Chanse gritted his teeth. How could he argue when he thought the same? When he intended to return home to England soon. But what of Arabela? "Taking the right path is never easy."

"That path would be easier if I knew where we were going or what your intention is."

"If by some unfortunate circumstance we are caught, and you are asked for that information, you'd have no choice but to share it."

She frowned. "I would never betray your confidence."

Surprise rolled through Chanse even as warmth spread through him. "I appreciate that more than I can say." He cupped his hand along the softness of her cheek, all too aware of what harm might befall her if she had to face Rory and his questions. "But you would have little choice." He touched her bruised arm to make his meaning clear.

The realization had her eyes widening. He detested seeing the fear she fought back. It made him all the more determined to make certain they weren't caught.

"We must take care with our path," she whispered.

Did that mean she was willing to accompany him regardless of whether she knew their destination? He hoped so.

"Aye. We will take great care."

The sound of Matthew speaking with Edith brought Chanse back to their surroundings.

"Let us have something warm to eat. That will make us all feel better." He raised a brow and she nodded, taking his offered arm, and they turned toward the camp.

Edith stirred the soup over the fire. At their approach, she looked up, studying her mistress. "I believe the stew is ready."

Chanse nodded his approval as she reached for the bowls to dish out the steaming broth.

Matthew's gaze swung between him and Arabela as he cut thick slices of the bread and set one on each bowl, but he said nothing despite the questions in his eyes.

They sat on the log near the fire, quiet as they enjoyed the meal.

"Tasty fare as always," Matthew told Chanse between spoonfuls. "So much better than what we've been eating."

"I don't think I've ever tasted anything so good," Arabela said.

"Nor I," Edith agreed.

Chanse chuckled. "'Tis easy to please others when they're no longer picky."

"You're far too modest," Arabela countered, her smile more genuine than it had been a few moments ago. "I don't know what you put in the stew, but 'tis wonderful."

He smiled, pleased at her praise. Now if only he could also convince her to trust him to see to her wellbeing.

CHAPTER 8

Arabela shifted on her blanket, unable to find a comfortable position. She rested on her side, the soft glow of the low fire offering comfort but not bringing peace.

The hoot of an owl echoed along the cliffs where they made camp, the eerie sound causing her to picture some unsuspecting creature stilling in its tracks. How long would she be like that poor animal, forever looking over her shoulder? Forever in fear. The daunting thought caused her to shudder.

The night was cool, making her grateful for the extra blanket that covered her. Edith snored softly nearby. Matthew kept watch somewhere amid the trees. Chanse lay behind her.

But she was certain he didn't sleep.

That was the cause of her restlessness. She became convinced of it as more stars bridged a path across the night sky. If she turned over, she had no doubt she'd find Chanse less than an arm's length from her.

Did he stay close because he feared she'd attempt to leave? Because he was growing to care for her? Or did he do so to protect her? She truly wanted to know. It shouldn't matter, but it did.

Unable to take the ache in her hip from the hard ground any

longer, she rolled onto her back. She told herself to keep her eyes closed, but curiosity had them popping open. Before she could stop herself, she'd turned her head to look at him.

The glow from the fire cast light over the planes and angles of his face, but his eyes remained in shadow. Did he sleep?

"Is something amiss?" he whispered.

She nearly jolted at his words. Nay, he didn't sleep. Unfortunately, the realization made her heart pound. "Merely attempting to find a comfortable position."

"It takes time to become accustomed to sleeping on the ground."

If only that were her problem. Between her circling thoughts and Chanse's presence, rest seemed impossible.

She couldn't imagine returning home to face her father and Rory's anger nor could she imagine what the coming days would bring. She despised the idea of anyone being placed in danger because she'd chosen to leave. Was she making the right decision?

Chanse rose onto an elbow to look at her. "Care to share what's troubling you?"

She closed her eyes at the temptation. Becoming dependent on this man would be a mistake. He had but one goal in mind. Any remarks he made were colored by that goal, by what *he* wanted. Her wants and needs mattered little if at all. Why did she have such a difficult time believing that?

"I don't think any purpose would be served in doing so," she said as she opened her eyes.

"As you wish." He lay back down and settled into place.

The idea that he was untroubled and acted as if he'd be able to sleep only made her feel worse. He was the one who'd caused much of her problem. Her tired mind argued that he should share in her sleeplessness. But the reality was that she didn't want to be alone with her thoughts anymore. "Do we travel to Edinburgh?"

With a sigh, he propped himself onto his elbow once more. "Nay."

"Then where?"

"The destination makes little difference to our plan. We are traveling away from your father's holding. That is all that matters." He glanced at Edith's sleeping form before leaning close to whisper even more quietly, "I will do all I can to keep you safe."

His words reassured her. She didn't know why, but they did. She studied his features. The strength in his face came as much from his physical form as from his character. He was even more appealing when he wasn't displaying the charm she'd come to expect.

His gaze moved over her face, and she wondered what he saw. When he looked at her lips, she couldn't help the warm flush of longing that swept through her. *Aye*, she wanted to whisper. *Kiss me, please.*

As though he heard her wish, he eased closer until she felt the heat of his body envelop hers. Her heart pounded, and she had to clench her fist to keep from reaching for him. Then his mouth captured hers.

Lovely.

He deepened the kiss with a gentle firmness that caused heat to spread low in her belly. Passion built, rising inside her until all else fell away. So many different emotions swelled through her that she could barely register one before another took its place. The strongest one of all was desire.

Did he feel any of the same things as she?

He eased back, his finger tracing the side of her face. "You are strong. Beautiful. Do not worry so. We'll manage this together."

For how long? she wanted to ask but was too frightened of his answer. "I'd just like to know where—"

"Arabela, I've told you that we'll adjust the plan as we travel, depending on those who pursue us. Telling you more could place you in danger." The intensity in his eyes softened as he continued to look at her. "I know 'tis much to ask, but I request it of you all the same. Trust me."

The idea of simply agreeing was tempting, but she had more than just herself to consider. Was what he wanted best for the people of her country? How could she trust him when he wouldn't confide his intentions? What if he decided this plan was too difficult after all and chose to abandon her somewhere along the road and return to his own life?

She swallowed hard at the thought.

Arabela couldn't deny her attraction to this man, but she had to guard against becoming overly dependent on him. Once they arrived at a city of some size, she'd make her own path. She refused to be used to control her father, and she had to guess that was what Chanse intended.

All the more reason she couldn't grow to rely on him. She needed to keep her bearings, both emotionally and physically. Chanse might be handsome and charming, but was one of the reasons he wouldn't share his plans because he knew she wouldn't agree with them?

She'd take this time with him to learn all she could about traveling without shelter and with few supplies so when the day came—and she knew it would—she'd have the skills to survive on her own.

Rather than respond to his request, she turned away from him to face the fire. Mayhap he'd be left wondering as to her thoughts much as she was left wondering about his. She closed her eyes, holding the small victory in mind as she sought rest. She knew she'd need it to face the days ahead.

CHANSE ROSE from where he'd sat against a tree the last few hours keeping watch. The light of dawn made it possible to see better, but still he listened for any sounds that didn't belong in the woods that were awakening with the morn.

He stretched his back and shoulders, hoping the short amount of sleep he'd managed would be enough to see him through this day. Normally, he was able to function for several days with little to no rest, but with Arabela along, he needed to keep his wits about him.

Her wavering emotions made her unpredictable, something he hadn't expected. His attraction to her complicated things further, making him second guess every word that came out of his mouth —and hers.

He wanted to protect her yet how could he when she kept pushing him away? Nor could he trust himself to make the right decision based on logic. Her presence shifted his thinking in ways he hadn't anticipated. His desire to please her warred with his need to keep them safe.

With a sigh at his circling thoughts, he walked the perimeter of the area slowly, stopping to listen several times. His senses were on high alert this morn, but he couldn't determine the cause. Unease filled him, causing him to return to camp to make certain all was well.

The sight of the empty spot where Arabela had slept sent his heart thundering. A quick glance about the area didn't reveal her or any clue as to her whereabouts. Edith still slept. Surely, she wouldn't have left without her maidservant. Her bag sat nearby as well. He strode forward to touch the blanket she'd had covering her and found it still warm.

With nerves on edge, he roused Matthew. The knight woke quickly, one hand reaching for his sword.

Chanse held a finger to his lips to request he keep quiet then pointed to Arabela's empty spot.

Matthew's eyes widened in alarm, and he was on his feet in a moment, his gaze sweeping the camp.

Though it was reasonable to think she might have stepped away to relieve herself, Chanse's senses said otherwise. He and Matthew started into the trees in different directions just as the snap of a twig sounded.

Chanse turned to see two men enter their camp, one behind Arabela with an arm around her neck and a knife in hand. His stomach curdled with fear. He glanced over his shoulder to see Matthew had stopped as well.

"Release her," Chanse demanded, a hand on the hilt of his sword even as his gaze searched the woods behind the two men to see if others followed. Had her father's men discovered them?

Edith released a startled scream before Chanse shot her a look of warning to remain where she was.

Finding the woods empty, he studied the intruders. Neither was dressed as men-at-arms. Rather, their simple clothing suggested they endured a rougher existence.

"We'll be taking any valuables ye have," the man holding Arabela said. "By the looks of ye, ye have some to spare."

"We won't be sharing anything with you." Anger turned Chanse's blood cold as he noted the fear in Arabela's expression. The men would pay for causing her such angst.

"Ye wouldn't want any harm to befall the lady, now would ye?" the man asked.

His companion looked less certain. His worried gaze swung between Chanse and Matthew as though unsure who would attack first. His simple homespun brown clothing was worn and filthy, but his body was plump enough to suggest he was well fed.

Chanse glanced at Matthew and tipped his head to the side. Matthew understood and took several steps to the side while Chanse did the same. That made them more difficult to watch. The two men had to continually look between them to keep them in sight.

The girdle Arabela normally wore low on her hips that held her knife sat on the ground near where she'd slept. She must've removed it to sleep.

"Here now," said the man making demands. "Both of ye stand next to the fire else I'll be forced to hurt her." The confidence in his expression shifted to wariness.

Good. Chanse wanted him to understand the terrible mistake he'd made by putting his hands on Arabela.

"Release her," Chanse repeated as he drew his sword. He refused to negotiate.

The sight of his blade unsheathed had the companion taking a step back as though ready to run.

Even better, Chanse thought. Let them try.

"Drop your sword." The man's breath came in short breaths with his order, his chest heaving with panic.

Arabela tugged on the arm at her neck as the man tightened his hold, leaving her gasping for air.

That was the last straw for Chanse. The idea of Arabela being in pain or distress was more than he could bear, and it would end now. He lunged forward, slicing the hand grasping the knife, his movement sure and steady, a movement he'd practiced many times before.

The thief's cry was satisfying in the terrible moment, making Chanse wish he'd severed his hand, for then he'd have no choice but to release Arabela. However, that would only bring her more distress.

The man shoved Arabela aside to grab his injured arm. She fell to the ground and scrambled away.

Matthew easily disarmed the other man. Chanse paused to see what the injured thief would do.

The leader glanced at his companion who held his hands up to signify he intended no harm. When the man who'd held Arabela turned back, Chanse could tell he would not give up so easily. Still, he waited, not wanting to make the first move while Arabela watched. He scowled when he realized her presence changed his actions. Yet the idea of her thinking of him as some cold-blooded killer was unappealing.

It only took a moment for the thief to draw a blade from the sheath at his belt. The act gave Chanse permission to do what he'd wanted to do since the man had entered their camp holding Arabela. Chanse knocked the knife out of his hand with the flat of his blade then ran it through his chest, unwilling to allow him to live to threaten them again.

The companion had made a similar mistake, reaching for his blade. The movement sealed his fate as well at Matthew's hand. His body crumpled to the ground beside his fellow thief.

Arabela's gasp was all Chanse heard in the silence.

It took a moment for him to gather the courage to look at her, afraid he'd see disgust in her eyes. He dropped his bloody sword on the ground and moved toward her, fearing what her expression would reveal. "Are you well?"

She raised a hand to her throat, drawing deep trembling breaths. She nodded, and at last he risked looking at her, wanting to make certain she was unharmed.

"Are you sure?"

Shock glazed her eyes. He hoped it wasn't because of what he'd done. "I only stepped away to..." A flush washed over her face, much better than the paleness of a moment ago. "To relieve myself. I didn't see him until he grabbed me."

Edith hurried forward, the older woman's concern etched in her face. "Milady, ye took five lives from me. I've never been so scared." She put a comforting hand on Arabela's shoulder. "Are ye certain ye're well?"

The next breath Arabela drew was steadier. Her gaze shifted to the dead man. Blood seeped slowly across the front of his brown tunic. His eyes stared sightlessly at the sky. She swallowed hard then glanced to where Matthew stood over the other dead man before quickly looking away.

"Let us prepare to leave," Chanse said, ready to allow Edith to comfort Arabela while he and Matthew dealt with the bodies. The longer she stared at them, the more upset she was becoming based on her expression.

He rolled up the blanket and gathered the supplies he'd left near the fire and packed them back in the saddlebags with quick, efficient movements.

Matthew did the same, and then they readied the horses. "Shall I dig graves for the pair?" he asked.

Chanse considered their options. Digging required tools and time they didn't have. "Our best option is to try for a shallow grave with rocks to cover the bodies. But we'll do it away from camp. No point in drawing attention to where we stayed."

"Why don't you proceed slowly," Matthew suggested. "I'll remain behind to deal with the bodies then catch up with you."

They discussed the general direction in which they intended to travel. Chanse assisted Arabela and Edith onto his horse. Matthew would keep his steed so that he might catch up to them more easily.

Already Chanse could feel the weight of Arabela's gaze. She glanced back several times at the bodies, but her attention came back to him. Did she now believe him to be as much of a brute as Rory was said to be?

It couldn't be helped, and in all honesty, 'twas probably for the best. He didn't want her to become overly dependent on him, and heaven forbid if the attraction between them developed further. That would be a mistake. He intended to return home before snow came to this rugged country.

What of Arabela?

He shut off the thought before his mind could latch hold. She'd planned to leave before he interfered. He'd see her safely settled at a place of her choosing before he left.

More than ever, he wanted to return to Berwick. Braden would be of help with the situation. Ilisa, his wife, might be of assistance to Arabela since she'd spent most of her life in Berwick.

Arabela's life afterward wasn't his problem. His goal was to stop the wedding, and he had. The other details weren't his concern.

If only he could convince himself of that.

ARABELA SWALLOWED hard against the lump in her throat as they wound their way through the trees. Chanse searched the area continually as they traveled.

She tried to do the same, but being on constant watch was exhausting, especially with her legs still trembling. Heavy in her heart was the knowledge that she'd already failed miserably at it.

She should be relieved to ride with Edith for a change. Being in such proximity to Chanse only upended her emotions further. After what had occurred, she didn't need more reason to be upset.

As they plodded along, Arabella's thoughts returned to what had happened when she'd awakened earlier. She'd noticed Chanse's empty blanket and known he was on guard. Perhaps that was why she'd felt safe. She wasn't about to find him to tell him that she had to relieve herself. That would have been far too embarrassing. She hadn't gone far. After all, she knew people searched for them.

The idea that someone had been watching her, and she hadn't realized anyone was even nearby shook her. One moment she was lifting her skirt, and the next an arm had been wrapped tightly around her throat, choking her.

Even more frightening was that for the briefest of moments she'd thought that arm belonged to Rory.

She closed her eyes at the memory of the fear that had taken over, paralyzing her. She hadn't been able to move, to think, to cry out for help.

The more she relived it now, the angrier she became with herself. How could she possibly survive the next few days let alone the next few months if she couldn't take care of herself? She touched the knife sheathed in her girdle, determined to carry it with her at all times from this moment on.

Those men could've used her to force Chanse and Matthew to hand over all they had. It would've been her fault if they had lost the few items they carried with them. The realization sent a wave of shame washing over her. If she couldn't find a way to improve her skills, she might as well return home. She'd never make it. Not only was she dependent on Chanse, but she wouldn't survive without him.

Somehow, she needed to learn to fight back if—no, when—that situation occurred again. Surprise would be on her side as most men didn't expect women to protest let alone put up a fight.

The idea of drawing her knife hadn't crossed her mind. How stupid of her. She put her hand on the small hilt, trying to imagine how she'd use it to gain her freedom if she had the situation to live through again.

"Are ye truly well, milady?" Edith whispered from behind her. "Ye're awful quiet."

Aware that Chanse could no doubt hear every word, Arabela reached out to pat Edith's leg. "I'm well. Thank you. It could've ended much worse." The thought sent a shiver through her.

Chanse drew the horse to a halt. "Don't step away from the rest of us under any circumstances in the future. Is that understood?" A glint of anger flashed in his eyes as he looked at both of them.

As if she needed to be told that after what had happened? As if she wanted to repeat that situation? Yet how could she blame him for being angry with her when she was angry with herself?

"Would you teach me?" The question popped out, surprising her.

He frowned. "Teach you what?"

"To defend myself. To know what to do if I ever find myself in similar circumstances." The idea took hold. This would be the perfect way for her to gain some of the skills she needed to survive. If he could teach her how to find what direction she was traveling, couldn't he also teach her other things?

While she would never wield a sword, she had limited skills with her knife. Surely Chanse could show her how to better protect herself with it.

He shook his head and started walking again, dashing her hopes. Did he think her so incompetent that no point would be served in teaching her?

That only angered her more. But before she could protest, he stopped again to look up at her.

"You must avoid placing yourself in the position of needing protection."

"That seems impossible. I wasn't even safe at my home." Tears clogged her throat at the situation. How could she protect herself if no one would teach her?

She knew she overreacted but couldn't help it. She was tired and scared and had no idea what new challenges the next hour would bring. Added to that was the feeling that she'd disappointed Chanse by being caught. She hated that sensation worst of all.

Chanse looked away for a moment before turning back to study her. "There are a few simple things you could do that might aid escape. But the most important trait you can do is to become more aware of potentially dangerous situations."

"Such as?"

"Never walk alone." He led the horse again.

She thought to rebuff his advice, but he was right. She was used to having the run of her keep and being able to go where she chose within its walls. But nowhere was safe now. She had to remember that. She needed to think differently starting now.

"What else?" she asked.

Chanse kept walking but glanced at her with a frown. He obviously had expected her to argue with his remark.

"I should've advised you of my intent this morn," she added. "It won't happen again."

He nodded. Had she convinced him of her willingness to learn? If not, she'd find a way to show him through her actions that she wouldn't be caught so unaware again. Edith depended on her, and she didn't take that trust lightly.

Never again would she put those who traveled with her in danger.

CHAPTER 9

Chanse thought his emotions had settled by the time they stopped for the midday meal. Yet as he lifted Arabela from the horse, he realized that wasn't quite true.

Matthew had caught up with them earlier and once again rode with Edith.

"Hold," Chanse muttered to Arabela before taking her arm. He ignored Matthew who watched with interest, then escorted her into the woods to have a few words in private.

"What is it?" she asked as he drew her along. She suddenly felt incredibly fragile to him.

The memory of her at the wrong end of the thief's knife sent his frustration high. Determining they were far enough from Matthew and Edith, he stopped and turned to face her. "Do you have any idea how close to death—or worse—you were?"

She bit her lower lip and nodded. The vulnerability in her eyes stopped the lecture he'd been prepared to give.

With a groan he took her in his arms and held tight, needing a physical connection to reassure himself that she was alive and well despite the near miss. The warmth of her body against the length of his slowly seeped into him, chasing away the chill that had lingered since the thief threatened her.

His heart lifted when she wrapped her arms around him and returned the embrace. He pressed his cheek against the top of her head, breathing in her scent.

"You scared the hell out of me," he whispered, half hoping she didn't hear him. He didn't want to admit how deeply the situation had affected him.

"It frightened me as well."

He leaned back to look into her eyes. "I don't want that to happen again." He couldn't admit anything more. The odd feelings he had for her were merely protectiveness. She was his responsibility until he found a place where he could safely leave her. Anything more was out of the question.

Was this how his father had felt when escorting his mother to her guardian when she didn't want to go? This terrible mix of duty set against...longing for something more? He wasn't prepared to put a name on it. That would only end poorly.

"Nor do I," she admitted. "Which is why I'd like you to teach me to better protect myself."

He frowned as he again considered her request. He'd been mulling over the idea during their ride. The thought of her attempting to save herself with nothing more than her small knife on her girdle set his teeth on edge. Doing nothing was far worse. He'd witnessed that for himself. Surely, he'd sleep better in the days after they parted if he knew she wasn't completely without defenses.

"Very well. But I was serious earlier. Your best hope is to avoid any situation that might put you in harm's way."

"I will do my best to watch for those. I won't be without my knife, small as it is, again." She released him and took a step back. "Show me what I should've done."

"Did he capture you from behind?" The idea of the thief doing so brought a wave of hot anger he had to shove back.

At her nod, he moved behind her and wrapped his arms around her tightly. "Like this?"

"Aye."

"Bend your knees, stay low, and try to wiggle free." He realized his mistake too late when she did as he requested. The feel of her moving within the circle of his arms made him think of things he shouldn't be thinking. *God's teeth.*

His distraction allowed her to twist away before he could regain control of his thoughts.

Her delighted smile pleased him. "How was that?"

"Good." In more than one respect. He gave himself a mental shake, willing his wayward thoughts to behave. "Let's try it again."

She turned her back to him, and he reached for her, unable not to notice how her curves fit against him, especially as she moved, attempting to break free.

"If he doesn't release you and you can't reach your knife, go limp. Carrying off someone who does so is difficult."

She did as he suggested and sank to the ground before he could catch her.

"What more should I know?" she asked, her expression even more determined.

Damn if that didn't appeal to him.

"If you're approached from the front, the best option is to kick or knee him between the legs. That will more than likely injure him more easily than trying to use your knife." He didn't want to say anything to offend her, so hopefully, she knew to what he referred.

"Show me."

He moved within arm's length. "One of the most vulnerable places on a man is here." He spread his fingers over his groin. "If you kick or knee him there, or use a well-placed elbow hard enough, you'll render him useless for a brief time and give you the opportunity to run."

Arabela frowned as she stared at his groin. Heat filled him despite the fact that she stared at him for a completely different reason than his body seemed to think. If only she considered it for a purpose other than something to harm. But it didn't matter as his manhood rose to attention regardless of her intent.

"Truly?" The look she gave him suggested she thought he jested.

"Truly." Anxious for her to look somewhere else before she realized just how she affected him, he shifted the conversation. "If he's too close for that and you can't reach your knife, poke him in the eye." He held up his finger.

She copied his action, staring at her finger as if wondering if she could truly harm another person.

"Remember, your life is in danger. You must do harm. Jab him as hard as you can."

She frowned. "I'll try."

"We'll practice." He gestured for her to turn around. "Show me what you'll do when you're grabbed like this." Again, he wrapped his arms around her. The scent of her enveloped him. The feel of her wriggling her way free made him grit his teeth.

She spun to face him, a delighted smile on her face at her success. He reached for her again, this time from the front.

She froze, and he could see her mind processing her choices.

"Act quickly before he can guess your intent," he urged her. He growled, hoping to press her into a decision.

He was too close to kick, so she raised her knee with enough force to have him jumping back just in time to save himself from harm.

"Oh," she said with surprise. "Was that right?"

"Aye. You would've easily dropped me to my knees if I hadn't backed away. But you must be quick, or he'll have a chance to guard against your move."

"I haven't had experience with...any of this." She gestured toward him, then herself, her face flushing a delicate rose.

The urge to kiss those pink cheeks nearly overwhelmed him. Touching her had caused different problems than the one he'd hoped to solve.

"We'll go through a few other ways you might protect yourself this evening." He needed to stop this training before he did something he shouldn't. He offered her his elbow, and she took it, her lashes guarding her thoughts. "Let us have something to eat before we resume our journey."

Matthew raised a brow when they returned as though to inquire if all was well. Chanse nodded then took some of the dried meat and a piece of the bread before sitting near his friend. Arabela and Edith sat a short distance away, speaking between themselves.

"She wishes to learn how to defend herself," he whispered.

"If Sir Rory finds us that will do little good."

"Always expecting the best, aren't you?" Chanse shook his head. "It can do no harm. We must make certain neither Rory nor Graham discover our whereabouts."

"Which brings up the question of where we go from here."

Chanse ate while he considered the best direction. A straightforward journey to Berwick was out of the question. Nor did he want to travel in the opposite direction to throw off any pursuers. That would take them too far from their true destination.

"Somehow, we need to make it appear as if we're not going to Berwick."

"We left a false trail to Edinburgh," Matthew said. "That should aid us."

"True. They could spend weeks searching there for us. Or they could decide that's too obvious of a place for us to remain and start to look elsewhere."

Matthew scowled. "I wondered about that as well."

"If we skirt Edinburgh then head southeast, that might be the best choice." Chanse pondered the idea as he ate the rest of his simple meal. "I don't want anyone to believe we're riding toward the border. That will cause more harm than good."

"Graham might think Englishmen are aiding his daughter?"

"Exactly. Which would only worsen relations between the countries and possibly bring about the war we're trying to prevent."

"But riding northeast makes Berwick appear the obvious destination."

"What about Dunbar?" Matthew asked.

"Where is that?"

"A few hours ride. 'Tis of some size from what I've heard."

Chanse looked at Matthew. "I'll rely on your opinion. You know this area better than me."

"I can't say I've ever ventured there, but if we don't like what we see, we can move on."

"'Tis a temporary destination, but I still don't want either of the ladies to know our plan."

"Are you certain 'twouldn't be better to simply tell them? They might know that particular place."

"Nay." Chanse didn't consider it for even a moment. Trusting anyone who hadn't proven themselves held too great a risk. Added to that was the knowledge that what they didn't know they couldn't tell even if forced.

He might be attracted to Arabela, but that didn't mean he trusted her despite a voice inside him that suggested otherwise. Those were two completely different things.

"If you're sure." Matthew lifted a shoulder as though it didn't matter, but Chanse knew he wasn't convinced.

That was of no concern. Chanse was certain this was the right path.

∽

Lord James Graham paced the solar of the Hawkswood Inn on the outskirts of Edinburgh, waiting impatiently for news of Arabela.

"'Tis a disaster," he told Donnan, his new steward, who stood nearby. "The guests who came for the wedding are no doubt spreading the news far and wide of this failure."

Donnan offered neither agreement nor protest. A wise man, thought James, though he itched for a reason to release his temper.

His previous steward had given him such hope with his crazed insistence that Sir Hugh had a secret gift James could use to show the people of Scotland that he, Lord Graham, was destined to be king.

Alas, the revelation that day forced James to find another way to guide his country. Rory wasn't the man he would've picked to rule, but his loose ties to one of Scotland's greatest kings was perfect. Rory's coarse behavior could eventually be refined with James's assistance.

However, Arabela's disappearance had temporarily stolen the opportunity to direct Scotland's future. Thus far, they'd found little to track her departure. Had someone taken her captive? Had she left of her own accord? If so, who aided her? He couldn't believe she'd managed to elude them this long on her own.

"Where's Sir Rory?" James asked.

"He's still meeting with Lord Basset, as you instructed."

"A damned Englishmen. I don't know that anything constructive will result, but there's a chance he might know something."

Lord Basset was governor of Edinburgh, but his English blood made him useless to James, who refused to ask for the man's help because of that. James had convinced Rory that meeting with Basset would be his first attempt at gaining political support under the guise of making inquiries about Arabela.

James paused his pacing before the steward. "Are you certain Arabela asked about Edinburgh?"

"Aye, my lord," Donnan said. "She asked how long it might take to ride there."

"Yet she didn't take her horse."

Donnan looked less certain at that reminder. "Mayhap she had someone's aid?"

"Who would bother to help her?" James returned to pacing. He doubted her ability to plan her departure let alone arrange for someone to help. Which made it more likely that someone had taken her. But who? Until he knew more, he didn't want to declare she'd been taken captive. If it turned out that she'd left on her own, he didn't want to look a bigger fool than he already did.

"We should hear news soon," Donnan added, whether to reassure himself or James, he didn't know.

James had men searching in all directions. He'd expected word of her location by now. The longer finding her took, the more severe her punishment would be. Though he supposed he could leave that to Rory. Mayhap he should warn the man not to strike her in the face. Leaving marks for all to see was never wise.

A knock sounded on the door. James nodded for Donnan to

answer. When the door opened to reveal his wife, James could only stare in shock. "Whatever are you doing here?"

She looked at him, her gaze wary but determined and clear for the first time in a long while. "I've come to see what you've learned of Arabela. I'm anxious for word of her."

He glanced at Donnan. "Leave us."

"Of course, my lord." Donnan bowed then left the solar, closing the door behind him, careful not to look at Rhona.

"I've been worried," his wife continued. "Is she here? What have you learned?" She lifted her chin, a gesture that reminded him of Arabela.

"Nothing!" he shouted, enjoying the tremble that shuddered through her. "We've yet to find a sign of her. I've no doubt this entire affair is *your* fault." He drew closer, watching her reaction even as a dark need swirled through him, stirring his senses. He relished the feeling as it happened so rarely these days.

"How so?" Her bewildered look lit a fire within him. It reminded him of the first time he'd taken her, all confusion and innocence. Damn if that hadn't been enjoyable.

"You obviously didn't know her thoughts," he accused.

Guilt flooded her expression before she could halt it.

Sensing he'd struck a chord, he pressed harder, enjoying the game. "'Twas the eve of her wedding. Did you not speak to her of what was to come? Reassure her that all would be well?"

"I-I had previously."

But he could see from her darting eyes that she hadn't.

"What kind of mother doesn't have a word with her daughter on such a night?" He shifted closer still, his gaze sweeping over Rhona's body, still firm and slim for a woman of her age. He couldn't think of a better way to release the anger inside him.

"I did, I tell you." Fear lit her eyes as she at last realized how aroused he was.

"You're lying. Liars must be punished." He reached for the fastening of his chausses.

"James. Nay, I beg you." She held her hands before her as though to hold him off.

Aye, fight me, he wanted to say. But he bit back the words, hoping that for once she'd be able to read his thoughts and act accordingly.

~

THE NEXT TWO days passed slowly for Arabela. The novelty of being somewhere different wore off as exhaustion set in. The countryside was unfamiliar, but the numbness of her bottom was not. She was sore in places she hadn't realized could hurt.

She admired Chanse and Matthew for their stamina, especially when she knew they'd be traveling faster if it weren't for her and Edith. Though her maidservant made no complaint, the lines of fatigue bracketing her eyes said it all. They needed to rest for a time and have a decent meal.

Chanse had avoided making a campfire the past two evenings to elude discovery. Or mayhap to ensure they didn't encounter another situation like they'd found themselves in previously. She didn't want to repeat that either. Though she liked to think she was better prepared after Chanse's lessons, she didn't know for sure how she'd react.

He'd surprised her several more times by wrapping his arms around her since those lessons. The first time she'd thought he was being affectionate, much to her embarrassment. Only when he'd urged her to break free did she realize his intent. Her face heated at the memory.

Since then, she'd become adept at gaining her freedom and hadn't repeated the mistake of thinking he couldn't keep his hands off her.

Riding with Chanse left her far too much time to think. She was accustomed to being busy with chores and activities to fill her days. Though she tried to keep her senses sharp and watch their surroundings for anything out of the ordinary, she was growing too weary to pay it much notice.

A red squirrel with its tufted ears twitching chattered at their passing, but even the sight of it didn't amuse her for long.

How much farther could they possibly ride? Surely, spending a night at an inn with a real bed wouldn't hold much risk now that they were so far from her home. Assuming they were far from her home. In truth, she didn't know. Thanks to Chanse, she had a general idea of their direction, but without knowledge of what towns or villages were in the area, it did little good.

"Is all well?" Chanse asked from behind her.

She stiffened at the question, realizing her shoulders had slumped in defeat. She straightened deliberately and reminded herself how difficult this journey would've been without his escort. How could she complain when she wondered if she would've simply given up by now if she'd have been by herself?

"Aye." She bit her lip to stop from saying that she was tired. He knew that. No doubt he was as well. Speaking of it would change nothing.

"Matthew says there's a village not far from here. We'll get some supplies."

She nodded as she closed her eyes with relief at the idea of eating something other than the limited fare they had. If there was an inn there, mayhap they'd spend the night. A giddiness filled her at the thought. At this point, she'd be pleased to have something to look at other than the countryside.

"He'll see what he can find for us," Chanse continued.

Arabela's hopes plummeted at his words. She looked over her shoulder at him. "Can't we all go?"

"That carries too much risk."

"What if Matthew goes first to make certain no danger is there?" The idea of waiting in the woods, when real food and a bed were nearby, was too painful to consider.

"Nay."

When they were within sight of the road, Chanse drew the horse to a halt and waited for Matthew and Edith to ride alongside. "I'll keep watch over the women if you want to proceed to the village."

Matthew's gaze swung to Arabela. "I believe there's an inn if memory serves me. If all is well, mayhap we could spend the night."

Arabela couldn't help the hope that spread through her at the thought. But she held her silence. She had no sway over Chanse's opinion. Arguing would serve no purpose. Perhaps he'd listen to Matthew.

"Let us see how your foray goes. Then we'll discuss it."

Matthew nodded. "I'll return as quickly as possible."

Arabela watched him disappear into the trees before emerging onto the road in the valley below. She could only hope he returned with good news. It shouldn't make any difference where she slept, but it did.

They dismounted as they waited. And waited.

Chanse said nothing but Arabela knew he watched the surrounding area closely. As did she. She didn't care to be taken by surprise again.

Chanse tensed as his gaze shifted to the other end of the road where it emerged from the woods.

Arabela looked to see a family walking beside a cart pulled by an ox. A man, woman, and three young children trudged along with two more riding in the cart. Their haggard appearance suggested far too long on the road. Suddenly, the beast pulling the cart stopped, and no urging from the man changed its mind.

Then the reason the ox stopped became apparent. The shifting of the animal caused the cart's wheel to fall off. One of the children in the cart started to cry at the unexpected lurch.

"We should assist them," Arabela said. Even from this distance, she recognized the exhaustion of the family. They looked like she felt. The father stared at the broken wheel for a long moment, hands on hips, as if the idea of repairing it was beyond him.

"They're not far from the village," Chanse said. "Help will come."

"But we haven't seen anyone pass while we've been watching. We could aid them now. Think of those poor children." The crying child tugged at her heart.

Chanse didn't answer but watched the scene unfold with a frown.

The father reassured the crying child who was now in the mother's arms. When the child's cries had calmed to sniffles, he returned his attention to the cart. He lifted the other child out to stand him near the others. Then he unhooked the ox, led it to a nearby tree, and tied it there. He searched the ground, picked up a large rock, and hauled it to the cart, using it to prop up the broken axle. The mother did her best to calm the children, but the one in her arms continued to fuss.

"They need help." Arabela said it as much to herself as to Chanse, but she turned to look at him to see his reaction.

"I'm not leaving you here."

"Good. Edith and I can assist with the children while you help the man." Before he could respond, she strode toward the road that wound through the valley.

"Arabela," he called, but she ignored him. She couldn't stand by watching when someone needed assistance.

He hurried forward to catch her, leading the horse, Edith directly behind him. "Arabela, we can't do this."

She paused to look at him, determined to help despite his words. "Should we use different names to be certain we're not recognized?"

"We shouldn't be going to aid them at all," Chanse protested, though he kept walking. "'Tis too great a risk."

"We won't linger." She continued to lead the way toward the family, pleased Chanse hadn't stopped. "Edith, don't say my name and I won't use yours."

"As you say, milady," Edith said.

"Don't call me that either," Arabela advised. "We must take great care not to reveal our identities."

Edith nodded.

Chanse merely growled his displeasure, but since he continued walking, Arabela considered her mission a success even though they hadn't yet reached the family.

The mother caught sight of them first, her expression wary as though uncertain if they were friend or foe. She still held the youngest in her arms and took the hand of one of the others. The oldest boy stood next to his father beside the broken wheel.

When the mother murmured something, the father quickly rose to face them.

"Looks as if you could use some assistance," Chanse called out.

"If ye've a mind to," the man said with a smile. "Worst luck when we're so close to the village."

"Indeed." Chanse looked at the oldest lad. "Might I request you to hold the reins of my horse?"

The boy's eyes lit with excitement, and he eagerly stepped forward to take the reins. He reached out a tentative hand to rub the steed's nose, delighted when the horse bumped his hand.

"What handsome children you have," Arabela told the mother. "How old are they?" She reached out to trail a finger along the babe's soft cheek.

After a brief conversation, where the mother revealed they'd had little food of late, Edith retrieved the rest of their meager supplies and gave the items to the children.

They ate eagerly, and the food quickly disappeared though there wasn't much of it.

Chanse assisted the man in propping up the cart so the wheel could be reattached to the axle. Chanse didn't seem to let his guard down for even a moment. He continually looked up and down the road to see if anyone approached.

They'd nearly finished when the sound of thundering hooves caught Arabela's notice. Four men riding hard over the rise approached. Her heart echoed the same beat as the horses as a terrible feeling came over her.

She tore her gaze from the terrifying sight to look at Chanse, hoping her fear was mistaken.

But his expression hardened into the warrior she knew him to be, and she realized her instincts were right. They'd just been caught. And she was to blame.

CHAPTER 10

Chanse didn't need to recognize any of the men riding toward them to know from where they came. He knew it in his bones. Though he'd prepared for this moment, the reality of their precarious position made his plans impossible. He never could've guessed they'd be in the middle of a road with a family, including young children. The circumstances narrowed his options considerably.

If he managed to get Arabela and Edith on his horse, he would be left on foot. While his horse was strong and could possibly carry the three of them for a short distance, they'd never be able to outrun the men. If he put Arabela on the horse and bid her to ride, she wouldn't. He knew she'd refuse to leave her maidservant behind. Then what?

Four against one. The odds were not in his favor. And there was the family's presence to consider as well. He wouldn't allow the children to come to harm because of his actions.

When his gaze met Arabela's, he saw panic along with fear. The sight of those emotions tore at him in a way he hadn't expected. Every instinct within him wanted to protect her.

But how?

"Pretend you don't know them even if you recognize them," he told Arabela and Edith. "Act casually and avoid looking directly at them." He glanced at the child Arabela still held. "They won't expect you to be holding a child."

Arabela nodded, but her expression still reflected fear.

Chanse turned toward the man. "Those men mean the lady harm. Act as if she's been traveling with you if they ask any questions."

"Of course," the man agreed, frowning at the approaching men.

Chanse returned to his work on the cart, pretending as though the men riding toward them didn't alarm him in the least. But he kept his hand free, so he might draw his sword if needed to save Arabela.

Out of the corner of his eye, he watched her draw up the hood of her cloak to cover her hair and shield her face. She returned her attention to the child in her arms. Edith bent over the cart as though digging through the supplies inside, hiding her face from view as well. The mother moved closer to Arabela and fussed with the child's clothes.

The men slowed as they approached.

"State your names and your business," one of the men demanded, eyeing Chanse's horse with a frown.

"Who's askin'?" the father replied while Chanse continued to work on the wheel.

"We search on behalf of Lord Graham who seeks his daughter, Lady Arabela."

"Why would you seek her here?" The father glanced about the deserted road as if to make his point.

"Have ye seen her?" the man replied with impatience.

"I don't know any who go by that name."

Chanse respected the man for avoiding an outright lie. If he were found out, things would go much better for him. He had no reason to protect Arabela, other than the fact that she'd been nice to his wife and children.

"Ye there." The rider studied Chanse. "What name do ye go by?"

Chanse glanced over his shoulder, still holding the wheel. "Not Lady Arabela."

Two of the other riders chuckled at his response until their leader turned to glare at them.

Realizing he had little choice as ignoring the question would only make matters worse, Chanse set down the wheel and rose to face them, dusting off his hands. His attire and horse already declared his position. "I'm but a humble knight on my way to Peebles when I came upon this family in need of assistance."

The leader's gaze narrowed. "Ye were at the tournament Lord Graham held two months past."

"Aye, I was."

"Then ye know Lady Arabela."

"I met her." He tried to think of what he might say to keep their attention on him and not on the ladies. "You may remember I won that tournament. I'm in search of another." Already the man's gaze shifted to the women. *Damn and blast.* "I don't remember how you fared in the competition."

That brought the man's attention back to Chanse. He shifted uncomfortably in his saddle even as one of the men behind him grinned knowingly. "I hardly think that matters. I had an injury that held me back."

"I'm sure." Chanse smiled politely, doing his best to keep his actions casual.

"All of ye are with the cart?" he asked.

The child Arabela held started to fuss, and she gently bounced him on her hip to quiet him. If Chanse didn't know her so well, he would've missed how stilted her movements were.

"Perhaps you'd like to lend a hand," Chanse suggested to the men, hoping they'd refuse and ride away.

The leader ignored him and continued to stare at the women. "Let me see yer faces."

Chanse tensed but could do nothing.

The mother moved to stand beside her husband as she shifted her hood and looked at the leader.

Edith turned away from the cart to look at Arabela. No doubt the leader would recognize her. Arabela gave a barely perceptible nod. She and Edith faced the man at the same time though Arabela didn't look up at him but continued to look at the child.

"Lady Arabela." The leader appeared astounded that he'd actually found her. His gaze swung between her and Edith as though unable to believe his eyes. Then he looked at Chanse as though uncertain if he had anything to do with her presence.

"Geoffrey, I have no wish to return to my father," Arabela said. "Be on your way, please." She looked toward the man at last, raising her chin as her hood fell back. Suddenly she appeared a noble lady, one brow raised as if daring him to disobey her command.

"But my lady, everyone searches for ye. Sir Rory is beside himself." Chanse noted he didn't say with worry. No doubt because his primary reaction had been rage. "As is your sire."

"You and I both know why they're displeased with my absence. No one need know you saw me. Ride on and I will tell none that we happened to meet on this road."

Geoffrey's mouth gaped as he tried to determine a response to her request. Then he stiffened and pressed his lips together. "I cannot do that, my lady. My orders are clear. I'm to return you home." Again, he glanced at Chanse as though uncertain what to do with him.

Chanse's stomach clenched. To have come this far and fail was not an option. Yet he could think of nothing he could do that wouldn't cause far too much bloodshed and put the family in danger. His best hope was to make certain they didn't take him as well. That way he'd be able to gain her freedom. Or at least try.

"And if I refuse?" she asked.

The man scowled. "Then I take you by force. Apologies, my lady, but I have my orders."

She handed the child back to his mother. Was she simply going to go with them? While that would be for the best as he didn't want to see her hurt, the idea still stung. The reason was one he preferred not to consider too closely, but damn if he hadn't come to care for her.

Arabela turned back to face Geoffrey, not looking at Chanse. "I ask you again to leave."

"I cannot do so, my lady."

Edith stepped close and wrapped her arm with Arabela's, showing unity with her mistress.

"We're not coming with you," Arabela said.

Chanse's heart thundered even as he was filled with admiration for her pluck.

The leader turned to two of his men and tipped his head toward the women. Both men hesitated before dismounting and walking to Arabela and Edith.

"I'm afraid ye are," Geoffrey said, his gaze sweeping the others near the cart to make certain none intended to put up a fight. "Don't make this harder than it already is."

"Nay." Arabela glared at the men before her, both of whom shifted uncomfortably. Obviously, they were reluctant to place their hands on the women, but she wasn't giving them any choice.

Chanse appreciated her stubbornness, especially when it wasn't directed at him. But the time for such behavior was over, and he hoped she'd give in to their demands before she was hurt.

The men took hold of her and Edith and drew them forward. When Arabela jerked away, one of the men half carried her forward. Her gaze flew to Chanse, and he shook his head the smallest amount. Now was not the time for her to use one of the methods she'd learned to escape. The other man escorted a reluctant Edith to his horse.

"Take care not to cause them harm," Chanse warned. When the leader narrowed his eyes at Chanse, he lifted a shoulder. "I wouldn't want to be the one to tell Lord Graham you injured his daughter."

Geoffrey didn't seem to appreciate his advice but called to his men to be careful all the same.

'Twas all Chanse could do to stand by and simply watch as the two women were placed on the horses and the men mounted behind them.

"I'm assuming ye had nothing to do with the lady's arrival here," Geoffrey said to Chanse. "And I trust ye won't follow us."

"Four against one? I don't care for the odds." Chanse raised a brow. "Unless you'd like me to come along to make certain the women don't escape?"

Geoffrey scowled. "We'll manage without your help."

"Good luck."

Arabela looked at Chanse at last—or rather, glared. Did she believe he would let her go? Then she didn't know him well. The change in the identity of her captor was only temporary.

The group rode back the way they came, the leader sending several glances over his shoulder as if he half expected Chanse to pursue them.

Chanse would follow, but first, he needed to finish getting the wheel on the cart and find Matthew. He had no doubt they'd catch up with Arabela well before nightfall.

～

ARABELA SWALLOWED back her fear as they rode away. Chanse's lack of concern at her departure shocked her. Had he decided she wasn't worth the bother of fighting for? He'd acted as though he didn't care that she was returning home. She thought they'd formed a bond of sorts, but mayhap that had only been one-sided.

His shake of the head suggested he might have a plan, yet how could he with such poor odds?

She shook her head. The true issue was that she would now be forced to face both her father and Rory, neither of whom would be pleased with her. She drew back her sleeve to see the yellow shadows of what had been bruises there. The idea of enduring Rory's anger had her shifting uneasily.

Was this it then? The end of her bid for freedom? She couldn't help but turn to glare at Geoffrey for not listening to her, though she hadn't expected him to do so. Better that she latched onto anger than the hopelessness threatening to overwhelm her.

She eyed the men around her. Could any of them be convinced to aid her? She knew two of their names, but they hadn't been at their holding long enough for her to know if they could be swayed. She tended to keep her distance from the garrison and those who stayed there.

As Chanse had said, the odds were not favorable. Edith's presence was more hindrance than help at the moment, but she had no intention of leaving her behind.

Assuming she could escape.

The more she pondered the idea, the more appealing it became. If she were caught, they wouldn't beat her, only restrain her. Whereas if she returned home, she had no doubt she'd suffer physical harm and her chance to escape again was nil.

The cover of darkness might aid her. But more importantly, she needed to make certain she went in the right direction. That would be a difficult feat in the dark.

She glanced over her shoulder to note the scenery, hoping for some landmark to help guide her. Following the road would only lead to her capture. She'd need to use the terrain to hide as well as track her progress.

Edith frowned when Arabela looked back again, which caught Geoffrey's notice. He looked over his shoulder with a quickness that might've been amusing under other circumstances. Did he fear Chanse would follow?

Tears threatened once more at the thought of him. How had she allowed herself to become attached to the man so quickly? Mayhap this situation was a reminder she couldn't depend on anyone but herself.

The next few hours passed slowly. Geoffrey had a nasty habit of spitting that she found disgusting, especially when she happened to see a few droplets in his beard. She hadn't realized how nice it had been to ride with Chanse until now.

"Can't we rest?" she asked for the third time. The less progress they made toward home, the better, as far as she was concerned. "Edith and I are exhausted."

Geoffrey scowled but acquiesced, and one of the men rode ahead to find a suitable place for them to spend the night a short distance from the road.

Another man started a fire, but none of them made an effort to cook a meal or hunt to provide supper. Instead, they made do with stale bread and cheese. That only made her miss Chanse all the more.

Was she a fool to miss someone she didn't even know if she could trust?

The possibility of seeing him again seemed more unlikely as the night grew long. The sooner she put him out of her thoughts the better.

Only she couldn't. She missed him with an ache that surprised her. Edith was ordered not to approach her but attempted to do so anyway. Each time, one of the soldiers grabbed her arm and pulled her back.

Arabela forced herself to eat a few bites, knowing she'd need strength for the journey to come. Their bags remained with Chanse and Matthew, so Geoffrey had two of the men hand over their blankets on which to lay near the fire.

"I couldn't rest without knowing Edith is close," Arabela protested when Geoffrey requested they lay on opposite sides of the fire.

"Very well. But no talking," he said.

Arabela and Edith rested within an arm's reach of each other. Arabela closed her eyes while her thoughts raced on how to proceed.

The idea of walking back the distance they'd ridden was exhausting. But she avoided those thoughts and focused on how she'd escape. It made little difference that the day's travel had been wasted. What was important was that she achieve her goal of avoiding marriage to Rory.

"Markus, you keep watch first," Geoffrey ordered.

Markus didn't seem pleased with the idea but walked a short distance from camp to find a place to sit. Arabela hoped the spot was overly comfortable and the guard fell asleep.

There were fewer trees in this area and more hills as the road rose from the valley floor. She had a good idea as to which way she needed to go but doing so in the dark would be a challenge. The image of an angry Rory filled her mind, and she used it to give her strength.

She evened her breathing in an effort to pretend sleep, waiting for the sounds of the men to quiet around her. Then she waited longer, wanting to be certain all were truly asleep. Based on the snoring, it sounded as if everyone slept.

She shifted from her side onto her back, opening her eyelids only enough to view those nearby. Once she determined they slept, she turned her head to study Geoffrey, who rested against his saddlebags. The fading glow of the fire revealed that his eyes were closed. He jerked in his sleep then settled into slumber once again. She couldn't see Markus as he was some distance from the fire. She hoped he slept as well.

As quietly as possible, heart thudding dully, she reached over to touch Edith. Her maidservant's eyes fluttered open, then widened with surprise as Arabela held a finger to her lips and gestured for her to rise.

They crept away from the fire and the sleeping men, moving in the opposite direction where Markus watched. With luck, he'd fallen asleep.

Nerves pulled taut as she took one careful step after another, certain a demand to halt would break the quiet, she and Edith eased away from the fire into the dark night.

Arabela slowed as the darkness blinded her, blinking with the hope that her eyes would quickly adjust. She took several more steps, shapes finally becoming clear.

A warm, strong hand grabbed her wrist and pulled her forward. Before she could scream, a hand pressed against her mouth. "Where do you think you're going?"

She knew him even in the dark, even though he only whispered. Emotions swelled up—relief, joy, and something she couldn't name. She launched herself into his arms, holding tight until her world settled.

Chanse hadn't let her go after all.

His arms held her so tight she could hardly breathe. He smelled good and felt so right that she didn't want to release him. The tight band of fear across her chest loosened.

"Christ," he muttered in her ear. "I missed you."

"Mayhap we should be on our way." Matthew's whispered words jolted her back to reality.

She eased back as Chanse dropped his arms, only to take her hand firmly in his as though he wasn't ready to part again either. Her stomach dipped at the thought.

They didn't speak again but hurried over the ridge and down the other side to where the horses waited.

"You made rescuing you much easier," Chanse said as he lifted her onto the horse.

"Once again, I didn't need rescuing," she protested with a smile. "I rescued myself."

"I still prefer to think of you as my captive." He swung onto the horse behind her and reached around her for the reins, once again holding her tight.

Dear heavens. Heat pooled deep within her at his claim. Why did his words sound more like a promise than a threat?

He glanced over his shoulder to make certain Matthew and Edith were ready then prodded his horse into motion, allowing it to pick its way in the dark.

The moon had already started to rise, its delicate light both a blessing and a curse. Not only did it light their way, but it would also light their pursuers' path if they woke and realized she and Edith were gone.

But for the moment, Arabela refused to worry. She was in Chanse's arms once again, and it felt so right.

CHAPTER 11

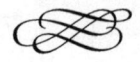

Arabela swore she was going to hurt him. Badly. How she thought she'd missed this bull-headed, stubborn, arrogant man was beyond her.

They'd ridden through the night, through the dawn, until the sun rose high. Still they rode on until exhaustion was all she knew. Their course had wound through the woods, backtracked along hillsides, the pace unrelenting.

Weariness dragged at Arabela as if she were wading through the deep waters of a loch. She asked to halt several times, but Chanse refused, insisting it was too dangerous. They'd only paused long enough to allow the horses to water and eat a small amount of oats.

She understood the pace. Truly. But they'd ridden for so long now. She couldn't bear it another moment.

"Only for a short while?" she asked again. "If I could just stretch my legs."

"Nay," he said, his tone flat as he pushed the horse harder. "The farther we go now, the better chance we have of escape."

She nearly growled in frustration. The man was as unyielding as the blade of the sword he carried.

While she had no desire to be caught again, her body ached from head to toe. She knew Edith must be even more tired than she. But still they continued.

A good portion of the day had passed when she caught the tired look on Edith's face. The poor woman appeared to be barely hanging on.

"I cannot keep this pace," Arabela told Chanse. "Surely we've eluded them enough to rest for a few moments." The hopeful look on Edith's expression when she overheard Arabela's remark made Arabela more determined.

"Let us ride a little farther," Chanse said. "Sleep on the horse."

"Nay." She turned to glare at him, wanting to be certain he heard her refusal. "I insist we halt." Her tired mind searched for an excuse he couldn't ignore. "I have to...relieve myself." She faced forward, heat flooding her cheeks.

"Humph."

Though uncertain what that meant, she couldn't bring herself to look at him after sharing such a personal admission. To her relief, he eased the horse to a halt.

Despite her embarrassment, she couldn't manage to swing her leg over the horse to dismount. Her hips and legs were too stiff with fatigue.

Chanse reached for her, not meeting her eyes. Her heart tugged. Where was the man who'd seemed so pleased to hold her last night? The stern one who'd taken his place made her want to cry.

When she reached the ground, she bit back a groan as needles pierced her legs. He held her a moment to make certain she had her balance before releasing her.

"Don't be overlong."

She tamped down her frustration at his coolness and walked slowly toward Edith. They stepped into the trees to see to their needs.

"Ye must be weary to the bone," Edith said on their way back.

"And you as well. I realize we must hurry, but I confess I can't do this much longer."

"Surely after another day at this pace, we can rest." Edith reached out to squeeze her shoulder. "Try to hold on."

When they returned, Arabela left Edith with Matthew and approached Chanse, prepared to battle on her maidservant's behalf. The older woman wouldn't last much longer at this pace. Edith and Matthew were talking a short distance away, giving Arabela a moment to speak with Chanse in private.

"Would it be possible to find a place to stay the night? An inn, perhaps?" she asked.

The bland look he gave her was answer enough. "Nay. The last time we considered doing so, you insisted upon helping that family and the result was less than desirable."

She shifted uncomfortably at the reminder, well aware she was to blame though it would've been impossible to watch the family's struggle and not offer aid. "I don't regret helping them. You can't tell me you do either."

His scowl suggested otherwise, but she refused to believe it. He was only angry they'd been caught.

"We had a temporary setback. That's all," she argued. "Geoffrey and his men don't seem to be in pursuit. No harm was done."

Chanse scoffed, hands on hips. The pose only made his shoulders look broader and his hips narrower. The sunlight glinted off his hair. He looked perfect while she felt dusty and tired and positively bedraggled from not only the sleepless night but so many days on the road.

"'Twas far more than a setback," he said. His eyes met hers for the first time in a long while, the intensity in their depths surprising her. "I almost lost you."

Her heart dipped at his words, but she couldn't believe he meant what he said in the way she wished.

"That was a reminder to us all to take greater care," he continued. "Or you'll be standing at the altar with Rory, saying your vows."

Her stomach clenched at the thought. She knew he was right and couldn't help the defeated slump of her shoulders. Despite the reminder of why they were riding so hard, she heaved a sigh. "I would've really liked a bath." She said the longing so quietly that she was certain he hadn't heard her.

"You're concerned about washing when we're trying to escape?" His seemed astonished.

She should've known he wouldn't understand. "That is only one of many concerns I have at the present moment." When he only stared at her with disbelief, she felt compelled to continue for both her own and Edith's sake. "I'm tired. I'm hungry. I'm sore." She swallowed against the lump in her throat, trying desperately to hold onto her anger. "Need I share more?"

Chanse glanced at Matthew as though wishing he'd come to his rescue. Matthew gave a small shake of his head and backed away, suddenly busy with his horse. Edith kept her gaze fixed on Matthew's movements. If she weren't so tired, Arabela would've been amused at the pair's determination to stay out of the conversation.

With a sigh, Chanse came forward to take her hands in his. "This evening, we'll camp near a stream or river or some sort of water. You can rinse off at least. We'll make something warm for supper. Matthew has proven himself an excellent hunter. Will that do?"

She appreciated his attempt to appease her. She nodded, receiving a squeeze of her hands in return. Her heart bumped in response.

"For now, we'll have a quick meal and be on our way."

Arabela smothered a groan. Both Chanse and Matthew seemed to have the same unfailing stamina as the horses, and she envied them for it.

"After this evening, you'll feel much improved," Chanse said with a crooked smile, a reminder of his usual charm.

"Surely you jest." Blast him and his ability to enchant her. She'd never admit that she liked it.

"You'll retire this evening after washing with a full stomach beside a warm fire and sleep like a babe."

"We shall see." She released his hands before she gave in to the temptation of stepping into his arms and allowing him to hold her. That would never do. But she much preferred this side of Chanse even if it did make her long for things that couldn't be.

Matthew brought her a piece of dried meat, but she waved away the dried bread he offered. How Chanse thought to make stew with the few supplies they had was beyond her.

"Can you last a while longer, Edith?" Arabela asked when she walked over to where the older woman stood.

"Of course, my lady. But like you, I'll be grateful to wash and sleep somewhere other than on a horse. I hope we're able to do so." She glanced around the area as though expecting pursuers to emerge at any moment.

The idea had Arabela looking about uneasily as well but riding for the remainder of the day was nearly as unappealing.

In far too short of a time, they were back on the horses. Arabela didn't bother to determine what direction they were going. She couldn't bring herself to care. She dozed as the afternoon wore on, waking to find Chanse's arms around her.

Though she righted herself, aware of how difficult it must be for him to hold her on horseback, he nudged her back against him. "Rest if you can," he whispered. "I've got you."

The words comforted her, and she dozed again.

When she next woke, they were riding through a meadow surrounded by trees. The sun had set, but dusk lingered in the sky. The area was beautiful even to her tired eyes.

"We'll stay here this evening." Chanse brought the horse to a halt at the edge of the trees.

The gurgle of a nearby stream greeted her, making her smile.

"I promised water, did I not?" Chanse asked.

"You did."

Chanse dismounted then helped her down, while Matthew aided Edith. Arabela and the maidservant gathered wood, which gave them a chance to ease the aches and pains as they moved about.

Chanse tended the horses, and Matthew left to hunt for something for supper. The idea of a warm meal made Arabela's stomach growl. After starting the fire, Chanse pulled the spit from his saddlebags along with the pot and bowls.

Determined to do her part, Arabela studied the small clearing as they gathered more wood, searching for roots or anything that could be added to the pot.

"Are those apples?" she asked Edith as she stared in disbelief at several trees a short distance away.

"I believe they are." The maid's eyes lit with delight. "We'll have something sweet to add to our meal."

They returned the wood to the fire and advised Chanse of their find. He walked to the trees with Arabela while Edith rinsed out the bowls in the stream.

"What a lucky find," Chanse declared as he plucked several apples from a tree.

Arabela took one and polished it on her kirtle before taking a bite. The sweet tartness of the juicy apple tasted like heaven. "Delicious," she said around another bite. Without thinking, she offered it to him.

He took a bite, his gaze holding hers with a heat that stirred her senses. "Excellent."

They picked nearly a dozen to have a supply for the days ahead. Arabela knew they wouldn't taste as good as they did at this moment. The carefree time, however brief, eased the tension she'd felt since things had gone so wrong the previous day.

"Now then," Chanse said with a look at her, "let us see what we can do about washing."

She nodded even as her cheeks heated. She'd never bathed anywhere but the privacy of her chamber. As dusty as she felt, she was prepared to set aside her modesty in return for feeling clean.

They left the apples near the fire, and Chanse paused to add more wood. Then they walked to the stream a short distance away, meeting Edith as she returned to the fire.

"I'll gather our things and return," Edith told Arabela.

When they drew close, Chanse tested the water. He lifted a brow. "'Tis cold," he warned her.

"I don't care. As long as 'tis wet."

Chanse chuckled. "No worries on that. Let us find a place where the water is deep enough to make it easier."

They walked a short distance along the gurgling stream, the idea of washing growing more appealing to Arabela by the moment.

"This might have to do," Chanse advised as he eyed a bend in the stream that created a shallow pool. "What do you think?"

Though it didn't appear to be deeper than mid-thigh, Arabela thought it would work, especially considering how cold the water was. She didn't need to immerse her entire body to wash. "This will suffice."

She might want to take a true bath and sleep in a bed, but she wasn't ready to risk being caught to do so.

Chanse walked a wide circle around the area, even crossing the stream on a fallen log to make certain the area was safe. Satisfied, he returned to her side. "I'll keep watch between here and the fire. You need only call out if you have need of me."

At her nod, he walked back toward the fire.

The idea of him nearby helped ease her nerves. Edith returned with a small bit of soap and a bone comb. She helped Arabela loosen her plaited hair and remove her kirtle and chemise.

Arabela stepped into the water, the cold stealing her breath. She made quick use of the water and the soap. She washed her hair as best she could as well. The water wasn't so bad after she grew used to it. Feeling clean again after a sennight of traveling was marvelous.

Edith shook their kirtles to remove some of the dust from the road. Then she washed as well while Arabela donned a clean chemise and kirtle. Edith did the same, and the two women returned to the camp, feeling refreshed.

Chanse stood in the trees, waiting for them.

"Go ahead and warm by the fire," Arabela told Edith. She wanted a moment to speak with Chanse.

Chanse's gaze swept over her, taking in her damp hair, eyes darkening at the sight. "Feel better?"

"So much better. Thank you for making this happen."

"'Tis the least I could do for pushing you so hard." He reached out to trail a finger briefly along her cheek. "I'm sorry. I wanted to put enough distance between Geoffrey and us that I could be assured they wouldn't catch us."

She still didn't understand the change in his behavior, but for now, his gentleness was enough. "Washing felt wonderful."

"I believe I'll do the same."

"'Tis cold but worth it," she said with a smile. "You might want this." She handed him the piece of soap she carried.

He took it with a smile. "I'll meet you by the fire shortly."

She nodded, the idea of him washing in the stream bringing to mind inappropriate images of what those broad shoulders might look like without the tunic covering them. She walked slowly toward the fire, enjoying a moment alone.

The evening was a fine one, especially when she felt refreshed and knew a meal awaited her. The smell of roasting meat taunted her senses.

Arabela couldn't help a smile at the sight of four rabbits roasting on the spit over the fire, thanks to Matthew's efforts. "Meat and apples. We will truly feast this evening," she told Matthew.

"The rabbits are plentiful here."

She settled near Edith next to the fire. Within a short while, Chanse returned, his hair wet, framing his freshly scrubbed face.

Arabela's heart did a little flip at the sight.

Matthew went to the stream to wash as well while Chanse added some dried vegetables to the pot of steaming water. "We had a few dried vegetables left. We'll use them to make soup to go with the rabbit."

"It already smells heavenly." The warm look he gave her curled her toes.

"I try to deliver on my promises."

Should she worry that his words brought something completely different to mind? Chanse was changing her ideas of what her future might look like. She could no longer imagine it without him in it.

CHANSE TORE his gaze from Arabela for the twentieth time as they ate. Something about her damp hair and the thought of her freshly washed curves roused his senses in a way that was becoming familiar.

He didn't know if he preferred the anger that had filled him at the near miss from their encounter with Geoffrey the previous day or this awareness that refused to release him. He'd been so relieved to have her back in his arms, but then the realization of how close he'd come to losing her had sunk in, making it impossible to look at her without fury at the situation filling him.

But all that had fallen away when she'd said how much she wanted a bath. The idea of her naked form had swept away his frustration, leaving only desire in its place.

Now as he watched, her loose braid fell over her shoulder, the dark strands shining in the firelight. Her cheeks glowed with good health, much different than the paleness that had filled them earlier.

He hated to push her so hard but doing so was for her safety as much as to reach his goal of reaching Berwick and Braden. Would this evening provide enough rest to allow her to continue at this pace?

The realization that her father's men had caught them bothered him more than he cared to admit. Failure was never an option, but especially not with this mission. Far more lives were at stake than his own and Arabela's. He needed to keep that uppermost in his mind.

But how could he do so when all he truly wanted was to draw her into his arms? He wanted to hold her, kiss her, reassure her that all would be well. Yet he refused to make such a promise when he wasn't certain he could keep it. The only thing he knew without a doubt was that he would do all in his power to make certain Rory never had her.

They finished their meal and Matthew took the bowls and pots to the stream to rinse, refusing to allow Edith to help. The maidservant's exhaustion was obvious. With Arabela's assistance, they spread the blankets near the fire to prepare for the night.

"Rest, Edith," Arabela insisted, a gentle hand on her shoulder.

The maidservant didn't argue. She lay down and was soon asleep.

"I'm going to walk a bit before I turn in," Chanse advised Arabela once Matthew returned, not trusting himself to be alone with her.

"I'll accompany you."

He nearly groaned but couldn't bring himself to argue. Not when the memory of her absence was still so fresh in his mind. He didn't care to relive those hours while she'd been gone when his thoughts had been filled with the fear that he wouldn't be able to free her.

With a stern reprimand to keep his hands to himself, he moved toward the edge of the trees with her at his side. They'd taken no more than a few steps when he felt the warmth of her hand on his arm.

"Thank you." They were still in sight of the fire. She looked up at him, one side of her face lit by the soft glow of the flames while the other remained in shadow.

"For what?" He fisted his hand so he wouldn't give in to the temptation to touch her soft skin.

"For this evening. The bath, cold as it was, the meal, the fire, time to rest. 'Twas just what I needed."

"I realize this journey has been difficult, but we don't dare let down our guard for even a moment with so many searching for us."

"Which makes this evening all the more precious." She lifted up and kissed his cheek, leaving him momentarily speechless, his heart thundering. "You have my gratitude."

He clenched his teeth to keep from saying that wasn't what he wanted, to keep from pulling her into his arms. But what he longed for was impossible. Nothing good would come from sharing his wishes. He didn't know if that time would ever come. His mission was far more important than his own desires.

But still, his breath caught at the thought of how much he needed Arabela. His brief time away from her had proven that.

"You're welcome," he managed at last. Then he turned and offered his arm, and they continued to walk along the edge of camp, the silence companionable.

He did his best to pay attention for any unusual sounds and was somewhat reassured when they heard nothing. Matthew was adding a few more pieces of wood to the fire when they returned, and his questioning gaze swept over them. No doubt his friend wondered what he was doing. That made two of them.

As Arabela sought her blanket, Chanse moved to where Matthew stood.

"Is all well?" his friend asked, a brow raised.

"Aye. I'll take the first watch." Heaven knew he wouldn't be able to sleep until his thoughts—and his body—settled. His emotions were another beast entirely, and he was no longer certain he could deny them when it came to Arabela.

CHAPTER 12

The next two days slowly passed as they made their way in the general direction of Berwick. The journey began to wear even on Chanse. While he'd traveled farther distances, it hadn't been with the worry of pursuit constantly hanging over him, causing him to look over his shoulder time and again.

They'd backtracked on more than one occasion, returning to hide the horses' prints in the dirt in several places, and rode in circles three times to throw off anyone who tracked them. But Chanse was no longer certain their efforts would be enough.

Normally, he might've made this into a game of sorts. He and his brother, Braden, would've wagered on their success or who chose the path they took. Damn if he didn't miss Braden at the moment. His steadiness was something Chanse depended on more than he'd realized. While Chanse was pleased to have Matthew at his side, it wasn't the same as having his older brother there.

In truth, what troubled him more than anything else was Arabela's presence. He might've been able to ignore her if she rode on another horse. But having her in the circle of his arms, day after day, where he felt her warmth, caught the sweet scent of her hair and spoke with her for many hours of the day caused him to feel emotions he'd never imagined. 'Twas unsettling to say the least. Yet he couldn't bear the idea of her riding with Matthew. What was going to happen when the time came for them to part ways?

She was much different than the spoiled, sullen woman he'd thought when he first met her. Her understanding of the challenges facing her country and how they might be solved showed a quick intelligence he wouldn't have guessed she possessed. To his surprise, they agreed on many issues. While she also wanted a Scottish king on the throne, as did her father, she had no illusions as to the trouble Rory would cause in the position.

"Rory stated the first step to resolving Scotland's issues with England is to gather every Englishman in the country and send them back across the border," she told Chanse with no small amount of disgust edging her tone. "How would that settle anything? The two countries are neighbors and forever will be. Differences need to be worked through, not ignored."

Chanse appreciated her opinion but refrained from telling her that he and Braden were two of those Englishmen. Though the information was on the tip of his tongue, he held back. He was coming to trust her, but if Rory or her father caught her and forced to speak of her ordeal, the less she knew the better. Too many times, he'd thought someone trustworthy only to be proven wrong when they used him to get to Braden. So he kept quiet.

As the day progressed, he couldn't shake off the idea that they were being closely followed. He didn't know what caused the sensation, but it lodged like a knot in the pit of his stomach. Mayhap he had a bit of his cousin's second sight. Whatever caused the feeling, he couldn't ignore it. When they stopped for a brief break at midday, he pulled Matthew aside.

"I'm going to retrace our steps to see if someone is in pursuit," he told the other knight.

Matthew studied him but didn't question his intent. Did that mean he felt it too?

"I want to see if I can catch sight of anyone," Chanse continued.

"Knowing how close and how many there are will help us decide how best to proceed."

"I'd be pleased to take a look," Matthew offered.

Spending time away from Arabela, however briefly, would be wise, Chanse decided. Mayhap it would help him remember that being in her company was only temporary. Coming to care for her more than he already did would be unwise. Now was not the time for emotions. Logic needed to rule his thoughts and actions.

"I'll go," Chanse said. "We should be within a hard day's ride from Berwick. But no purpose would be served in allowing any pursuers to follow us there."

"I agree."

Chanse took one of the last few pieces of the dried meat from Matthew. "I'll catch up with you as quickly as I can. Well before nightfall I'd expect, if not earlier."

"And if you don't?" Matthew asked.

"Ride to St. Mary's, the convent outside of Berwick. The prioress knows us both. I have no doubt she'll aid us." Prioress Matilda had sheltered them more times than Chanse could count, especially after she realized how hard he, Braden, and their cousin, Garrick, were trying to keep England from invading Scotland once again. And now Matthew as well.

Matthew nodded but still looked concerned.

"Do not worry," Chanse told him, forcing his customary grin. "I'll return before you have a chance to miss me."

Matthew shook his head but smiled all the same. "I have no intention of missing you."

"Where are you going?" The alarm in Arabela's voice had Chanse turning swiftly to find her directly behind him.

Did he tell her the truth? Or would that worry her unnecessarily? He decided on a partial lie, a method with which he was becoming far too familiar. "I'm going to do a little scouting but will return soon."

"Why?" Her eyes narrowed with suspicion.

"To find the best path to take to our destination."

"You mean Berwick?"

He scowled, realizing she could only be guessing but regretting his lessons on how to tell directions all the same. "I'll see you soon."

He mounted his horse, not looking back as he rode away. His focus needed to be on the mission, not on whether her feelings were hurt by his behavior. Yet he couldn't forget the look she'd given him that suggested she wanted more than he could give. He was no hero, only her temporary captor.

Taking a different path over the terrain than they'd previously ridden, he wound his way over two ridges, keeping a careful watch and pausing several times to listen. When his horse's ears perked up, Chanse reined back, not far from where he'd left Matthew.

Chanse waited, listening for riders. Several long moments passed before he caught the sound of the hooves followed by the creak of saddles.

Five men rode over the ridge moving slowly as the one in the lead watched the ground. The man gave a muffled call, which brought the group to a halt. As Chanse watched from his hidden spot, the man slid off his horse to more closely examine the ground.

That was the place where Matthew had brushed a branch over their tracks as the bare ground made it far too easy to track them. 'Twas good to know their efforts paid off in at least slowing the pursuers.

However, those men held the advantage of carrying one rider per horse. This wasn't the same group Geoffrey had led, making Chanse wonder how many men pursued Arabela. Their odds were worsening.

He'd known this mission wouldn't be easy, but he cursed himself for not considering the details more carefully. Graham would pursue his daughter with every resource he could gather, for all his plans were doomed to fail without her.

These riders were closing in on them, slowly but surely. Chanse hated the doubt spiraling through him at the odds of successfully leading his group to any sort of safe haven before the men caught up with them.

He eased back until he was out of sight then galloped in the direction he'd left Matthew and the women.

With a curse, Chanse pulled on the reins and made a few twists and turns, hoping to make pursuit more difficult. He wanted to believe it would be enough to allow them time to reach Berwick but was no longer sure.

It didn't take long before he caught up with his companions. Matthew walked alongside his horse at a brisk pace, allowing the women to ride.

Matthew immediately grasped what Chanse's quick return meant. "How many?" he asked after he'd handed Arabela the reins and stepped over to Chanse.

"Five." Chanse kept his voice down but knew he'd have to tell Arabela of the situation. "Close."

"Damn." Matthew strode back to his horse and assisted Arabela to dismount.

"What's wrong?" she asked as she hurried over to Chanse. He offered his hand, and she took it, gracefully mounting before him with his assistance.

Once she was settled, he urged his horse forward. "A group of pursuers is gaining ground on us."

"Is it Geoffrey?"

He shook his head. "None I recognize."

"Rory?" He couldn't mistake the worry in her voice. Her fear of the knight along with the memory of the bruises on her wrist angered Chanse.

"I don't know what he looks like." There had been one man dressed more finely than the others. Could that have been Rory? In truth, who they were mattered little to Chanse at the moment. His goal remained the same—evade them.

"What do you intend we do?" she asked.

"Hope we can escape them until we find a shelter that offers some protection."

She glanced back at him with a frown, but her fear was visible just below the surface. "Do you have a place in mind?"

"Depends."

With a mutter, she made her displeasure with him clear. "If you'd tell me, I might be of some assistance. I can at least help look for whatever it is we seek."

"I'll advise if you can be of help." This time, his reason for not telling her more was because he didn't know. It truly depended on how soon the five men reached them.

He pressed his horse faster, glancing back to make certain Matthew and Edith followed. No time could be wasted with those men gaining ground. Nor would he push his horse to the breaking point. The steed had served him well despite the challenge of carrying two riders most of this long journey.

Chanse studied their surroundings as they rode, hoping for a place to hide, yet fearful of being forced to hand over Arabela if they were discovered. The thought had him riding even harder. His instincts suggested they make for Berwick, but was he right? Or was his desire to gain Braden's assistance overriding his logic?

Then the answer came to him.

He drew back the reins to allow Matthew to ride alongside them. "We're going to have to split up."

"Nay," Arabela protested.

"If we want to keep you safe, we have little choice," Chanse argued. "We must do it before they catch sight of us." That much he knew for certain.

"What?" Arabela sounded horrified, whether it was at his statement or at the idea of being caught, he wasn't certain.

"We cannot outrun them, and they're gaining on us." He reached forward to place his hand under her chin so that she would look at him fully. "There's a chance they're going to catch us."

Her eyes went wide with panic even as Edith gasped.

"If they do, they're going to take you, and there will be little I can do to halt them. Rory will want to marry you as quickly as possible before something happens to you again. You are the key."

"The key?" She blinked back tears as her wild-eyed gaze held his.

"Aye." He swallowed, realizing she was quickly becoming his key as well. He shoved aside the thought. Now was not the time for emotions. Why couldn't he set them aside? "None of their plans will succeed without you. Rory needs to marry you no matter the cost."

Her breath hitched as she faced forward again. He felt the tremble of her body against his and wished like hell he could reassure her. "What do you want me to do?"

"I want you to fully understand what's at stake."

She glanced briefly at him, her tears gone. "I do. My life."

"Do we have a plan?" Matthew asked before Chanse could respond.

"Edith, raise your hood to hide your hair," Chanse said. "Arabela, do the same. With luck, they won't know which horse to follow. Matthew, ride south. Make a wide circle. If no one follows you, meet me at the convent."

"The convent at Berwick?" Arabela asked.

Chanse didn't answer. Now was not the time.

"See you soon." Matthew spoke the words like a vow, his gaze meeting Chanse's. It reassured Chanse. Slightly.

He wheeled away as Chanse did the same. A ridge soon hid Matthew and Edith from view.

Chanse found a path through the woods but rode off to the side of it—anything he could do to prevent their pursuers from easily tracking them.

"Are you certain this is the best course of action?" Arabela asked.

"Do you have a better idea?"

The hair on the back of his neck stood upright. *Damn.* He knew all too well what that meant. As though sensing the nearness of their pursuers, the horse galloped even faster when the terrain allowed it.

Chanse directed the steed deeper into the woods, hoping the cover of the trees would aid them. The horse leapt forward even as Chanse heard the thunder of hooves behind them.

"Hold tight," he told Arabela.

The landscape roughened, filled with rocks and shrubs, slowing their progress. Chanse eased the horse down the hill then turned, allowing his steed to pick the best path. Shouts came from above them. No doubt the men were studying the tracks, determining which set to follow.

Chanse didn't bother to try to watch them through the trees. Nothing mattered except continuing forward. They reached a clearing, but he kept to the cover of the trees. His horse lurched. He leaned over to see if it limped, rubbing the top of its leg in encouragement. An injured horse would quickly end this chase.

A thwack struck the tree nearby. He jerked in surprise. Were they so desperate to catch them that they'd risk hurting Arabela?

Another arrow flashed past. Arabela's scream rent the air, curdling his blood. He straightened, only to find Arabela bent forward, an arrow protruding from her shoulder.

His heart stopped at the sight.

CHAPTER 13

Arabela felt as if someone had struck her shoulder with a hammer. Pain rippled across her back. A glance over her shoulder revealed the shaft of an arrow.

Sticking into her.

She couldn't catch her breath. Disbelief slowed her thoughts. She reached back with one hand to remove it, desperate to halt the crippling pain.

"Arabela. Nay." Chanse took her hand and gently lowered it. "We must wait until we can remove it properly." His stiff tone surprised her.

But she didn't answer. Words weren't possible. Not when she couldn't draw a breath. The jarring motion of the horse as they galloped reverberated through her.

Another thwack sounded to her right, the sound terribly familiar, especially now that she knew what it meant.

"Stay low," Chanse urged as he bent forward with her.

Her body complied, her mind blank. The hand of her injured shoulder released the pommel, and she couldn't get it to grasp it again. An odd numbness spread across her shoulder, allowing her to breathe.

"You will be well," Chanse said, his voice commanding, a balm over her panic and fear. "Do you hear me? You are going to be well. Just hold tight."

It sounded like an order.

Her mind gripped his words, and her body did as he demanded. With one hand holding the pommel, she stayed low and used her legs to help keep her seat. The idea of falling off the horse with the arrow stuck in her back was horrifying.

Chanse guided the horse along the edge of a steep ravine where the shrubs were thick. "Damn," he muttered. "I have an idea, but I can't say that I like it."

"What?" she asked, the effort to speak allowing the pain to seep back.

"We can't outrun them. Not with two of us. I'm going to leave you in the ravine."

His words sent fear spiraling through her. The thought of being left alone to face the men who chased them caused her body to go rigid. How could she defend herself when she could hardly breathe?

"The brush is thick here. Our pursuers will follow me. Once I lose them, I'll come back for you."

"What if you don't?" Tears choked her at the thought.

"I will. Trust me." He drew the horse to a halt, then lifted her leg over the horse so she sat sideways, facing the ravine. He kissed her hard. "This is going to hurt."

Before she knew what was happening, he'd taken hold of her good hand and eased her off the horse, sliding her down its side and into the ravine.

She gritted her teeth with the pain the movement caused. Her feet didn't reach the ground. Panic filled her when she realized Chanse was going to have to drop her.

"Hide," he ordered as he released her.

She slid a short distance into the ravine, landing on her feet. The bank was half again as tall as she and thick with shrubbery. The brush caught on the arrow, and she whimpered in response. Her vision narrowed, darkening as she nearly passed out from a wave of pain. She blinked to regain her senses, Chanse's order ringing through her mind. *Hide.*

She knelt in that very spot, staying low and hoping the brush hid her. She looked up to see if Chanse approved.

But he was already gone.

And she was alone.

The realization brought forth a sob and tears filled her eyes. She pressed her good hand over her mouth to keep her cries back. The arrow hurt more than anything she'd endured before, but the larger threat at this moment was being captured.

Shouts filled the air above her followed by the snorts of horses and the pounding of hooves as the riders advanced. Was Rory among them? The thought made her want to cry more. Instead, she clenched her teeth and hugged the bank, making herself as small as possible. With a shaking hand, she drew the hood of her dark cloak over her hair and held still as the men drew closer.

And closer.

Until they were directly above her.

Bile rose in the back of her throat. She swallowed hard. Using her good hand, she gripped the root of a plant growing out of the bank to help keep her position, praying the thick brush in the ravine hid her.

"Where did they go?"

"Find them!"

Oh! The men were directly above her. She held her breath, but the idea of the arrow clearly visible protruding from her added to her fear. Surely she'd be discovered at any moment.

As much as she wanted them to ride on, she wanted Chanse to have time to gain some ground. Now that his horse carried only one rider, he had a better chance of escape.

Tears ran down her face as she pressed her cheek into the damp earth of the bank and held tight to the root, hoping it wouldn't give way. Her breath came in tiny gasps, the shallow breaths less painful.

She said a silent prayer that the men would leave her and Chanse would escape. Asking for both outcomes seemed an impossible request. How could both come true?

The men rode back and forth along the ravine's edge as though searching for tracks.

"What is that?" one asked.

An image of her footprint on the edge of the bank popped into her mind. Had she left a sign of her hiding spot? Nay, she reassured herself. Chanse had dropped her down here.

She whispered a prayer that they hadn't spotted the arrow.

Based on the sound of the voices above her, their words muffled, the men had spread out as they searched the area for evidence of their passing.

A shout from some distance away caught her notice.

Then another. "Over there!"

The noises above her faded, but still, she held her place, unwilling to risk revealing her position.

"Blast." A muttered curse from nearby reached her ears.

Her body trembled at the sound. It seemed as if one man had remained behind to continue the search. If she'd moved...

Arabela closed her eyes, unable to complete the thought.

She held her breath until at last the shouts, the jingle of the reins, and the thud of hooves faded.

Silence.

She drew a slow, shuddering, painful breath. Then another. At last, the normal chirps and scuffles of the woods filled the air. But she continued to hold in place, too frightened to risk moving.

As fear slowly receded, pain took its place. Each breath she drew hurt. Yet what could she do? The idea of reaching back to try to pull out the arrow crossed her mind, but she quickly dismissed it. She doubted she could reach it, and she knew how much it would hurt. Additional pain was something she couldn't consider at the moment.

If Chanse were caught—

Nay, she couldn't think like that. Mayhap the delay of the riders searching above her had allowed him to make good his escape so he could return for her.

And what of Matthew and Edith? Were they well?

Her fingers gripping the root felt numb. She tried to release her hold but couldn't. Her fingers refused to cooperate. Part of her illogically insisted that releasing her grip would somehow announce her presence to the pursuers.

So she held on.

Her tears dried, but her body began to shudder. The shivers only caused more pain, yet she was helpless to stop them. All she could do was focus on drawing one breath at a time, her senses still on high alert for sounds of those in pursuit returning.

She had no idea how much time passed as she sat there, cold seeping into her body from both the damp earth and the events that had transpired. The sun wasn't visible from the ravine, but the fading light suggested darkness wasn't far behind.

Despite the pain, a heaviness came over her limbs and weighted her lids. She leaned against the bank and closed her eyes, her thoughts on Chanse with the wish that he was somewhere safe. He'd promised to return for her, and deep inside, the knowledge that she trusted him to keep his word gave her hope.

∼

CHANSE COULD WAIT NO LONGER. He'd already left Arabela far longer than he intended—several hours had passed—but it had taken time to lose the men following him.

Dropping her into the ravine, injured and frightened, had been one of the hardest things he'd ever done. He'd gone over his options again and again since that moment but still feared he'd chosen wrong.

He couldn't outride the men with two people on his horse. While he hoped to confuse them by splitting off from Matthew, he hadn't wanted them to follow Matthew and Edith either. His friend was in no better position to protect the maidservant than he had been to protect Arabela. But from what he could tell, the men had split into two groups and followed both of them.

Chanse had used the terrain as best he could to lose them, hiding in the tall, thick brush along a riverbank at one point as they passed within a stone's throw. Though tempted to draw his sword and kill each and every one of them for the harm they'd caused Arabela, he'd restrained himself. He couldn't take the risk of something happening to prevent his return to her.

The arrow that had struck her had been meant for him. If he hadn't bent over at that moment, it would've hit him. They would've more than likely been caught. But that didn't mean he liked the turn of events that had occurred.

Now with dusk approaching, he rode back to the area he'd left her, praying she hadn't given up on him and started out on her own. The thought of her injured and trying to find her way in the unfamiliar landscape chilled his blood.

The arrow had struck Arabela high, he told himself. It hadn't hit her lungs or heart. Only muscle and bone. He'd seen enough injuries on the battlefield to be fairly certain. As long as she didn't pull it out, bleeding would be minimal. He needed to determine if the arrowhead had lodged in the bone. If it had, removing it would be more difficult. Leaving it in held risk as each time she shifted, it might move the head and cause more damage. He wished Braden were with him to make certain of her recovery.

At one point, he'd considered riding for Berwick to get his brother. But that would take too long. There was always the risk the men would circle back and somehow manage to find Arabela. Or that she'd try to find help on her own.

His steed had to be tired despite resting a few times while they'd hidden. Chanse had pushed him harder than he'd wanted. But now the horse seemed to sense Chanse's urgency and kept a steady pace back toward the ravine.

The dimming light changed the appearance of the terrain, and Chanse hesitated several times before finding the area where he'd left her. Then he began to search in earnest. The ravine ran the length of the hillside, deeper in some places than others.

"Arabela?" he called softly.

A KNIGHT'S CAPTIVE

Nothing but silence and the hoot of an owl greeted him.

"Arabela?" Still nothing.

Panic filled him as he called several more times with no answer. Surely, this was the right place. He slid from his horse to have a better look, noting the numerous hoofprints back and forth along the edge. The men had searched here for some time. Arabela must've been frightened out of her wits.

Dear God. Despite his efforts, had they somehow found her?

Heart hammering, he looked harder. Though tempted to bellow her name, he held back. He didn't know where their pursuers were. Nor did he want them to return. Not until he'd found Arabela.

"Arabela," he called again, this time a little louder, desperation filling him.

An odd sound broke the stillness, one he didn't recognize. Could it have been her?

"Arabela," he said. "'Tis Chanse." He found the place he was certain he'd left her and leaned over the edge of the ravine, the fading light hiding shapes, tricking his senses, causing doubt to bloom.

There! A movement.

"Arabela?"

The answer was part gasp, part whimper. But 'twas all the answer he needed.

He released the reins of his horse, certain it wouldn't wander. Then he scrambled down the steep bank, anxious to reach her.

"Chanse?" Though no more than a whisper, he heard her as clear as day. The sound of his name on her lips pierced the doubt, allowing him to breathe.

"Here." He eased forward, relieved at how well hidden she was. She would've been difficult to find even in the light of day. He reached for her, but she didn't move.

"I-I can't seem to r-rise," she said. She sat on the ground, tucked tight against the bank, the blasted arrow visible even in the dim light.

"I've got you." He knelt beside her, emotions welling up inside him as he took her outstretched hand in his, dismayed at how cold it was.

"I didn't think you were coming back." The hopelessness in her voice destroyed him, making his eyes sting.

"My apologies for taking so long. I didn't mean to frighten you. Those men were persistent." He drew her hand against his chest to warm it, moving slowly to make certain he didn't cause her pain. What he wanted more than anything was to take her in his arms and never let go, but that would have to wait. "How badly does it hurt?"

"Hurts. Thirsty," was all she managed.

"Let us get you out of here. I have water." He took hold of her waist and helped her to rise.

She groaned at the movement.

He could only imagine how much more it was going to hurt to lift her out of the ravine. Doing his best to keep the worry out of his voice, he asked, "Can you take a few steps? 'Tisn't as steep over there."

"Aye."

He was almost glad he couldn't see her face. He feared the pain it revealed would break him. That wouldn't do either of them any good. After giving her a moment to adjust to standing, he squeezed her waist reassuringly. "Here we go." He eased her forward, his hold gentle.

Her steps were halting, but she followed his lead.

"I'm going to lift you to sit on the edge of the bank."

She nodded even as she cried softly. Were her tears from relief or pain?

Bracing himself, he grasped her hips and lifted her, taking care to avoid anything hitting the arrow. She sat, one hand holding onto his arm.

"Stay right there," he ordered as he released her to vault up beside her. The light was better here, and he could see her tear-streaked face. The sight of the arrow made his stomach clench. He cupped her cheek. "So brave. I'll get you the water."

He retrieved the flask from his saddlebag and knelt to hold it to her lips.

She drank greedily.

"I'm going to break off the arrow, then take you somewhere safe and see to your injury." Trying to do anything more here in the dark with the threat of the men returning was too dangerous.

She nodded. "Chanse?"

He met her gaze. The feel of her trembling hand along his cheek nearly made him lose his resolve.

"I'm so pleased you're here."

His heart thudded dully at her simple words. He placed his hand over hers and moved it to his lips. He kissed the palm of her hand, emotions swirling, making words difficult. "I am too. We'll make it through this. Together."

A hint of a smile curved her lips. But he knew she wouldn't be smiling for long.

He rose to a kneeling position and pressed her hand to his waist. "Hold tight to me." Wanting this moment over, he took hold of the arrow with both hands and snapped it in two.

"Oh!" Her body stiffened even as he lowered to sit beside her, drawing her in his arms.

"All done." *For now.* He didn't mention the pain would be worse when he pulled the arrow. But he needed better light to do so along with something to wrap over her wound to stop the bleeding. It would have to wait until they found shelter.

She leaned against him, her face tucked against his neck, taking a shuddering breath. After a few moments, to his surprise, she eased back. "Let us go before they decide to return."

"Excellent notion." Urgency filled him as he lifted her in his arms and onto the horse. She hissed with pain but said nothing as he returned the flask to the saddlebag and leapt up behind her.

Careful of the broken arrow, he reached around her to settle her into his arms, pulling her cloak over her. Never had she felt as good before him as she did at this moment.

"Here we go," he said softly. "You've done well, Arabela." He eased the horse forward, trying to think of where best to take her. Would he be able to remove the arrow? Should he risk somehow getting word to Braden? Where could they go that their pursuers wouldn't find them?

Nothing held his thoughts more than the woman in the circle of his arms. He eased her good shoulder back, so she leaned on his chest. "Sleep if you can. I've got you now, and I'm not letting go."

Her shuddering sigh tugged at him. She'd endured far more than most had. Now 'twas up to him to help her recover.

But where?

CHAPTER 14

Chanse rode through the night with Arabela in his arms, a bright moon lighting the way. Though tempted to venture to Berwick or the convent, the closer he drew, the more convinced he became both would be watched. No other towns were nearby, narrowing his choices.

If *he* knew that, their pursuers would as well.

Then where? He'd already pushed Arabela more than he'd intended. She stirred restlessly in his arms. The pain would keep her from truly sleeping. If he stopped to try to take out the arrow, he risked the possibility of the shaft coming free, leaving the arrowhead behind. The heads were often attached to the shaft with sinew or tendon that could loosen and stretch when damp. That would mean he needed something with which to dig out the head. He needed to remove the whole damned arrow, head and all, as quickly as possible, let her rest, then find some food.

And hope she healed.

But where?

The answer came to him as dawn cast a hint of rosy light along the horizon, making the fading star-filled sky look endless. He'd followed the river for a time, but now that daylight threatened, he took to the trees as he rode toward his destination.

Berwick called to him since 'twas close and familiar and Braden was there, but he knew this was a better option. The men who chased them could very well have taken shelter at the convent, regardless of whether the prioress wanted them to. Riding there could prove to be a fatal mistake, and he refused to risk it. He hoped Matthew came to that conclusion as well and remained hidden. His friend had spent the last few weeks in the area and knew it well.

Chanse stopped his horse at the edge of the clearing and studied the small cottage nestled on the opposite side. It looked much as it had last spring when he and Braden had brought their cousin, Garrick, here. Smoke curled out of the hole in the thatched roof. Hilda must be home.

Relief filled him. He glanced down at Arabela, whose head rested against his shoulder. "Nearly there." He pressed a kiss to her forehead, something he'd done frequently throughout the night. Then he guided the horse into the meadow, watching the trees to make certain no one waited for them.

The healer was an odd sort, but she was the next best thing to having Braden assist Arabela. Even as his horse entered the clearing, the cottage door opened to reveal Hilda who stared directly at him as if his presence was no surprise.

Chanse could only shake his head. How the old woman knew the things she did was beyond his ken. But much like his brother's gift, there were some things in this life one didn't question, for there was no logical answer.

Hilda waved him forward as if to suggest he dallied overlong. Her long gray hair was plaited, leaving several strands around her wrinkled face.

"Good morn, Hilda," he called softly when he drew close, wondering if she remembered him.

"Madainn mhath," she replied with a nod. "Bring her in. See ta yer horse after." Her thick accent made the words difficult to understand,

and she often sprinkled Gaelic words in her speech, but he caught the gist of her meaning.

No questions. Just an order to bring Arabela inside. He might've found the situation amusing if he weren't so worried.

He dropped the reins then drew Arabela into his arms, taking care to avoid her shoulder. With her securely in his embrace, he slid to the ground.

Her eyes fluttered open as she gasped with pain.

"I've got you." He'd repeated the phrase throughout the night as it seemed to reassure her each time she woke.

"Where are we?" she whispered as her gaze swung about.

"A safe place with someone who can aid you." Now that daylight was approaching, he could see the pain etched clearly in her features.

Hilda held open the door, and Chanse crossed the threshold with Arabela in his arms. A fire burned in the hearth with two pots hanging above it. By the aromatic smell filling the cottage, at least one held pottage. Chanse hoped the healer had sensed their arrival early enough that she'd made plenty of the thick soup. Bundles of dried herbs hung from the rafters. The small cottage had changed little since his last visit some months ago.

The healer gestured toward the neatly made bed, and Chanse carried Arabela there and gently laid her on her side.

"Och." Hilda grimaced at the arrow, touching the shaft. Then she pointed to the knife at Chanse's waist and gestured for him to cut Arabela's kirtle and chemise along the side seam from her hip to her shoulder.

A glance at Arabela showed her eyes were closed, so he didn't attempt to explain what he was doing. After doing as Hilda bid him, he cut the material away from the arrow shaft, moving slowly so as not to bump her.

Hilda returned to the bed carrying a steaming bowl of water with several scraps of linen over her arm. She gestured for him to clean his knife in the steaming water then set her things on the table nearby. With a gentle hand, she slightly twisted the shaft.

Chanse took the movement as a good sign, suggesting the arrowhead wasn't stuck in the bone.

Hilda nodded and released it, her gaze shifting to Chanse. She gestured for him to pull out the arrow, and held her fingers together, seeming to suggest he use his knife to aid it.

As though it were that simple.

His stomach tightened at the task before him. He'd known this moment was coming and that he would be the one to pull out the arrow. But now that the moment was here, he dreaded it. Then again, he didn't trust anyone else to do it with more care than him. If all went well, the head lodged in her shoulder would come out with the shaft. If it didn't...

He didn't finish the thought but gave the healer a reluctant nod to confirm he understood what needed to be done. He would wager that he'd seen more arrow wounds from the battles he'd encountered than Hilda had. Plus, he wondered if the older woman had the strength needed to do it.

Hilda stepped around the bed to grasp Arabela's upper arm and shoulder then grunted at Chanse as though suggesting he move quicker.

He drew a deep breath to brace himself then took hold of the shaft as close to her skin as possible. His other hand held his knife tight to the shaft. Leaning close, he probed the wound to find the arrowhead so he could use the knife tip to aid its exit. "God be with us," he prayed then pulled.

Arabela's cry filled the air.

"Hold on, Arabela," he said even as Hilda tightened her grip. But he didn't stop in his task.

He focused on drawing the wood straight out the same direction it had come in, hopefully doing as little damage as possible. The head resisted, forcing him to press harder with the tip of his knife to loosen it.

Arabela groaned, her body trembling beneath his hand, and it was all he could do to force himself to continue. Should he have pushed it forward through her chest to remove it? Nay, it had been less than halfway through her body. He didn't think it had pierced her lung based on her breathing. Yet he worried he did more harm than good, despite Hilda's guttural sounds of encouragement.

At last, the blasted thing came free, the head included, still attached to the shaft. Arabela went limp. He hoped she remained so until they finished. Even so, he couldn't resist leaning over her, pressing his cheek to hers. Somehow the gentle contact settled him. Though she couldn't hear him, he whispered, "'Tis all done. The arrow is gone."

Hilda pressed one of the damp linen strips against the wound to wipe away the blood. Then she moved back to the fire, selected some of her herbs from the various boxes stacked on the table, added a bit of steaming water, then ground the mixture into a thick paste before adding honey.

Chanse sat wearily on the edge of the bed, keeping a hand on Arabela, not questioning his need to reassure himself that she'd recover.

Hilda picked up the arrow he'd dropped and studied it. Chanse realized she was checking to see if any part of the shaft was missing, which would mean it remained in Arabela. He knew from experience that such things could cause wounds to fester.

Seeming satisfied, she drew closer with several supplies. With quick, efficient movements, she threaded a bone needle and stitched the wound closed. Next, she applied a thick layer on the stitches and placed a folded strip of linen over the poultice, gestured for Chanse to hold it in place, then wrapped Arabela's shoulder with the other strips.

Arabela's eyes fluttered open. Chanse reached for her hand, wishing he could offer her his strength. "We're nearly done. Then you can rest."

Arabela nodded, her face pinched with pain, and her cheeks pale.

Hilda muttered something unintelligible as she raised a cup half full of a dark liquid toward Arabela.

"Drink this," Chanse said, interpreting the older woman's meaning as best he could. "'Twill ease the ache."

At Hilda's nod, he supported Arabela to help her into a sitting position, keeping the bed linen covering her. She took a sip only to grimace. "'Tis foul."

Hadn't Garrick complained of the same thing? Chanse was sure of it. "If you can bear the stuff, it will greatly aid you."

Arabela tried again, swallowing with effort several times before waving it away. "No more."

Hilda nodded, accepting her response, but when Arabela's eyes drifted closed, Hilda clucked in protest. "Och. Eat. A few bites, eh?" She moved to the fire and ladled a small amount of pottage into a bowl.

Chanse's stomach growled at the sight. The sound brought a hint of a smile to Arabela's lips.

"Mayhap you should eat first," she whispered.

"You first," he replied with a smile. "Let me know if 'tis edible," he teased, hoping Hilda hadn't heard him.

Arabela's lips curved at his jest though he knew she was in pain. "I'm to be your food taster?"

"Aye."

Hilda ignored their conversation and handed Chanse the pottage. "My thanks," he said. He dipped the spoon and offered it to Arabela.

Her gaze swung to the healer, noting she'd turned away to reach for another bowl. Arabela sniffed the pottage then ate the spoonful Chanse offered.

"How is it?" Chanse asked in a whisper.

"Better than the drink." She ate several spoonfuls before shaking her head, her smile faded. "I'm tired."

Chanse quickly set aside the bowl and helped her to lay on her side once more. Her puckered brow noted her pain even if she held her silence.

He gently placed the covers over her then brushed several loose strands of hair from her cheek. "Rest," he said though her eyes were already closed. He waited a few moments to make certain she appeared comfortable before rising.

"Eat?" Hilda asked, gesturing toward the pottage.

"I would see to my horse first." With one last glance at Arabela, he stepped outside to find his horse where he left it.

Hilda had no stable as she had no livestock, but a lean-to on the side of the cottage sufficed. He removed the saddle, rubbed the steed down with some straw, and took some grain from the saddlebag. A bucket of water sat outside the door, and he gave some to his horse.

At last, he returned to the cottage to find Arabela still sleeping. Hilda handed him the bowl, which he quickly ate. She refilled it without a word and offered it again.

"My thanks to you," he told the healer as he ate. "For everything." He glanced over at Arabela.

The healer nodded and gestured toward the bed. "Ye rest as well, eh?"

Chanse needed no further invitation. Exhaustion took hold as he moved to the bed and removed his boots and sword, keeping the weapon within reach. He hoped he'd hidden their path here well enough that they wouldn't be discovered.

He settled onto the bed facing Arabela, watching her closely. He couldn't resist reaching out to touch her, if only to reassure himself that she was here, safe and sound.

To his surprise, Arabela shifted closer to rest her hand on his chest. Her touch was all he needed to close his eyes and sleep.

~

ARABELA WOKE, surprised to find bed linens against her cheek rather than the dirt of the ravine bank. Even better, Chanse slept beside her.

But the pain in her shoulder throbbed insistently, reminding her of their precarious position.

Unwilling to move for fear of hurting more, she studied the cottage, noting the healer's absence. That left her free to study Chanse.

While hiding in the ravine, fear had filled her that Chanse wouldn't return. Even now, that terrible hopeless, helpless feeling caused tears to sting her eyes. She'd imagined him injured—or worse.

To know that he'd come back for her and brought her to someone who could help her, caused a warmth in her heart she couldn't explain. Far more than simple gratitude. Far more than relief.

But her thoughts weren't clear at the moment, whether from the pain or the mixture the healer had given her to drink, she didn't know. Now was not the time to examine her feelings for the knight. Nor was she going to worry about where they were going next.

Before any of that concerned her, she needed to recover. Her shoulder still felt as if the arrow protruded, and it was all she could do not to look.

Instead, she shifted closer to Chanse, allowing his presence to ease her mind. She focused on his strong arm as she wrapped her hand around the muscle there. On the broad shoulder next to her. On his handsome profile as he slept.

For now, that was enough to allow her to sleep again.

***

CHANSE SHUT the cottage door behind him, not surprised to see the day was waning. He'd slept like the dead and had woken to find Arabela sleeping soundly beside him. He wasn't certain if Hilda had given more of her remedy to Arabela. The healer wasn't anywhere in sight to ask.

Chanse checked on his horse, pleased to find its oat bag full. Hilda must've replenished the supply. The animal bumped its nose against him as though to reassure him that all was well. Chanse looked over its hooves and ran a hand along each leg to be certain nothing needed immediate attention. Satisfied, he left the horse to rest then walked along the edge of the meadow to clear his thoughts from the fog of sleep.

Though he wanted to send a message to Braden, he had no way of doing so. Not when that meant leaving Arabela. There was still a chance they'd be discovered here. The idea of her alone and injured, facing Rory, was enough to make him stay within sight of the cottage.

His only choice at the moment was to watch over her until she recovered enough for him to venture to the convent. He'd ask the prioress to send a message to Braden.

He returned to the cottage to find Arabela sitting up in the bed with a worried expression. That worry eased as she watched him enter.

"All is well?" she asked.

"Aye, though I can't say where Hilda has gone."

"Do you know her well?"

"Nay. She's a gifted healer who aided us in the past." He sat on the edge of the bed, studying her. "How are you faring?"

"Better without the arrow." He appreciated her attempt at humor.

"I'm sure." He glanced away for a moment, guilt settling heavy on his shoulders. "That arrow was intended for me. If I hadn't bent over—"

"You're welcome."

He looked back to find humor lighting her eyes. "Those men were stupid fools to take the risk of shooting arrows at us."

"It could've been much worse."

"Aye, but it shouldn't have happened at all."

"I suppose 'tis a good reminder of how determined they are to stop us." Worry returned to darken her eyes. "At any cost."

"We didn't need that particular reminder." Chanse scowled, unable to remove the image of the arrow striking her from his mind.

"What will we do next?"

He covered her hands which rested in her lap, appreciating the contact. "We return you to good health. That is our only priority."

"But I—"

"Nay. That is all that need concern you at the moment." He didn't want her to worry. Discussing how they might proceed would surely upset her. "We are close to Berwick, so getting supplies shouldn't be a problem."

"Won't they be looking there for us?"

He cursed himself. Why hadn't he realized even those sort of details would cause her concern? "We'll find a way." He glanced about, wanting to change the subject. "Are you thirsty? Hungry?"

"Thirsty."

He found a cup and poured some water out of the pitcher on the table. She drank the entire cup.

Her face was still pale, and each movement of her arm caused her pain. She seemed ready to rest again and settled under the covers once more.

"You'll be here when I wake?" she asked.

"Of course. Else I'll be right outside."

Relief filled her expression, and she closed her eyes.

Her even breathing reassured him that she truly rested. He stood, wondering how he might be able to repay Hilda for her help. One of the options made itself clear when he stepped outside. Her woodpile was sadly lacking.

He found several downed branches in the woods and pulled them to the cottage. Chopping wood seemed as good a way as any to pass the time, plus it provided a way to focus on something other than what the next day might bring.

After checking on Arabela several times to find her still sleeping, he again stepped out of the cottage to see Hilda emerging from the trees, a bag over one shoulder. He strode forward to take it from her.

"Supper." She pointed at the bag.

He took the liberty of looking inside to find freshly caught fish. The river wasn't far from here. No doubt she'd traded her services in exchange for the fish.

"Shall I clean them?" he offered.

She nodded and left him to it while she entered the cottage.

He hurried with the task, hoping to see how Arabela's wound was faring. He assumed the healer was changing the bandage and applying a fresh poultice.

Fish in hand, he entered the cottage only to stop short at the sight of Arabela's bare back as Hilda unwound the bandage.

Unable to tear away his gaze, he followed the curve of her back, the swell of her hip, wanting more than anything to trace that curve with his hand. Or even better, his tongue. Her alabaster skin was smooth and perfect. He had no doubt it was as velvety soft as her cheek. Hilda shifted, moving the bedding out of her way, which gave him a hint of how lovely her bottom might be.

Hilda's gaze found his, and she chuckled as though finding his desire for the lady amusing.

When Arabela started to turn to see what caught Hilda's notice, he quickly looked away, his hands full of fish. He closed his eyes, but the memory of Arabela's lovely back and hips, and especially her bottom, wouldn't leave him in peace.

With a sigh, he set the fish on the table and quickly left to wash. He hoped Arabela's recovery didn't take overlong else he'd be driven mad with desire.

∼

ARABELA STIRRED RESTLESSLY, unable to sleep. She'd offered to give Hilda back her bed after supper, but the healer had insisted she remain where she was. The older woman had made a pallet by the fire and slept soundly, based on her soft snores.

The empty place beside her was the cause of her unease. The hour had to be late. Where could Chanse be? Had he changed his mind and left her after all? The thought sent her heart racing. 'Twas only because she hurt that she felt so uncertain without him. She was in a strange place and—

She stopped before she could tell herself any further lies.

With a sigh, she eased up on the bolster, careful not to lean against her shoulder. The wound hurt like the devil.

The sound of the latch rattling gave her a start. Chanse entered the cottage, his tall form casting shadows as he closed the door behind him.

He had said little during supper. With Hilda there, Arabela hadn't wanted to ask what caused his silence. He'd left right after the meal and only returned now. Where had he been? What had he been doing?

His gaze swung to her, his brows lifting at the sight of her sitting up. He stepped closer and leaned down. "Is something amiss?" he whispered.

"I was wondering where you were." She kept her voice low, not wanting to wake Hilda.

"Just...outside." He gestured toward the door as if she didn't know where 'outside' was.

"Are you coming to bed now?" she asked, still uncertain why he acted so oddly.

"Bed?" He glanced at it as though he'd never seen it before. "This bed?"

"Where else would you sleep?" Did he prefer to make a pallet so that he might sleep near Hilda instead of her? The thought hurt.

"I-I—" He frowned, staring at the empty space next to her.

She couldn't imagine what was wrong, but she'd had enough of it. She knew she wouldn't sleep without him nearby, so she patted the place beside her. "There's plenty of room."

He nodded. After taking a deep breath, he sat to remove his boots and his sword, the mattress dipping under his weight. He laid down on top of the blankets on his back, his hands at his sides. "Sleep well."

She could see he had yet to close his eyes. After only a moment's hesitation, she scooted close to rest her head on his arm.

"Here," he said and lifted his arm to fit her along his side, her head resting on his chest.

She placed her hand on his, appreciating the feel of his steadily beating heart beneath her hand. The physical connection to him was just what she needed. The tension in her body eased. She felt warm and safe.

The word 'captive' now held a different meaning to her. She'd become his captive in an entirely unexpected way. At peace now that he was at her side, she drifted to sleep, Chanse's scent following her into her dreams.

CHAPTER 15

By the afternoon of the second day, Arabela woke feeling better. Whatever Hilda had placed on her shoulder had kept it from festering. Added to that was Chanse's tender care. Each time she'd woken during the night, he'd been there, offering a comforting hand or a sip of water. The thought of his gentleness brought a warmth in her heart she couldn't easily dismiss.

She glanced about to find the cottage empty. With care, she sat up, taking measure of how she felt. While her shoulder was still painful, it had shifted from a throbbing ache to something duller, depending on how she moved. The time had come to rise and take a breath of fresh air.

The problem with venturing outside was that she was only wearing her chemise. Dressing was more than she could manage. Her cloak hung by the door. That would do for the brief time she'd be out.

She stood, pausing a moment until the light-headedness subsided. She drew her cloak over her shoulders, then managed to slide into her shoes and open the door.

The bright daylight caught her off guard after the dim interior of the cottage. But not nearly as much as the sight of a shirtless Chanse carrying two buckets of water toward her from across the meadow.

Her mouth went dry at the sight even as weakness threatened her knees. She remained in the doorway, her gaze drinking its fill of his powerful body as he strode forward, unaware of her presence in the doorway. The corded muscles of his shoulders and arms were what she'd expected, but the rest of him was so much more. Broad shoulders. Narrow hips. All of him covered by a fine coat of sweat, his skin kissed by the sun, suggesting this wasn't the first time he'd gone shirtless. She sighed. He was a sight to behold.

The muscles of his stomach appeared as though stacked on top of one another, lined up neatly in two rows. Her fingers itched to explore them. A dusting of dark hair covered his chest, tapering down to a narrow path that disappeared into the top of his chausses.

He carried the buckets to a large wooden barrel at the side of the cottage. After setting them down with his back toward her, he poured one into the barrel then most of the other before dumping the remaining water over his head. The water splattered over him before he shook his wet hair and wiped off his face. His back was as impressive as the front, all of him rippling as he moved.

The thought of running her hands over those defined muscles caused her stomach to dip. Would his skin be warm from the sun or cool from the water?

Suddenly, he turned as if sensing the weight of her regard. His eyes widened as his gaze slid down her body. Her nipples tightened at the intensity of his expression.

Only then did she realize she'd released her hold on her cloak, which had puddled at her feet. She now stood in the doorway in nothing but her thin chemise.

The heat in his gaze kept her from bending to retrieve the cloak.

"Arabela." His nostrils flared as he said her name. Heat pooled low in her belly. She couldn't have looked away if her life depended on it. "Are you well?"

He walked toward her, one hand reaching for her as if he expected her to fall. Droplets clung to his face and lashes. He blinked when he touched her as though unprepared for the contact.

As was she.

The touch that had given her such comfort since her injury was now anything but. Instead, a spark flew up her arm and lit the liquid gathered in her body, causing a heat unlike anything she'd experienced.

"Oh." The feeling was unexpected and...wonderful. And she wanted more.

She tentatively placed her hand against his bare chest. "So warm."

"I was chopping wood." His gaze searched her face, though she wasn't certain what he looked for.

She traced the muscles of his chest, fascinated by their definition, all thoughts of her injury falling away. Then with one finger, she touched the tip of his nipple. He jerked in response, and she raised her gaze in surprise.

The spark in his eyes burned brighter.

She couldn't resist doing it again to see his reaction.

With a muffled oath, he leaned forward until he was no more than a breath away only to stop. She offered her mouth, wanting nothing more than to kiss him.

So she did.

Her good hand moved up to his shoulder as she lifted to her toes and pressed her lips to his.

With a groan, he placed his hands on her waist with such gentleness that she melted from the inside out. But his lips were far from gentle. They ravished hers as though he couldn't get enough. When his tongue invaded her mouth, she welcomed it, the sensation deep inside her making her ache.

She cupped his jaw with her hand, enjoying the stubble there.

He moved his lips down to press a kiss on the sensitive spot just below her ear and along her neck. Slowly, his hand shifted, the warmth of it reaching her through her thin chemise. His thumb rose to touch the lower curve of her breast.

Her breath caught with the hope that he'd touch her nipple as she'd touched his. As if he understood, he cupped her breast, molding it to the shape of his hand before releasing it, then repeating the motion.

When his thumb moved over the tip, she gasped at the pleasure that filled her.

"Chanse," she whispered, enchanted by the feelings coursing through her.

"So sweet." He kissed her again, his tongue swirling with hers before he eased back to study her. "So brave. So beautiful."

Her heart squeezed at his words. She winced when she moved her shoulder but ignored the pain, not ready for this moment to end. "And you are so strong." She touched him as she'd longed to earlier, running her fingers along the muscles clearly visible, pleased to find his skin still damp.

"Then why do you make me feel weak?"

Before she could think of a reply, he kissed her again, tenderly this time, as though treasuring the moment. As though he'd never let her go. How she wished that were true. Why couldn't *he* have been the man her father had chosen? She shoved aside the idea as quickly as it came, not wanting to think of anything except Chanse and this stolen moment they had together.

When his hand brushed across her breast again, she had her wish. All thought fell away at his touch.

Then he reached for the ribbon that held up the neck of her chemise and tugged the bow loose. His gaze met hers for a brief moment before he lowered his head. His warm lips trailed a path along the opening of her chemise, then near the binding on her shoulder, before his clever fingers freed her breast.

"Arabela," he muttered. The kisses he pressed to her sensitive skin sent need spiraling through her until the apex of her thighs was damp. When he took the tip of her breast in his mouth, she gasped, surprised at his action as much as she was at the way he made her feel. The sight of his dark head against her pale skin should've shocked her. But the feelings he evoked were too good to stop.

"Perfect." He raised his head to hold her gaze.

"Indeed, you are," she said, wanting to make him feel at least a portion of what she did. She ran her hand along his shoulder then cupped his cheek before dropping it to his chest. If only she had both hands with which to explore him.

"Arabela." She loved the sound of her name on his lips, especially when it was laced with need. "You tempt me beyond measure."

Good, she thought. Why shouldn't they have these moments together? After all they'd been through, this seemed like a fitting reward for what they'd endured.

"You should be resting." He heaved a reluctant sigh, sending wariness flooding through her. He tugged the chemise into place, tightening the ribbon, before gently pulling her into his arms to hold her.

She placed her head on his shoulder, wishing she could tell him what was in her heart. But his desire didn't mean his plans had changed. She had to find the strength to guard against the urge to depend upon him. For all she knew, their time together was nearly at an end. Until he trusted her enough to tell her of his intentions, she had to take care.

As the passion burning within her banked its flame, she pressed a kiss on his bare skin then eased back. She avoided looking at him for fear of what she'd see there.

"I'm going to rest," she whispered. Then she turned and went back inside to lie on the bed, allowing her eyes to drift closed.

On the morrow, she'd ask him one last time to tell her his plans. If he refused, she'd have her answer. Without trust, they had nothing.

Why did the freedom she'd dreamed of now stretch before her like an empty path?

∼

It didn't matter how many times Chanse told himself he'd done the right thing by letting Arabela go back into the cottage the previous day, he still felt regret.

Nay. More than regret. He felt down to his bones that he'd missed an opportunity he might never have again. One that could've changed the course of his life. She was a special woman who moved him in ways he'd never expected.

He scoffed as he brought the axe down on a piece of wood. Who was he trying to fool? She stirred him in all ways—mentally, physically, emotionally.

But that was also the problem. He was allowing desire to cloud his logic. That logic would keep them both alive in the days to come. Leading with emotions might get them killed. They were safe for the moment, but they couldn't remain at Hilda's much longer.

Somehow, he needed to determine a way to get them into Berwick without being discovered. Once he reached Braden and reviewed the situation with him, he'd better know how to proceed, where to go. If only he could trust himself the way he trusted Braden.

He couldn't think properly with the temptation of Arabela just inside the cottage. Lying beside her on the bed the previous night without touching her had nearly killed him. The sooner they left here, the better.

Or was that being illogical?

With a groan, he lifted the axe and struck another piece of wood.

"That'll do," Hilda said.

He glanced up in surprise, not having heard her approach. He shook his head at his failing. How could he think to protect Arabela when an old woman could approach without him noticing?

The healer, a bag in her hand, looked from him to the large pile of wood he'd chopped in the past two days.

As he followed her gaze, he realized he might have overdone the chore.

With a puzzled look at him, she went inside, leaving the door open as the day was a fine one. The sound of her talking with Arabela carried out to him. At least Arabela spoke to Hilda. She hadn't said more than three words to Chanse since he'd kissed her. No doubt he should apologize for his behavior, but how could he when his regret stemmed from an entirely different reason?

The sight of her in nothing other than her chemise as she stood in the doorway, staring at him, had been more than he could resist. She was a beautiful woman with a good soul. It would take a stronger man than he to withstand the interest that had glistened in her eyes. Not that he'd seen it since. He should be grateful for that, but he wasn't.

He couldn't make out their words, but that was no surprise as he had difficulty understanding Hilda even when she spoke directly to him.

On the morrow, they'd go, he decided as he stacked the chopped wood along the side of the cottage. Arabela could have one more day of rest before they ventured to the convent. Prioress Matilda would know whether it was likely he could enter Berwick without gaining notice. Though she rarely left the convent, she knew most everything that occurred in the city.

The trick was to make certain no one watched the nunnery. He considered the options as he worked. Traveling at night was possible as it wasn't far, but the convent locked its gates at dusk. Going in the daylight gave too much of an advantage to any who watched for their arrival.

"How do I look?"

Chanse turned at the sound of Arabela's voice to see her standing before him dressed as a lad. Shock seeped through him at the sight of her legs clearly defined in chausses. The simple brown woolen tunic she wore hung loosely on her frame. Her beautiful hair was tucked into a soft hat.

Like a woman in a lad's clothes, he wanted to say. Though his mouth opened, no words emerged.

"Hilda says I'll pass for your squire in this attire." She raised a brow, waiting for his response. "We'll be able to travel to the convent without fear of discovery."

"Nay," he nearly shouted. "Absolutely not. Are you crazed?"

She took a step back before her chin lifted. Blast her and her stubbornness. "I think it will work well and so does Hilda."

Since when didn't his opinion matter? "Everyone will easily see that you're a woman."

"You only think that because you know," she argued. "People only see what they expect."

Her shapely body would shout it to all who looked. Of that, he had no doubt.

"Hilda is fashioning a sling for my arm. Not only will it be more comfortable, but it will also help explain why I don't aid you more. Because I'm your squire," she added when he said nothing.

The chemise had been revealing but seeing her in chausses played tricks with his mind. He could only think of her naked and in his arms. His manhood rallied at the thought, and he had to close his eyes for a moment to regain his senses.

"We can leave for the convent after the midday meal," she said.

"You aren't going anywhere dressed like that," he said, daring another look at her.

She held out her good arm and looked down at her attire. "'Tis rather comfortable, much to my surprise."

Could she not hear him speaking? He strode forward to stand before her only to realize he'd made a tactical error. Being this close only gave him a better view.

The long sweep of her lashes, the curve of her cheek, the flutter of her pulse at the base of her neck. Nothing about her looked like any squire he'd seen.

"Hilda says a squire would normally run alongside your horse, but surely it would suffice if I walked." She glanced up at him from under those lashes, sending his pulse hammering.

"Nay." There. This time he said it more firmly.

She frowned up at him. "But running wouldn't do my shoulder any good."

He nearly groaned in frustration. "You're not walking or running anywhere dressed as such."

"Chanse." She reached up to place her hand on his chest close to his heart. Or was she already touching it more than just physically? He swore as he felt it expand at the thought. "You and I both know we can't stay here. They'll find us sooner or later, and I don't want to put Hilda in danger after all she's done to aid us."

"But—"

"Hush," she said as she lifted that hand to hold a finger over his lips. "Hilda believes I will pass for a lad as do I. No one will look twice at a knight and his squire on the road. Hilda says 'tisn't far to the convent. We need only use the disguise for a short while."

She was right, though it didn't please him to realize it. Hadn't he just been trying to think of a way to get there without gaining notice?

As though sensing his reluctant agreement, she stepped back. "Do boys swing their arms when they walk?"

He watched with a scowl as she turned and strode back to the cottage, swinging her good arm. But 'twas the swing of her hips that truly caught his notice.

"Damn me," he muttered.

CHAPTER 16

Arabela swallowed hard when St. Mary's came into view as she walked alongside Chanse's horse. The convent was nestled a fair distance outside the city walls as though it preferred being independent. Would that be her new home from this day forth?

A tight knot formed in the pit of her stomach at the thought. Though she'd been certain the idea held merit before she'd left home, now that she faced the reality of it, doubts surfaced.

Would living within its walls be so different than living behind the confining parapets of her father's holding? She hadn't had freedom there either. Being of service to others was a notion she welcomed, yet the idea of taking vows to remain part of the convent for the rest of her life when she'd finally had a taste of the world gave her pause.

She shook her head. The world wasn't a safe place. She need only move her shoulder to remember that. The idea of continuing to evade her pursuers for the foreseeable future held no appeal. That wouldn't be a life at all.

With a deep breath, she shifted her attention to her surroundings. Walking in chausses was a new experience. She liked to think she acted the part but wasn't certain. Her hat was pulled low over her brow, and her arm was in a sling. The journey hadn't been a long one, but she already felt herself tiring.

Arabela risked a glance at Chanse on the horse. He frowned as he stared at the convent. Did he intend to leave her there? Would he be pleased to see the last of her along with all the problems that accompanied her? He hadn't spoken more than a few words since their kiss other than his heated protest at her attire. Did he regret their kisses so much then? The idea placed a weight on her chest that caused her breath to hitch.

She hadn't worked up the courage to ask him what his purpose for her was. Not when she'd find out upon their arrival at the convent. Mayhap it was better that she didn't know.

Her consideration of remaining at St. Mary's might collide with his ideas if he intended to use her somehow to force her father to halt his plan.

She had to find a way to release her desire to hold onto Chanse. He wasn't hers to keep. They shared an attraction, but that meant little to men from what she knew.

No matter how much she'd come to care for him, she wouldn't be any man's pawn. She steeled her resolve at the thought.

As they turned a bend in the road, the gate of Berwick came into view as well. The sight caught her full attention. Berwick, a market city, sat on the north bank of the River Tweed. A few fishermen in their boats were sprinkled along the river just above the place where the river met the sea. The wide expanse of the North Sea stole her breath. The horizon appeared never-ending. Longing pierced through her at the beauty of the area. What would it be like to live here?

Her gaze shifted back to Berwick, its secrets hidden by the walls that encircled it. Only a hint of buildings appeared above the enclosure, including a church tower and a few roofs. If she were to take her vows at the convent, would she eventually be able to visit the city, once the search for her settled down?

A line of people waited on the road that led to the gate's entrance, which was flanked by watchtowers. Was the length of the line normal or the work of her father?

"They closely search all who enter," Chanse said, confirming what she'd feared. He seemed displeased at the realization.

"Does that affect your...plans?" She couldn't help but ask.

"Mayhap. I won't know until I've spoken with Prioress Matilda."

"What's she like?"

He looked down at her as though surprised she'd asked. She wanted to tell him that he wasn't the only one who could keep secrets. She'd felt no need to share her desire to join the convent since he failed to tell her of his plans. Now was a good opportunity to discover more about the woman who might soon be in charge of her life.

She drew a deep breath at the thought.

"She's clever and intelligent," Chanse advised, unaware of her concern. "She understands the problems the country faces better than most."

Hope lit Arabela along with nerves. Mayhap that was the card she could play with the prioress. With no dowry to bring, the woman's concerns might be the leverage she needed. Aiding in stopping the alliance from occurring might take the place of the payment normally given upon entering a convent. Surely the woman would understand how terrible it would be if Arabela married Rory, not only for Arabela but for the country.

If Arabela kept her emotions in check and focused on logic, she might be able to convince the prioress to allow her to become one of them.

"I believe you'll like her," Chanse added.

Touched that he'd think to reassure, she smiled up at him.

"Careful to keep your face hidden," he warned. "We're about to pass someone."

Other travelers on the road had been few until now. Luckily, she was on the opposite side of Chanse's horse, and those passing would see little of her up close. She was careful to make her stride longer and keep her face turned away.

All too soon, they were passing through the convent gate. Fatigue pulled at Arabela as Chanse dismounted and led his horse into the nunnery, her at his side. Several of the sisters passed by. One nodded politely while another giggled as she waggled her fingers at Chanse. Apparently, they knew him from a previous visit.

He offered one of his charming smiles, making her realize how long it had been since she'd seen it. Before she could decide whether that was a good thing, they crossed a courtyard, where Chanse tied the reins of his steed to a post. Then he escorted her to one of the buildings and held open the door.

Arabela regretted her attire. How terrible that she was going to meet the prioress for the first time dressed as a lad. Never mind that her shoulder ached, and tiredness pulled at her thoughts.

She placed a hand on Chanse's arm. "I'd prefer to change clothing before—"

"Sir Chanse, is that you?" One of the sisters hurried forward. "We've been so worried."

"Sister Maude, 'tis good to see you. I'm hoping to have a word with the prioress."

"Of course," she said as she turned. "She'll be pleased you're here."

Arabela was surprised when the sister didn't even acknowledge her presence. Was her attire that effective? Did she truly believe her a lad? Or was it the sister's infatuation with Chanse that prevented her from seeing anything beyond him?

It took a moment before Arabela decided to be amused by the sister's behavior rather than offended. She supposed it was much like the times she'd donned a servant's clothing at home. Any guests visiting hadn't looked beyond that.

They reached the door of a chamber, and the sister paused. "Would your lad prefer to wait in the courtyard?" She peered around Chanse to look at Arabela.

"He'll remain with me."

Arabela stared in surprise at Chanse. Why didn't he correct the woman?

He shook his head ever so slightly, so she kept her head down, wondering why they continued to keep up the deception.

The sister knocked on the door then entered and exchanged words with the occupant before turning back to Chanse. "She'll be happy to see you." The sister beamed brightly at him.

He used his charming smile once again. If his intent was to distract the woman so that she ignored Arabela completely, he succeeded.

After thanking the woman, Chanse held the door for Arabela to precede him. "The fewer who know of your presence, the better," he murmured.

"What a delightful surprise." The woman behind the desk rose and came around the side of it with hands outstretched.

Chanse took them and kissed each one in turn, causing the woman to laugh. Not the girlish giggle like Arabela had witnessed earlier, but a true laugh. The sound was foreign to Arabela's ears. There had never been much laughter at her home.

"We've been worried about you after your brother told us of your plans. I'm so pleased to see you're well."

"My thanks. I hope you are also." Chanse closed the door.

"Braden shared what you've been about. Quite bold of you." The woman shifted her attention to Arabela, and her blue eyes narrowed with curiosity. "Who do we have here?"

The prioress wasn't easily fooled. She seemed to look directly through Arabela's attire and expected an explanation for it. Her wise gaze swung back to Chanse, one brow raised in question.

"Prioress Matilda, may I present Lady Arabela Graham."

Arabela curtsied before realizing how odd it was to do so in chausses.

"'Tis a pleasure to meet you."

"The pleasure is mine," Arabela said.

The prioress appeared bemused by her presence and even more so by her clothing. "Is that how you managed it?" she asked Chanse.

"Nay. Only our brief journey this day. The lady already had plans to flee prior to my arrival. I merely convinced her to allow me to accompany her."

Arabela couldn't help but scoff.

The prioress's attention shifted to Arabela's arm in its sling. "You make it sound a simple task, though I'm certain it was far from it. I assume you encountered danger along the way?"

"Unfortunately," Chanse admitted, his expression dark as he, too, looked at Arabela's injured shoulder.

"I look forward to hearing the tale. But first I sense you have other matters on your mind." She gestured toward the chairs before her desk. "Tell me how I might be of service."

Though she'd only just met the prioress, Arabela had no doubt the woman only served those whom she deemed worthy and had a just cause with which she agreed. Arabela respected her already.

Chanse held the chair for Arabela then took a seat as well. He cleared his throat. It almost appeared as if he were hesitating. That caught her curiosity. "You mentioned Braden shared my plans?" he asked.

"Only that you intended to halt the wedding with the hope that Lord Graham wouldn't be able to place Sir Rory on the throne." She glanced at Arabela as she spoke.

"Yes. Exactly. I need to speak with Braden as soon as possible."

"We should be able to get word to him."

Disappointment welled up inside of Arabela. That was it? His only plan was to speak with his brother? She couldn't wait any longer to discover what Chanse had in mind. She had to take action now. She needed to present her wish first.

"If I might speak," Arabela said.

Chanse frowned at her in surprise.

"Of course, my lady," the prioress said, a polite, if curious, smile on her face.

"I'm not certain how much you know of my situation, but I seek to join St. Mary's." Her stomach lurched at her words, causing her to hesitate. Was she even saying it correctly? "I wish to take my vows. To become a sister. Here." Was that clear enough?

Heat filled her face as she felt the weight of Chanse's confused gaze.

"What is this?" He shifted in his chair to face her. "Whatever are you saying?"

The prioress's eyes rounded at his reaction, but she held her silence to give Arabela a chance to explain. Arabela didn't want to do so. She only wanted the prioress to agree. To say how delighted they'd be to have her join them. To have someone want her presence for more than a few days.

As the silence grew long, so did Arabela's concern. "I have given the matter much thought and believe I have a calling." She risked a glance at Chanse, the anger in his expression surprising her. She jerked her attention back to the prioress. "A calling to join the convent."

"You must be jesting," Chanse said.

Heat filled her face at the incredulity in his voice. Did she not fit his idea of a nun? Was he thinking of their kiss? Only it had been far more than a kiss. It had been touching and caressing and things a woman about to join a convent shouldn't want to do. Was that why he was so surprised by her request?

Yet what choice did she have? None that she could think of.

She lifted her chin, ignoring Chanse to hold Prioress Matilda's gaze. "If I marry Sir Rory Buchanan, my father intends to do all in his power to put him—or rather, us—on the throne."

"I see," the prioress said, casting a quick look at Chanse before returning her attention to Arabela.

Arabela licked her suddenly dry lips. "I believe that would have dire consequences and only add to the problems between England and Scotland. While I escaped the initial wedding, I don't believe Rory or my father will rest until I am found and forced to wed. So, you can surely see the need for me to join the convent as quickly as possible."

Chanse shoved back his chair and stood. "You didn't think to mention any of this to me before now?" The disbelief in his tone wasn't lost on her.

But she was having none of it. "Why would I? 'Twasn't as if *you* chose to confide any of your plans to me." She glared at him, daring him to disagree.

He scowled in return. "That's because my plans change." He

gestured vaguely in the air as he shifted his feet. "They depend on how things are progressing."

She rose in disbelief as the truth dawned on her. "You had no plans."

"I didn't say that."

But she could see she'd struck a mark.

"None of that matters at the moment," he said. "We're discussing you and your...request."

"What else could I do?" She lifted her arm in the sling to better make her point. "I can't travel about the countryside, trying to stay ahead of them for the coming months. I won't survive it."

"Arabela," Chanse said, his voice quiet, his expression softening. "That arrow was meant for me. You must know that I would never put you at risk."

"Wouldn't you?" As much as it hurt, she forced herself to ask the question. "If the outcome met your wishes, wouldn't you?"

"Never." He placed gentle hands on her upper arms. "I would never see you harmed."

Prioress Matilda cleared her throat, causing both of them to look at her. "Well then. That was quite enlightening, wouldn't you say?" Then she waved her hand in the air, not so different than Chanse had a moment earlier. "We would be honored to discuss you joining us, Lady Arabela."

Arabela's heart sank. What was there to discuss? "I realize I have no dowry, but I would be pleased to spend my life in service."

The older woman rose and reached for Arabela's free hand. "I appreciate that. I can already see that you have a good heart. There aren't enough of those in the world. All the same, we must consider all options to be certain as to what would best suit your situation and that of St. Mary's."

"Oh?" Arabela swallowed against the lump in her throat. Did the prioress not want her either? Then where would she go?

∽

CHANSE PACED the courtyard at St. Mary's alone, sorely regretting having ventured to the convent. He'd only intended to obtain an update from Prioress Matilda and request her assistance in sending a message to Braden.

Instead, he'd learned Arabela had been keeping a secret of her own. Become a nun? After the way she'd responded in his arms? The idea seemed a terrible one. Thank goodness the prioress had the good sense not to readily agree.

He scowled as he realized neither had she denied Arabela's request.

Before he could state the many reasons Arabela shouldn't join the convent, she'd been rushed away for a proper bath and rest as well as a change of clothing while Chanse was left to wait and wonder.

In truth, he was hurt that Arabela hadn't confided in him. Perhaps he shouldn't have revealed that he didn't have a fully developed course of action. Doing so had been a misstep on his part. It had shifted the conversation to him rather than remaining on Arabela and her request.

What was wrong with being able to adapt as they encountered new challenges? Journeying to Berwick could've proved impossible, and he would've changed their course if that had come to pass.

He halted abruptly and ran a hand through his hair. He was not in question here. Rather than concerning himself with Arabela's request, he needed to find a way to make certain Graham and Rory didn't find her. That might eliminate her wish to join the convent. The idea gave him a hope he didn't care to question.

But how?

He only knew he was done running. The time had come to move into the offense. His best hope was for Braden to arrive so the two of them could determine a way to halt Graham's plans to put Rory on the throne without further involving Arabela.

He rubbed his chest at the sudden ache there. Arabela become a nun? He didn't want to dwell on the reason the idea upset him so, yet he couldn't cast it from his thoughts.

Did she truly have a calling? Or did she feel she had no choice? If he had to guess, he'd wager on the latter.

There could be only one reason Arabela hadn't confided in him—she didn't trust him. How could he expect trust when he hadn't given her a reason to do so? He'd convinced himself that telling her anything would put any plans in danger if she were caught. While that had been true in the beginning, he should've shared his ideas with her as the days had passed. She deserved that much.

"Sir Chanse?"

He turned at his name to find Sister Catherine nearby.

"Your bath is ready."

He frowned. "I didn't request—"

"Prioress Matilda ordered it. This way, if you please." She gestured toward one of the buildings with a smile. "Will you need assistance?"

His face heated at the thought of the stout, older woman aiding him. "I believe I can manage. I must see to my horse first."

"The stable boy is already tending to him."

Before he knew it, he was alone in one of the small chambers with a tub of steaming water, a small pot of soap flakes, and linens with which to dry. His saddlebag sat nearby as well.

With a sigh, he unstrapped his sword belt then sat to remove his boots. This felt like a waste of time when so much was at stake. He paused to sniff his tunic, wondering if he smelled that bad. The odor he caught was less than ideal, so he made quick work of stripping then stepped into the water, determined to be swift.

A knock on the door had him sinking deeper into the small tub, his knees protruding, making him feel vulnerable.

Sister Catherine peeked around the edge of the door. "I've come to take your clothes for a cleaning." Without waiting for an answer, she bustled inside and gathered his things. "No doubt they're dusty from your journey."

"But I won't be long," he protested. Why didn't this chamber have a door that could be locked?

"Nor will I," she declared with a lingering look before she left, a broad smile on her face.

He scrubbed himself with a vengeance to try to work away some of his frustration and even washed his hair, using the bucket of clean water beside the tub to rinse.

Still confused to find himself taking a bath when he'd intended to merely gain some information and get word to Braden, he finished cleaning. Then he quickly dried himself, guarding against every sound for fear one of the sisters would enter without notice.

To his surprise, none of his clothes were in the saddlebags. Apparently, they'd been taken to be cleaned as well. Which left him with nothing more to wear than the linens with which he'd dried himself. How unfortunate.

He waited.

And waited.

When no one came with clothing, he cautiously opened the door, hoping to catch someone passing by. But the passage was empty.

Though tempted to go in search of someone, the idea of encountering any of the sisters when he was practically naked kept him in place.

At last a knock sounded on the door. Before he could answer, it opened to reveal his brother.

"Braden." Chanse had never been so pleased to see him and hugged him despite his lack of attire.

"Whatever are you doing?" His brother frowned, taking in his appearance after the embrace. "You took a bath?"

Chanse felt heat stain his cheeks. "I wouldn't say I had a choice in the matter. Did the prioress send word I was here?"

"Aye. Don't you want to dress so we can discuss a plan?"

"I have no clothes." Chanse gripped the linen tightly about his hips. "The sisters took them away to clean."

Braden shook his head as he closed the door. "Heaven knows when you'll get them back. No doubt they're hoping you'll come in search of them," he said with a laugh.

His mirth caused Chanse to scowl. "I do not find this amusing in the least."

"I do." Braden's smile made Chanse grit his teeth. "In truth, I'm pleased you returned safely."

"As am I," Chanse admitted, his ire easing. "Our journey nearly ended badly." He shared with Braden the events of the past few days, including Arabela's injury.

"I told you this was a poor idea."

"And I asked you for a better one that would halt the wedding," Chanse reminded him. "You had none."

"True. Sir Rory on the throne with Lord Graham and the Sentinels of Scotland behind him would be disastrous. We all agree on that."

"I have no doubt they still search for Arabela."

Braden nodded. "The guards at the city gate are closely checking all who enter on Graham's order. He's gained the agreement of Sir Gilbert to search everyone."

"That complicates matters even if it doesn't come as a surprise," Chanse said. Sir Gilbert de Umfraville served as governor of Berwick. They'd had an unpleasant encounter with him in the spring. The man might be Scottish but he had strong ties to England, which made his allegiance unclear.

"What's worse is that Graham is spreading word that his daughter was taken captive."

"Does he suspect who took her?" Chanse asked, not surprised at the news.

"Nay. But he's blaming the English. That will only aid the cause the Sentinels have to break all ties with them. Did Lady Arabela accompany you willingly?"

"Not exactly." He hated to admit how badly his charm failed him when it came to Arabela.

"Did she wish to marry Sir Rory?"

"Nay. I believe she had a plan of her own which I interrupted." Still displeased at the idea, he said, "She asked Prioress Matilda to join the convent. The prioress is considering her request."

Braden paused as though to weigh the merits of the idea. "That might be a clever solution to protect her from her father. I'd be relieved if she had a safe place to stay."

"Staying is one thing but joining the convent should not be an option." Chanse turned away to pace the room and back, the linen still wrapped around his waist. "I cannot fathom why Arabela suggested such a thing. 'Tis a foolish notion."

Braden smiled as though amused at Chanse's upset. "Prioress Matilda is a wise woman. She'll make the right decision as to whether Arabela would do well here."

"How can you even consider it?" Chanse's anger sparked. "The idea is a terrible one." It caused a weight in his chest for which he didn't care. He wanted to find Arabela and convince her that she had other choices. Yet his mind shied away from naming those choices.

Braden frowned. "How so? 'Tis a noble choice for many."

"Not for Arabela." Braden continued to stare at him. "Tell me you're jesting," Chanse said, not caring for the desperation that clawed at his throat.

"I'm not. Ilisa considered it for a time," Braden said. "Luckily, the prioress was wise enough to see that path was not for Ilisa."

"That was completely different. The prioress decided the two of you should marry instead since you were posing as husband and wife."

"Aye. She saw more of what was between us than I did." The look of satisfaction on Braden's expression spoke of a man pleased with how his life had unfolded.

"I cannot wait idly by to see if the prioress makes the right decision. I intend to find a way to stop Graham's plans. Doing so will allow Arabela to chose her own life."

Braden nodded. "I like it. How?"

Chanse was reluctant to admit that nothing helpful had come to mind thus far. "I'm hoping you and I can determine a way to do so."

"Hmm. A lack of ideas is what caused you to resort to taking Arabela captive," Braden pointed out.

With a groan of frustration, Chanse turned away. "I need clothes to continue this conversation."

"Will that improve your ability to think?" Braden's grin annoyed Chanse further.

"Nay, but mayhap it will keep you from wearing that smirk."

Braden only nodded, smirk still in place.

"I need to speak with Arabela," he said as he started toward the door only to turn back to Braden. "Perhaps you'd be so kind as to search out my clothes."

"I'll see what I can do." Braden walked toward the door. "Matthew arrived just before I did. He was quite relieved to learn you're here."

"He's well? And Edith, the maidservant, too?"

"Aye. He said the journey took an unexpected twist, causing you to split up."

"Our pursuers drew too close." His thoughts darkened at the memory. He caught Braden's eye. "Would you see to her wound?"

"Does she know of my ability?"

"Nay."

Braden nodded. "Let me first do what I can to find your attire. I'll return shortly."

The door closed, leaving Chanse alone with his thoughts once more, along with a sinking feeling in the pit of his stomach.

Arabela join the convent? He shook his head. 'Twas a terrible idea. Yet he wasn't certain what he could do to halt it. He only knew that he felt panicked at the thought of her spending the rest of her life within these walls, out of his reach.

CHAPTER 17

James sat in the back of a tavern in Dunbar, a cup of ale before him. Waiting.

His dark mood must've been reflected in his expression, for no one approached. Not even the maid had returned after serving him his drink, though she kept a watchful eye upon him.

Arabela had been missing for nearly a fortnight. Though Geoffrey had caught her briefly, she'd escaped once again. The knight had been questioned thoroughly but seemed at a loss as to where she'd gone. James still wasn't certain if she had help or if she made the journey on her own.

He shook his head, dismissing the latter. His Arabela wasn't strong enough to survive on her own. He didn't know who aided her, but they would soon pay. The question was where was she going? Rhona had gone on to their holding near Berwick, stating she was weary of travel and would await word from him there.

Rory had bumbled his way through inquiries in Edinburgh to no avail. They'd discovered nothing there. Dunbar had been the next possibility they'd chosen to search. The village was large, nestled on the coast not far from Berwick. James had taken it upon himself to speak to the local lord with no results. Rory was talking to a few of the shopkeepers to see if they'd noted anyone fitting Arabela's description.

The knight should arrive any moment.

In all honesty, James was no longer certain Rory was the best person to marry Arabela, let alone be king. His rough manners and lack of foresight posed a problem. Guiding him in decisions affecting the country would be no easy task. But James still believed he could control him.

None of those issues mattered if they couldn't find Arabela.

The door to the tavern opened, blowing in a few early autumn leaves and dust.

And Rory.

The man slammed the door shut, drawing the eyes of all the occupants.

James sighed. Rory seemed to do everything to draw notice, much like a child who acted out. With a scowl, James waved him over when he continued to stand by the door.

"Well?" James asked.

Rory drew back the chair next to him, scraping it along the floor before sitting heavily in it. "Not a damned thing. Did ye fare any better?"

"Nay." James took a sip of ale, trying to decide what should be done next.

Rory gestured for the maid to bring him some ale. She did so quickly, bending forward as she set the drink on the table before him, which placed her generous bosom on full display.

"Isn't that a pretty sight," Rory murmured as he admired her goods, reaching out a dirty finger to dip into the top of the woman's kirtle.

She giggled in delight.

"On with you," James ordered, annoyed with the both of them. "We have important matters to discuss."

The maid stood abruptly, her smile gone. She sauntered away as if to make certain Rory saw all she had to offer.

James tapped his fingers on the table while he waited for Rory's attention to return to him, certain his disapproval of the younger man's behavior was clear.

Rory held James's gaze, suggesting he didn't care what James thought.

"You may do what you wish in private," James said, leaning forward to issue his warning quietly. "But before the people, you will act with decorum and honor. Do I make myself clear?"

Rory lifted a casual shoulder. "My bride has vanished. Ye can't expect me to live as a monk while we search for her."

"Aye, I can and I do. At least in public." When Rory opened his mouth to protest, James raised a hand. "Doing otherwise will not endear you to those you seek to rule."

Rory leaned forward as well. "They don't have to like me in order for me to be king."

"Stepping onto the throne will prove much easier if they do." James unleashed his anger as he spit out the words. "You are nothing without me. Do not make me send you back from where you came."

Rory hesitated a long moment before he sat back in his chair and reached for the ale, wisely holding his tongue.

"Now then, we must decide where to search next."

Rory remained silent. Whether that meant he had no ideas on the topic or he was showing his displeasure at the reprimand, James didn't know. Nor did he care.

"I suppose we must venture to Berwick, though I hold a strong dislike of the place."

"Do you truly think she could've made it that far?" Rory asked.

"Not without aid. But that matters little at this point. Whoever assisted her will pay. But we must find her and quickly. Rothton has already ventured there to advise the governor of some of the details."

"When I find her," Rory said, "she'll regret this delay."

"When *we* find her, we'll make certain she doesn't escape us again. We'll place the blame on those who aided her and make an example of them."

That made Rory smile, and the brittle gleam in his eyes reminded

James his supposed heritage wasn't the only reason he'd chosen this knight for his plan. "The pleasure will be all mine."

～

"What could I say or do to convince Prioress Matilda to allow me to join the convent?" Arabela asked Sister Maude, who'd assisted her with her bath.

The sister's surprise to learn that Arabela was a lady rather than a lad had been amusing. Now Arabela sat before the narrow window on a bench as the sister combed through Arabela's damp hair, a task Arabela found impossible with her injured shoulder.

"I don't think anything on your part will make a difference, my lady. The prioress will pray on the matter and decide in time." The woman's calm demeanor made her easy to speak with, even if Arabela didn't always like her response. "We're rarely privy to God's plan."

Arabela bit her lip to keep from arguing that it wasn't God's plan that concerned her, but rather everyone else's, including the prioress's.

She understood why Chanse called Prioress Matilda a force. 'Twas true. And she was clever about it. One moment, Arabela had been prepared to launch her argument as to why she wanted to take her vows and the next she'd been escorted to a chamber to bathe and rest, all with the promise that they'd discuss the matter later.

The thought of Chanse's upset at her request caused a quiver in her belly that even now had her drawing a deep breath. She hadn't expected him to understand, but what choice did she have? Where else could she go that her father and Rory couldn't reach her other than St. Mary's?

While she appreciated all Chanse had done for her thus far, she didn't dare rely solely on him. Or care for him more than she already did. She touched her chest at the pang the thought brought. Denying her feelings for him seemed pointless, but that didn't mean she could allow her plan to change. She had to stay strong.

No doubt he had a life to return to now that he'd helped free her.

The rest was up to her. The only idea that held merit was to join the convent.

The prioress could surely be swayed by a logical argument. Arabela had hoped to gain insight from Sister Maude, but the woman had dashed those hopes. What more could she say to convince Prioress Matilda? Each day they waited put Arabela in danger of being caught by her father and Rory. She was already tired of running. If the prioress denied her request, then what could she do?

A knock on the door interrupted her worrying.

Sister Maude hurried to the door, spoke a few words, then opened it wide, revealing Edith.

Joy and relief filled Arabela as she rushed forward to hug her with her good arm. "I've been so worried. All is well?" She drew back to look over the maidservant from head to toe.

"Aye. Sir Matthew took great care to see me safely here with the hope you'd have already arrived." Edith frowned at the binding on Arabela's shoulder visible beneath her chemise. "What is this?"

"An arrow struck me. But 'tis mending quickly."

Edith was horrified, but Arabela managed to calm her as they shared the details of the past few days. Matthew and Edith had been pursued as well but narrowly escaped.

Sister Maude offered to help the maidservant clean up from the journey for which Arabela was grateful. Edith had to be exhausted from all that had occurred.

Arabela was left alone with the order to rest. But how could she when her future was so uncertain, and her heart hurt so much?

～

"We have a problem," Braden advised Chanse as he joined him in the passage that led to a solar near the kitchen where they were to share a meal that evening.

Chanse had requested a separate area from the sisters to dine so they could discuss their plans for the coming days in private. It would also give Braden an opportunity to heal Arabela without her knowing.

Though Chanse had considered telling Arabela of Braden's gift, that was a secret he closely guarded. Telling anyone went against his instincts.

"Another?" Chanse asked. "I believe we already have more than our share. Can you disregard it?" He was only half jesting. The situation already felt impossible. He couldn't imagine it growing worse.

"Nay." Before Braden could say more, Arabela appeared.

Her freshly washed skin and hair, as well as her clean kirtle, made her look much different from the weary, dusty woman who'd ridden before him for so long. Now, she looked much more the part of a lady yet still she stole his breath.

"Sir Hugh." She slowed her steps as she stared at Braden in surprise.

Chanse felt the weight of Braden's glare, guilt causing him to shift uncomfortably. Not only had he not told Arabela of Braden's gift, he hadn't shared Braden's true identity or any of the events surrounding their departure from the tournament her father had held to honor her birthday.

He'd done so purposefully, certain the fewer details she knew about his life, the better. But now as his brother stared at him, Chanse realized his mistake.

He'd held Arabela in his arms and kissed her. He'd done all in his power to save her life when the arrow had struck her. But he hadn't trusted her to share the truth. Worst of all, that truth involved her.

Why had he been surprised to discover she'd kept secrets from him? More importantly, why did it bother him so much that she had?

"Arabela," he began, wondering how to best explain the situation when it had become even more complicated.

"'Tis good to see you again, Lady Arabela." Braden bowed. "But I must confess that I'm not who you thought." He smiled, placing a gentle hand on her injured shoulder as he gestured for her to continue along the passage before him.

Chanse realized Braden meant to use her distraction at this news to heal her. Aware he needed to do his part, Chanse moved to her other side to take her good hand in his. "Sir Hugh is actually my brother, Braden, rather than my cousin."

She frowned, turning her head to look back at Braden who still had his hand on her shoulder.

"Allow me to explain," Chanse quickly said, not wanting her to watch as his brother used his special gift to draw out her pain and into himself, healing her.

Though Arabela's injury was well on the mend, Braden's touch would finish the process. If Arabela had been in a more serious condition, it would've been difficult for Braden to hide the healing as doing so took all of his focus and strength.

Arabela looked again at Chanse, her expression clearly telling of her displeasure. "Please do."

"Braden attended your birthday celebration to learn more about your father's activities. The only way he could do so was by taking the identity of a man your father knew who had received an invitation."

"What of Lady Cairstine?"

"She is actually Lady Ilisa," Chanse continued, as much to keep her attention on him as to explain. "Her older brother served as governor of Berwick but is being held prisoner in England since the siege of the city two years past."

Arabela's eyes widened at this news. "Is she Braden's wife or was that a lie too?"

Chanse frowned, wondering why it mattered. But the tone of Arabela's voice suggested it mattered a great deal. "They are husband and wife."

He didn't share that they'd only arrived at her father's as a married couple at the insistence of Prioress Matilda. Those details weren't his to give. Plus the entire story was complicated and better left to another time and place to tell, preferably not by him.

Chanse risked a glance at Braden to see he had his eyes closed, concentration etched in his face, his hand still holding Arabela's shoulder. Did she feel the sudden heat and release of pain those who benefited from Braden's healing touch often mentioned?

"Lady Ilisa is in Berwick at the moment," Chanse added, hoping to keep her from noticing overmuch. He and Braden had found that people often disregarded the sensations if they were distracted. Another moment and Braden would be done. "With luck, you might soon see her again."

"Is she well? I know she appeared to have an amazing recovery after that terrible fall on the tower stairs, but I've thought of her so often and wondered." Arabela drew to a halt and turned to look at Braden for a response.

Braden released her shoulder, opened his eyes, drawing a deep breath, his face paler than normal. But hopefully, Arabela didn't know him well enough to note any of those things.

"Ilisa is well," Chanse said, hoping that would prompt Braden to offer more.

"She will be pleased to see you," Braden added, his voice gravelly.

Arabela moved her shoulder as if noting a sudden difference in how it felt compared to a few moments ago.

"Let us discuss this further while we eat," Chanse suggested, moving once again toward the solar. "You spoke with Edith?"

"Aye. I'm so pleased she and Matthew returned safely. She's resting."

"Matthew will be joining us for the meal," Chanse said. He glanced over his shoulder to make certain Braden was recovering.

His brother nodded, seeming to gather his strength as he followed them.

Chanse knew if her injury had been worse Braden wouldn't have been able to act normally. He'd witnessed Braden nearly lose his life when he attempted to heal someone too near death. That fear terrified Chanse, as did the thought of someone wanting to use Braden's gift for their own purpose, much like Lord Graham had. The fewer who knew of Braden's ability, the better.

How could Chanse be blamed for carefully guarding secrets when so much was at stake? But that was a weak excuse now that he'd come to know Arabela. He should've told her more. Guilt weighed heavily on him but sharing additional details would have to wait until they had a moment alone. He could only hope it wouldn't be too late and that she'd forgive him for keeping his silence.

They entered the solar where a small table and benches awaited them.

"Dining with the sisters is enjoyable but given how much we have to discuss, I thought it best if we had some privacy," Chanse advised Arabela.

She nodded even as she released his arm to touch her shoulder.

"Did one of the sisters change your binding?" he asked.

"Aye. Sister Maude helped me with it."

"Chanse said Hilda tended your wound. She's a gifted healer." Braden sent a knowing look at Chanse. Giving credit to a healer was a good way to keep the attention of curious people away from him.

"Hilda helped our cousin, Garrick, this spring," Chanse added, unable to shrug aside his guilt.

Luckily, Matthew entered the solar, saving them from having to explain more.

"Lady Arabela," Matthew said, his gaze sweeping over her as he reached to take her hand. "When Chanse told me of your injury—" He shook his head as though unable to finish the thought.

"I'm doing well. Remarkably so." She moved her shoulder as though surprised at just how good it felt. "Edith preferred to rest rather than join us, but she told me you also had a challenging time of it."

They visited for a moment, giving Chanse the opportunity to speak with Braden. "How do you fare?"

"I'll be well soon enough."

"My thanks," Chanse added, clasping his brother's shoulder.

The questioning look Braden gave him made Chanse realize he was revealing more emotion than he'd intended. When Braden's gaze swung to Arabela, Chanse knew he guessed why.

He quickly took a seat at the table, not wanting to be questioned about his feelings for Arabela. Especially not by Braden. Not when he had yet to decide just *how* he felt about her. Now was not the time to worry over such things when they had larger problems to solve.

Two of the sisters brought in steaming trenchers made of bread and filled with a thick stew of roasted meat, onions, and turnips. Chanse and Arabela shared one while the other one was set between Braden and Matthew.

Though it might be unusual for an unmarried woman to dine alone with three men, Chanse hoped Arabela felt the sisters serving them would be sufficient to ensure they behaved with propriety.

As Chanse tore off a piece of the bread to sop up the stew, another sister arrived to set a jug of wine on the table and wooden cups. Braden poured for each of them. The conversation fell into easy topics for a time as they enjoyed the simple meal.

Arabela repeatedly shifted her shoulder as though puzzled by the change she felt. With luck, she wouldn't remove the binding for another day or so and therefore wouldn't be shocked to realize her injury had completely healed.

Another omission of his to add to the growing number. He shifted on the hard bench, guilt at his lies bubbling up no matter how he tried to quell the emotion.

"Is all well?" Arabela asked.

"Of course." He offered a smile.

Her eyes narrowed in response, almost as if she didn't believe him. Did she know him so well then? The idea both disturbed and thrilled him that she'd seen through his defenses.

"As we've mentioned, the city gate is being closely watched," Chanse began. "Braden can pass through easily enough, but the rest of us would have more difficulty."

"Do we have reason to venture into Berwick?" Matthew asked then took another bite.

"Actually, the answer to that has changed of late," Braden said.

"How so?" Chanse asked. Was this the bad news to which Braden had referred earlier?

"Ilisa sent word that she happened to see the Earl of Rothton pass through the market square," Braden said.

"That's rather surprising." Matthew looked up from the meal with a frown.

"Ilisa thought the same. She sent Alec to follow him. The lad managed to overhear that he's in Berwick for a meeting."

"Why is his presence surprising?" Arabela asked.

"He prefers to stay as far away from the border as possible from what we've learned," Braden advised.

"Do you think his presence has anything to do with Arabela's disappearance?" Matthew asked.

Chanse wondered the same.

"Alec eavesdropped in the stable when one of the earl's men saw to their horses," Braden continued. "It seems to be a mystery with whom the earl is meeting. Not even his men know the person's identity."

"Interesting." Chanse pondered the information. "Secret meetings in a location the earl normally avoids?"

"Which makes me think the purpose of it doesn't necessarily have to do with Arabela," Braden said.

"Our focus needs to remain on keeping Arabela safe." Chanse stared at the cup in his hands as he considered the matter. "For the foreseeable future, not just the next sennight."

"Do you have something in mind?" Braden asked.

"I'm done running," Chanse said. "The time has come to take the offense."

"How?" Arabela shook her head. "What could we possibly do that would make them stop looking for me?"

"Reveal Graham's secrets." Chanse watched her closely for a reaction.

"What secrets?" she asked.

Braden cleared his throat. "Not only is it his wish to place a man of his choosing on the throne, but he also leads a group of men who share the same idea. They call themselves the Sentinels of Scotland."

Chanse was pleased Braden had been the one to share this news. Mayhap Arabela would take it better from him than Chanse. Her eyes went wide, her gaze swinging to Chanse as if for confirmation that it was true.

"Many in Scotland would agree with their goal," she offered.

"True, but 'tis who they choose and how they do it that causes the problem." Braden kept his tone even.

"And if Rory is no longer an option, what will they do?" Matthew asked. The knight had learned of Graham's plans soon after he'd left the lord's service, so the news of the Sentinels was no surprise to him.

"I doubt they've abandoned Rory quite yet," Chanse said. "Not when Arabela might still be found, and their plan can be put in place."

"Then it becomes even more important that Arabela remain hidden." Braden shifted to face her. "Do you know with whom Rothton might be meeting? We know the earl is one of the Sentinels, but we're not certain of the other members."

Chanse watched as Arabela considered the question. He was amazed that she was willing to help rather than defending her father. 'Twas more proof that she was an intelligent person who placed the people of her country before her own concerns. His respect—nay, his feelings—for her only increased. As difficult as it was for him to confide in anyone, this woman deserved his trust.

"Rothton has visited my father more often of late," Arabela shared after a long moment.

"Do you know if they met with anyone else?" Chanse asked, desperate for anything that could help him end this.

"Nay, but the Bishop of Moray has also visited several times."

Chanse shook his head. "His activities have been examined, but nothing was found."

"I'd be curious to know why they meet in secret," Matthew added. "As Arabela said, placing a Scotsman on the throne would be welcomed by many. Why hide it?"

"Their methods are less worthy than their cause," Chanse said. "They've attempted to murder some they believed stood in their way. I'd wager they're not proud of that. Revealing who's involved in the group might be the information we need."

"My father has had many visitors in the past few months, some more secretive than others," Arabela said. "However, most attend meals and the like even if they speak in private."

"Does anyone come to mind?" Braden asked.

Arabela frowned. "Are you certain the bishop is not involved?"

"Aye, from what we know," Chanse advised. "If you think of anyone else whose beliefs might align with your father's, do let us know."

"If I saw the person meeting with Rothton, I might recognize him."

Chanse considered her suggestion. Though it had merit, how could they place her in a position to see the man if she couldn't get into Berwick? "That would have to be a last resort."

"With the guards searching those entering the city so closely, it would be a difficult task." Matthew's remark seemed to cut off Arabela's protest.

Silence fell as they sipped their wine, each in their own thoughts.

"You can't remain at St. Mary's forever," Matthew said.

"I can if Prioress Matilda allows me to take my vows," Arabela countered.

Chanse didn't care for the reminder.

"I didn't realize you were considering doing so," Matthew said, his surprise obvious.

As Chanse watched, color rose into Arabela's cheeks. "I have given the matter much thought and believe it might be an ideal solution for me."

Chanse couldn't help his scowl. That didn't sound like a calling to him. He was even more convinced that she'd arrived at this idea only out of desperation.

More than anything, he wanted her to have a choice. A future of her own design. Such an idea was a rarity for most, but if possible, he wanted to provide her that.

CHAPTER 18

Arabela woke the next morn, still reeling from all the information shared the previous evening. She'd lain awake late into the night, trying to match what she'd witnessed before she left home with what the men had told her.

Why hadn't Chanse shared any of this with her before? She closed her eyes as the truth struck her. The same reason he hadn't shared any of his plans—he didn't trust her.

The knowledge hurt more than she could say.

Her father's boldness should no longer surprise her, but it did. Now more than ever, she feared he wouldn't give up his quest as long as he yet breathed. She knew his hatred of the English drove his actions. He'd never liked them, something his father had taught him at an early age.

But dislike had bloomed into hate when her brother, Alistair, had died. She didn't know the details of his death. Her mother had told her at the time that it had been a tragic accident. The fact that he'd died during an argument with Sir William Douglas, the former governor of Berwick, a man who had ties to both England and Scotland, had enraged her father. He blamed Sir William for his son's death. From that point forward, he'd made his dislike of the English clear.

To learn that Lady Cairstine was in truth Lady Ilisa and sister to Sir William had stunned Arabela. Might Ilisa know how Alistair had died? Arabela intended to ask her if she had the chance.

She rose to prepare for the day, almost surprised to see the binding on her shoulder. It felt so much better—as if the arrow had never struck her. She moved her arm in every direction, shocked to realize she had no pain. Unable to contain her curiosity, she used her knife to remove the wrap. To her shock, only a small mark remained on her front. She dearly wished to see her back but from the way she felt, she already knew how it looked—healed.

Her thoughts raced. How was this possible? She had been on the mend but never expected this. It had been sore and uncomfortable the previous evening before supper. As she placed a hand over the scar, she remembered Braden's hand on her shoulder as they'd walked toward the dining room and the odd heat she'd felt.

Had he healed her somehow? She could think of no other explanation. If that were true by some miracle, what an amazing ability he had. Then she gasped as the memory of Ilisa's recovery came to mind. Braden must've healed her as well.

She blinked back tears at the gift Braden had given her. No wonder Chanse was so protective of his brother. Each time Braden healed, he risked someone learning of his skill and therefore trying to take advantage of him. She hoped she could find a way to repay his kindness as well as Chanse's. More than anything, she wanted to tell Chanse that his brother's secret was safe with her.

Her improved condition didn't resolve the question of what path her future should take. Would she have a chance to speak with the prioress about joining the convent this day? While having her life settled was something to which she looked forward, committing to St. Mary's caused a tightness in her body that made breathing difficult. Did she have any alternative? The idea of always looking over her shoulder in fear wasn't much of an option. Unfortunately, that didn't make the decision any easier.

A knock on the door revealed Sister Maude. "Prioress Matilda would speak with you. If you'd please follow me, my lady."

"Of course." This was her chance. Yet as she followed the nun through the corridors of the convent, she had to press a hand to her chest to slow her racing heart. Panic fought to break free, and it was all she could do to put one foot before the other. She had to find the strength to make her argument to join the convent. But the task felt more daunting with each step.

"Here ye be." Sister Maude gestured toward the prioress's door with a smile, seeming unaware of Arabela's angst.

"My thanks." Unable to calm herself, Arabela passed through the open door anyway, praying for guidance.

A woman stood with her back to Arabela, the hood of her cloak drawn over her head.

Arabela stopped in surprise, realizing at once it wasn't Prioress Matilda as the door closed behind her.

The woman turned. "Arabela."

"Mother?" Arabela could only stare, shock holding her in place, unable to understand why she was in the prioress's office.

"I'm so pleased you're well." Her mother blinked back tears as she held out her arms.

Arabela glanced about the small chamber for a sign of her father, but they were alone. "I don't understand. What are you doing here? How did you find me?"

Her mother slowly lowered her arms. "I intended to leave something with the prioress in case she had the opportunity to pass it to you. Imagine my surprise to discover you were here."

"That makes two of us. Where's Father?" A tumble of emotions swept through Arabela. Though her mother's eyes were clear, she recognized the fear in them as she'd seen it in her own reflection often enough.

"I believe he'll come to Berwick soon." Arabela's face must've revealed her fear, for her mother reached out a hand. "I won't tell him I saw you. I promise."

Arabela nodded, though her mother's words did little to reassure her. If her mother had managed to find her, her father would as well. That only made it more imperative that she join the convent as soon as possible. She now had to doubt if doing so would protect her. Her heart sank at the thought.

"I-I wanted to give you this." Her mother reached into the opening of her cloak, untied a small bag from her girdle, and handed it to her.

The weight of the coins surprised Arabela. This was a significant sum.

Her mother folded Arabela's fingers around the bag. "This could serve as your dowry to the convent. I want you to choose. To be free, if you so wish." Tears filled her eyes as her face crumpled. "I want you to have the choice I never had." Her words came quickly, her voice rough. "I'm sorry I wasn't stronger for you."

"Mother," Arabela began, blinking back tears of her own.

"You are so brave. I'm proud of you. You cannot marry Rory. No matter what it takes, do not marry that man."

Arabela reached to embrace her mother, wishing they could've shared this moment months ago. It would've changed everything. But what had caused her mother to take the risk of venturing here?

"Are you well?" Arabela asked as she leaned back to study her face.

"'Tis of no consequence." Which was all the answer Arabela needed. Something had happened.

"Stay. Stay here at the convent." Arabela hugged her mother again. "The prioress will protect you."

"Nay." Her mother pulled away, shaking her head. "That's impossible. And holds far too much risk for you. I must go before anyone notices my absence."

"If you would wait a moment and speak with Sir Chanse, he might be able to aid you."

Her mother's eyes widened with fear. "Nay. That's not possible."

"But Mother—"

"Nay." She placed her hands on Arabela's face, her gaze sweeping over Arabela's features as though memorizing them. "Stay strong, daughter. Follow your heart."

"Mother, wait—"

Her mother pressed a kiss on her cheek and reached for the door before Arabela could stop her. Then she was gone.

~

THE REST of the morn passed slowly, leaving Arabela far too much time to think. She returned to her chamber, relieved to find Edith elsewhere, which gave her the opportunity to gather her composure.

She berated herself for not pressing her mother about what had happened to cause her to take the risk of coming to St. Mary's on her own. Nor had she asked about her father's search for her or the details of her brother's death. She'd been so surprised at her arrival and worried her father would throw open the door at any moment that she hadn't said what she should've.

The bag of coins her mother had given her changed things, but still Arabela hesitated over what to do. When Edith returned, Arabela didn't tell her anything. She needed to sift through the options before speaking of them.

Unable to bear her thoughts or the idleness any longer, she worked in the garden for a time with Edith at her side, helping to harvest some of the vegetables. The sisters voiced their appreciation for the assistance, but Arabela had a difficult time imagining herself doing this in the years to come. She felt out of place.

If she didn't remain, then what did the coming days, weeks, and months hold?

Needing a moment alone, she left Edith with the sisters and walked around the grounds until she came to the front gate, approaching with caution to make certain no one was outside wanting in. She stared through the iron rails toward Berwick, feeling barred from both the city and the convent. She existed in a strange limbo where she couldn't move forward, nor did she wish to move back. She didn't belong in either location.

Which left her where?

She ventured to the stable to see if she could help with the horses, something she'd often done at home which brought her comfort.

"Good morn," she greeted the young stable boy.

He blushed at her greeting and dipped his head in answer.

"May I be of assistance with the horses in some way?" she asked.

The shock on his face was answer enough, but he stammered a reply. "Nay, my lady."

Disappointed, she walked into the stable, so she might at least visit Chanse's horse. But the steed was gone. The realization that he'd left surprised her. Hurt, actually. Why had he departed without telling her?

She shook her head at her tangled thoughts. Too many questions and doubts tugged at her. She'd only just told herself the previous day not to become too dependent on the handsome knight, nor give in to her attraction to him. Her focus needed to be on her future.

Therein was the problem—the months ahead were still hazy in her mind. If she could look around in Berwick, she might gain a feel for the city and determine whether she wanted to try to make her home there rather than at the convent. But doing so would be nearly impossible when her father and Rory searched for her. While she'd known they wouldn't let her go easily, she hadn't realized how difficult it would be to remain out of their grasp.

Arabela returned to the garden, hoping to work off some of her uncertainty with labor, only to be interrupted soon after she'd begun.

"Bela?"

She straightened to see a familiar face approaching. "Lady Cairstine." She stopped herself before she said more, realizing that wasn't the lady's name. "Or rather, Lady Ilisa."

Ilisa offered a rueful smile. "I hope you'll forgive me for the deception. We felt it necessary at the time."

Her words and easy manner put Arabela at ease. She'd liked the woman from the moment they'd met, and the dishonesty hadn't changed that. "'Tis truly a pleasure to see you."

"I'm pleased to see you too."

Remembering all too well the terrible fall that should've taken Ilisa's life, Arabela couldn't help but study her closely, especially given her own recovery. "You are well? Truly?"

"Aye. Recovered in full." To Arabela's surprise, she drew close to embrace her. "I believe I should be asking that of you from what Braden shared." Ilisa eased back and glanced at her shoulder. "You have been through quite the ordeal."

Arabela found herself swallowing against the lump in her throat at Ilisa's sympathy. "'Tis nothing compared to yours." She reached out to squeeze Ilisa's hands. "I still don't understand what happened when you fell from the tower stairs." Ilisa's miraculous recovery was a far greater miracle than the quick healing of Arabela's own wound. But Arabela couldn't bring herself to ask if Braden had the gift of healing. Somehow it seemed far too personal when he obviously wanted to keep it a secret.

Ilisa sighed as she wrapped her arm around Arabela's and pulled her forward to walk along the path that circled the garden. She waved at several of the sisters who greeted her. "Life is often more complicated than one expects. Do you find that to be so?"

Arabela nodded. "Especially of late."

Ilisa leaned close. "I must say how delightful it is to have another woman with whom to speak. I miss my sister more than I thought possible. The nuns at St. Mary's are very kind, but I'm not one of them and feel a little lonely even when I'm here."

"I understand. I feel much the same way thus far." She glanced around to make certain no one could hear them.

"Braden and Chanse suggested I speak with you about why Braden and I were at your holding as Hugh and Cairstine."

"Why do I feel as though I won't enjoy this story?" Arabela asked.

Again, Ilisa gave her arm a comforting squeeze. "That makes two of us." She drew to a halt to face Arabela. "But you deserve to hear the truth."

Arabela gathered her fortitude and nodded. "I appreciate that."

"Your father has sworn to kill my family, including me."

"Why?" A shiver of cold shock swept through her.

"He blames my eldest brother, William, for your brother's death."

Arabela sorted through what little she knew, but the news still surprised her. "What does Alistair's death have to do with you?"

"Nothing. But that doesn't seem to matter to Lord Graham. He made two attempts on my sister's life before she left the country. I only know what William told us about the matter, which was very little. But he said your brother's death was an accident."

"Then why does my father blame him?"

Ilisa shook her head. "If you don't know, we may not learn more unless we can speak with my brother or your father regarding the details."

"My father hasn't been the same since my brother's death. I fear it worsened his hatred of anyone with ties to England." Of that, she had no doubt. That hatred had shaded his opinion of people and formed his goals. Goals with which she had difficulty agreeing.

"Losing his only son must've been terrible for him and your mother," Ilisa said. "And you lost your brother. I feel as if I've lost mine too as he's locked away in England."

"That must be difficult." Arabela hadn't known her brother well as he'd been five years her senior and left to train as a page before she'd been old enough to remember him. His rare visits home had been brief and spent mostly with their father. That didn't mean she didn't feel his loss. Yet it would also be hard to bear if he were locked away where no one knew if he still lived.

"William was accused by some of allowing King Edward entrance into Berwick over two years ago when he laid siege to the city. The king ordered the River Tweed to run red with blood. Thousands died, including men, women, and children. But I know William wouldn't have opened the gate."

"I can't imagine what you went through during the siege." Arabela had heard of the march on Berwick as had everyone in Scotland.

"The English think him guilty as well. They accuse him of not aiding them when he should have," Ilisa said with a sigh. "They took his title and his son and our home. William has been locked up since. His son was taken to train as a page for an English lord." She shook her head, the situation obviously distressing.

"How frightening for you."

"Aye. 'Twas because of that situation that Braden and I came to your holding using different names. We hoped to learn more of your father's plans and who is involved in the Sentinels of Scotland. Their goal is to remove anyone with English ties by any means necessary."

"Was that when you discovered the Earl of Rothton was part of the Sentinels?" Arable asked.

"Aye, but there are others. We need to discover who."

Arabela held Ilisa's gaze. "I don't pretend to know what happened between our brothers, but I'm sorry my father believes you are to blame in any way for Alistair's death. I certainly don't think that. Your family has already lost so much."

"I appreciate your words, and I hate to ask more of you, but we need your assistance. Discovering the others involved in the Sentinels will help all of us."

"Except my father." Arabela felt compelled to point out that truth. While she didn't agree with her father's actions, was she willing to assist others who wished to stop him when she knew it would most likely end in violence? Possibly even his death?

"That's true," Ilisa said with a somber nod. "Mayhap we ask too much. But we're trying to do what we can to keep the people of Scotland safe. To keep war from killing more on either side."

Arabela considered her words for a long moment before she realized she had no choice. Her father was wrong. "I'm not certain how I can help, but I'll do what I can."

∽

CHANSE RODE TOWARD ST. Mary's with Braden and Matthew soon after midday, more frustrated than when he'd left. Obtaining information in this country was proving nearly impossible. He preferred to fight his foes on the battlefield where the objective was clear along with the enemy.

They'd spoken with several fishermen who'd heard rumors of Graham's efforts to place a person of his choosing on the throne, which led them to another who refused to share anything, and then another who told them they'd been misinformed. Making plans based on hearsay was impossible.

"I'm returning to Berwick to make certain all is well with Ilisa," Braden advised him as they neared the convent gate.

"I'll come with you and see if I can learn anything in the market square," Matthew said.

Chanse nodded as the two men continued down the road toward the city entrance. Neither would have any difficulty entering despite the extra precautions the guards were taking. But Chanse knew if Arabela tried to enter she'd be stopped as the guards were searching for any female matching her description.

He didn't want to venture to Berwick until he had a reason to, nor did he want to leave Arabela alone overlong. He worried she'd either depart on her own or manage to convince the prioress to let her join the convent. He didn't want her to do either though he knew he was being unreasonable when he didn't yet have another solution for her to consider.

After handing the reins of his horse to the stable lad, he searched for Arabela and found her working in the garden.

"What are you doing?" he asked, surprised she wasn't resting in her chamber.

She straightened and brushed off her hands. "Exactly what it appears I'm doing. Where have you been?"

He blinked at her tone. "I thought you'd still be tired."

Her glare suggested he was wrong about more than just that.

"I was with Braden and Matthew, trying to discover more information but with little success."

She said nothing, only continued to study him. Her displeasure with him was apparent, but he wasn't certain why.

Awareness dawned slowly. "I should've told you where I was going before I left."

"That would've been helpful."

He glanced about to realize several of the sisters watched with interest. Rather than give the curious nuns anything more to visit about, he pulled Arabela into the entrance of the nearby chapter house to provide them with privacy. "I wouldn't leave for any length of time without telling you."

A hint of worry flashed in her eyes and told him he'd struck a chord. "I'm pleased to hear that."

"Will you promise me the same?" he asked as he gave in to the urge to trail a finger along her cheek.

She looked at him, her gently arched brows lifted in surprise. "Where would I go?"

"I don't know, but you were leaving when I took you. You choosing to do so again wouldn't surprise me."

She hesitated longer than he would've liked. "I will do my best."

Her answer only worried him further. "I know the situation is difficult since we don't know what the morrow will bring. But know that I won't leave until you're safe."

She swallowed, drew a deep breath then gave a single nod.

Had his words upset her? How, when he'd meant to reassure her? Unless she chose to share her thoughts, he couldn't comfort her further. Or could he?

With slow, careful movements, he drew closer, placing his hands on her hips. His touch caused her eyes to widen but when she didn't pull away, he took it as permission to proceed. He kissed her, thoroughly, wanting to express how he felt. Especially since he didn't have the right words to describe it. For now, he hoped his affection for her was clear in his kiss.

The sound of voices approaching warned him their privacy had come to an end. He eased back though his body wanted nothing more than to draw her into his arms and hold her tight.

Sighing, he realized he needed to think of something to do for the rest of the day or he'd be seeking out Arabela again.

"I'm going to find something to eat then ride to your father's holding to see if there are any signs of his arrival."

"I'm coming with you," she said. Her chin lifted in a now familiar gesture that he admired, despite how much it frustrated him.

"Nay. Remain here where 'tis safe."

"Don't ask me to wait. I want to see for myself what you see. Waiting here, wondering, is already driving me crazed."

"I might not be able to protect you beyond the convent walls." He understood what she must be feeling and could empathize. However, more than anything he wanted her safe.

"I understand, but I can be of aid. I might recognize any guests my father has if he's there. If the Earl of Rothton is in Berwick, isn't it most likely that he'll venture to my father's holding at some point along with the person he's meeting?"

"We don't know that such a meeting will happen this day if at all," Chanse argued though he knew he was losing ground. She had a valid point, but more than that, he wanted to spend whatever time with her that he could.

"What if it did?"

He shook his head, annoyed at his inability to deny this woman anything. "We won't be traveling along the roads."

"Then there will be less chance of being seen."

"You'll need to remain hidden as best you can just in case."

"Shall I don my squire clothes?"

"Nay." The idea made him break into a cold sweat. "We won't be taking the road, only crossing it. We'll do so when few others are in sight and ride into the trees." The convent was far enough away from Berwick and the woods close enough that the likelihood of being caught seemed slim.

"Very well. I'll fetch my cloak." She smiled and turned away before he could determine a reason why she couldn't accompany him.

With a scowl, he made his way to the kitchen to coax anything he could from the cook—anything that didn't include stale bread, hard cheese, or dried meat. He quickly ate though it had more to do with who waited for him than the tastiness of the food.

Arabela lingered near the door when he stepped outside.

"Are you certain you wouldn't rather wait?" Chanse asked, hoping to change her mind. "You must still be tired. And you've had more than your fair share of time on horseback of late."

"I have already recovered."

Out of reasons for her to remain, he glanced at the darkening sky and latched onto the sight. "It might rain."

"Then I'll be wet."

"Don't say I didn't warn you," he said as they walked toward the stable, both relieved and anxious that she was accompanying him.

Soon she was astride his horse and pressed against him as she had been nearly all of their journey. Before they'd ridden out of the convent gate, he knew he'd made a terrible mistake. His feelings for her grew each day no matter how he tried to convince himself otherwise.

A hint of lavender caught his notice, the scent causing desire to smolder inside him. He appreciated the feel of her in the circle of his arms. The idea of leaning close and pressing his lips to the softness of her neck came to mind and wouldn't leave.

"Do you know where my father's holding is?" she asked, glancing over her shoulder at him.

"Aye. I'm told there's a ridge that runs along the south side of it that should provide a good view."

She ran her hand along the horse's neck then sat back, her body teasing his as she shifted into place.

He could only hope she didn't feel his manhood springing to life with each move she made. The remainder of the day stretched out before him, feeling as though it would be a tortured one with Arabela back in his arms. But damn if she didn't feel as if that was where she belonged.

CHAPTER 19

Arabela told herself to focus on the direction they were riding, the trees they passed, the rocky bank. Anything to keep her attention away from the man behind her.

She felt safe and protected riding with Chanse. But that was only part of what she felt. Awareness tingled from head to toe caused by her continually bumping against him as the horse made its way along the narrow path they took that meandered through the woods.

Though she knew it wasn't possible, she swore she could feel the hard muscles of his chest against her back. Mayhap because she remembered what he looked like without his tunic—all broad shoulders and sculpted torso. His strength was undeniable. But his impressive form was only part of the reason her heart beat faster when he was near.

He attracted her on every level. Physically. Emotionally. Mentally.

Was it because her life was so unbalanced that he felt like a safe anchor in a storm? She only knew her world righted itself when he was near, only to tip again when he touched her.

The time slowly passed as they rode, speaking little, the silence comfortable. She wondered what held his thoughts, but since she didn't care to share hers, she didn't ask about his. Though she longed to ask him about Braden and his ability to heal, she waited, hoping a more opportune time would arise.

At last, they topped a ridge, and a small holding was visible below. Chanse halted the horse within the trees, careful to stay out of sight.

The two-story stone manor was nothing compared to her home. A stable sat on one side and a large garden on the other. Several fields spread out on the opposite side of the ridge on which they stood, one with grazing sheep. The manor would be difficult to protect if threatened as it had little in the form of defenses other than the men who occupied it.

She resented the fact that her father had never brought her here. Was her mother here? Its proximity to the English border must annoy her father to no end as would its lack of defenses. Owning this holding might be convenient for any business he needed to tend to in Berwick but served little other purpose as he never ventured to England.

Servants worked in the garden. No doubt they kept a close eye on things as well as making certain the manor was prepared should her father pay a visit.

"Little activity on the grounds," Chanse murmured.

She blinked to clear her thoughts and studied the area objectively. Very few people walked about. Based on that alone, she had to believe her father had not yet arrived if he intended to come.

"Father normally travels with quite a few of his men," she said. "There's no sign of preparations being made, though I don't know if he'd bother to send word prior to his arrival."

"I suppose he wouldn't come this far without a better idea of your location."

She hesitated, the urge to tell him of her mother's visit surprising her. But if she didn't choose to confide in him, how could she expect him to do so?

"My mother came to the convent this morn."

Chanse's body tensed at her words. "How did she know you were there?"

"She didn't. She wanted to leave...something with the prioress for me in case I happened to come." Telling him of the dowry for the convent didn't feel like the right thing to do. Not when he'd already expressed his displeasure over her taking her vows.

"What did she say?"

"She believes my father will soon arrive but promised not to tell him she saw me." She swallowed against the lump in her throat. "She apologized for not being stronger."

He was silent for a long moment. Then he wrapped his free arm around her and held her tight, his cheek resting against her hair.

Her heart swelled at the gesture. How had he known the right thing to do?

"Does she intend to stay in Berwick?" he asked when he loosened his hold.

"She didn't say. She left before I could ask questions. I should've tried to gain more information." Again, she berated herself for not doing so.

"That would've been difficult when her visit was so unexpected."

She relaxed at his words, grateful he understood what a shock it had been.

They remained in the cover of the trees and observed for a time.

"I don't think she's staying here," Arabela said. "I'd hazard a guess that Father didn't know of her journey based on the way she acted."

The lack of activity supported her suspicion. If her father had arrived, there would've been more men and horses about.

"Braden learned of two cottages near the boundary of the land that belongs to your father," Chanse advised. "I thought we might try to locate the one nearest Berwick on our way back. I don't know if anyone resides in it but knowing its location could prove helpful in case a meeting is held there."

"Very well."

They watched for a while longer but saw little of interest. Though nothing had resulted from their outing, Arabela was pleased she'd come. Doing something—anything—felt better than simply waiting for news to arrive at the convent.

"Let's be on our way," Chanse said at last. "I doubt we're going to escape the rain." He studied the dark clouds that moved steadily toward them. They looked heavy and threatening.

"Mayhap they'll take a different direction before they reach us." Unfortunately, they looked rather ominous.

"Hmm. I believe I warned you it might rain," he said as he turned the horse back the way they'd come.

They took a slightly different route through the terrain, pausing several times for Chanse to study the area.

The clouds soon caught them. What started as a gentle sprinkle at first soon turned into a deluge. They waited out the worst of it under a tree but were still soaked before long. Then the wind picked up.

Arabela shivered from the chill. The cold didn't seem to bother Chanse. Then again, nothing did. His calmness under pressure and in difficult circumstances amazed her. What might it take to ruffle his feathers, she wondered?

"You're cold," he murmured and attempted to adjust her cloak. "And wet to the skin."

The mention of skin brought things to mind that heated her cheeks. "I'm fine," she said, but the chattering of her teeth belied her words.

"The tree is no longer serving its purpose. Mayhap we can make it to the cottage and wait out the remainder of the storm there while we dry off." He leaned forward to catch her gaze. "Shall we make an attempt?"

Another tremor passed through her, answering for her. With an oath, he kneed the horse, and they rode into the storm. Though the rain wasn't coming down as hard as it had earlier, the drops were steady. And cold. The temperature was falling, adding to her discomfort.

"Now do you wish you remained at the convent?" he asked.

"Nay." She decided against explaining further, partly because her chattering teeth wouldn't allow it and partly because she didn't want to tell him the truth. Any time they spent together pleased her. Unfortunately, those moments were most likely drawing to an end.

The realization made her want to make the most of every opportunity to be with him that crossed her path. Even if that meant being wet and cold. She was with Chanse, and that made a world of difference in her ability to deal with her discomfort.

The downpour increased, making it difficult to see. How Chanse knew where they were going was beyond her. But soon a small cottage came into view at the edge of a clearing similar to Hilda's. No garden surrounded this one, though it was evident one had been there in past years. The thatched roof had seen better days and looked in need of repair. The place had an abandoned appearance to it.

"I'd say 'tis free for us to borrow for a brief spell," Chanse said.

She nodded, not risking another response. The cold felt as if it had seeped into her bones, and she couldn't stop shaking.

He rode slowly toward the cottage, but no one came outside to demand what they were doing there, much to Arabela's relief. The idea of drying off and warming for a time held great appeal.

After halting the horse under the eave where they were out of the worst of the weather, he dismounted, tethering the reins around a post. "Wait here while I have a quick look."

She nodded, missing the warmth of his body already.

He knocked on the door then unlatched it. He called out as he entered, but no one answered. Within a few moments, he returned. "Looks as if the roof is holding well enough to provide temporary shelter for us."

With little effort, he lifted her from the horse, blocking the worst of the rain from her with his body. He escorted her inside, and she found herself standing there shivering in the mostly empty cottage. A fine layer of dust coated the table and two chairs that stood not far from the hearth in the center of the room. A bed sat in one corner with a chest at the foot of it.

"All the comforts of home," Chanse said. He moved past her toward the hearth where wood and kindling were stacked in a small pile. "There's more than enough to start a fire."

Within a few moments, flames blazed cheerily. Chanse pulled the two chairs forward for them to sit on.

"I'll see to my horse and bring in more wood."

Arabela nodded then sat stiffly and leaned forward to warm her hands near the fire. They were out of the rain and wind, but the interior of the cottage was cold and damp.

"Soon the cottage will be warm," Chanse said upon his return. He cast a doubtful glance at the roof as he set more wood beside the fire. Then he shifted closer to take her hands in his, holding them tight between his warm ones.

Her heart stumbled at his kind gesture, wishing he meant it in a different way.

~

CHANSE CURSED UNDER HIS BREATH. He'd promised himself to avoid touching her beyond when she rode before him on the horse. What else could he do when she was shaking with cold? Her hands felt like ice, but the feel of soft skin still stirred his senses.

He shoved aside his wayward thoughts and focused on getting her warm. The fire would help but not when her clothes were wet.

"Why don't you remove your cloak?" he suggested. "We'll hang it near the fire to dry."

She nodded, but her stiff fingers didn't cooperate.

He leaned close to assist her, her sweet scent wafting toward him as though released by the rain. He forced himself to concentrate on unfastening her cloak then removing it. After draping it over the end of the table to dry, he turned to face her.

Tremors shook her slender frame.

"I fear not only my cloak is damp," she said as she plucked the wet skirt of her kirtle with an attempt at a smile.

"You'd be better off removing your kirtle as well, else you'll never warm," he said. He swallowed hard at the thought. Yet the sight of her shivering left no choice.

She looked at him, her uncertainty obvious. "What of you? Your tunic is soaked as well."

He closed his eyes for a brief moment, telling himself this was best for both of them. The sooner they were dry, the better. "True. With luck, our clothes will be dry by the time the rain ends." He couldn't ignore the desire that simmered beneath the surface as he removed his tunic, making him all the more aware of her every move.

Just because they removed their wet clothes didn't mean anything would happen between them, he reassured himself as he placed more wood on the fire. He was a man of honor. Resisting this woman would be difficult but certainly not impossible. He moved to the chest near the bed and found two blankets to place on each chair.

Arabela turned away from him, revealing the laces that ran up the back of her kirtle. "Would you mind assisting me?"

Swallowing back the quickly forming ball of need that threatened to overpower him, he moved closer. The fabric wasn't nearly as damp here, but still his fingers fumbled with the ties until he loosened it enough for her to remove. He helped her pull the damp wool over her head, leaving her in her thin chemise. He couldn't help but think of the last time she'd stood in her chemise. The memory spiked his desire even more. The long plait of her hair fell over her shoulder and dripped onto the thin fabric.

"I suppose I should dry my hair as well," she said and turned to face the fire. With trembling fingers, she removed the ribbon that held the plait and loosened the long tresses.

He placed the kirtle beside her cloak then eased into the chair, unable to take his gaze from the feminine task her fingers performed. What might those clever fingers feel like dancing across him? He drew a deep breath at the thought, his mouth suddenly dry.

She continued her movements until that long dark hair fell in waves to just below her waist. She shook out the tresses a safe distance from the flames then did the same with her chemise, fluttering the damp fabric away from her body.

The sight was magical. In places, the linen clung to her skin to reveal tantalizing hints of her body. In other places, the fabric was nearly sheer and just as tantalizing. She turned in a circle beside the fire to warm each part of her in a slow, exotic dance, her movements heating him from the inside out.

"What of your chausses?" she asked, her voice barely above a whisper. "Would you prefer to remove them to dry?"

He shook his head aware his voice would fail him. If he removed those, heaven knew what would happen. And so did he.

"But aren't you chilled?" she asked as she stepped close. Close enough that he parted his knees to make room for her without thinking twice.

"A bit." No purpose would be served in lying though only his skin was cold. Inside, he was burning.

As if to make certain, she reached out a hand and touched his shoulder. "Aye, you are." A slight tremor shook her frame.

"And you're still cold." Reminding himself that his purpose was to protect her, not ravish her, he rose and drew her into his arms.

A delicious heat rose through him, tempting him to offer more. To take more. He clenched his teeth to keep a tight rein on his building desire.

But his traitorous hands refused to listen. They roamed over her back, seeking out the chilled places to hold there to warm her, then moving on to the next cold spot along her body.

She gently shivered in the circle of his arms, but only a small tremor this time. He considered that progress and continued his efforts until he realized his hands cupped the delightful curve of her cold bottom. His manhood surged, causing him to suck in a deep breath as his body tensed. Still his hands refused to listen to his silent demands to stop, instead caressing the mounds. He couldn't help but appreciate the way his touch pressed her against his hardness.

"Oh." Her breathlessness teased his senses. Then she lifted her arms to wrap around his neck, bringing her even closer.

Heat rose between them, swirling around them, and had little to do with the fire.

"Arabela?" He drew her name out, asking without words what he so desperately wanted. Needed.

She kissed his bare chest, and her fingers caressed him just as he'd imagined. Her tentative touch felt wonderful as she ran her hands along his shoulders, over the muscles of his chest then back up again.

His need for her built with each move. He grasped her waist then eased upward until his hands rested just beneath her breasts. Unable to resist, he shifted to hold those soft globes, remembering well the taste of them and longing to experience it again.

She eased back, the movement dashing his hopes. But then her hands lifted to tug at the ribbon that held up the chemise.

"Chanse," she began with a wrinkle in her brow. She pulled the edge of the chemise low to reveal a small mark—the only sign of her terrible injury.

Bless you, Braden, Chanse thought.

"I'd like to know how." Her eyes held questions he didn't want to answer. Not now.

"I'm sure you would." To distract her and please himself, he leaned close to press a kiss on the scar then continued upward along her neck and ending with her lips. He hoped the kiss held what he didn't say—that he cared for her and would do all in his power to protect her. When he shifted back, the crease in her brow was gone.

He held his breath as she completed the task, the linen parting to hint at the curves of her breasts, the tips just visible through the thin cloth. With a sigh of reverence, he raised a finger to caress first one tip, then the other, his touch bringing back her trembles.

"May I?" he whispered.

She nodded, her eyes darkening.

He loosened the neckline to reveal her breasts. The flames of the fire flickered along her curves, casting shadows only to remove them, another exotic dance for him to enjoy.

Need made his movements jerky as he took her mouth with his. His tongue pressed against the seam of her lips and gained entrance. The idea of what that represented made his body thrum with desire. Only for her.

"You are perfect," he said as he drew back to look into her eyes. "So beautiful."

Her soft smile caused his chest to tighten with emotion. She placed her hand along his cheek. "So handsome."

The tender gesture twined with her words made his heart thump alarmingly. He kissed her again, enjoying the feel of her, the taste of her.

She shifted closer and her bare breasts rubbed against him. His entire body tingled with need.

Passion bloomed, and he loosened his hold on it. With his hands on her waist, he moved his body against her curves. She moaned as though enjoying the sensation as much as he did.

"I ache for you," he muttered.

"As do I." She couldn't have given him a finer gift than that admission.

He eased up the back of her chemise, needing to feel her bare flesh beneath his hands. Her bottom felt like the finest silk. He lingered there, finding the delicate flesh at the back of the apex of her legs as he kissed her again.

Her sigh was all the encouragement he needed to continue his exploration. He could feel the dampness between her legs. That made him even harder.

With one hand on her bottom, he shifted the other to her waist, her belly, moving slowly, hoping she wouldn't halt him. When he touched the curls at her center, she broke their kiss with a gasp.

"Chanse."

To his surprise, she placed her hand on the front of his chausses, molding the fabric against the bulge there. He rocked his hips as his body surged. Then she lifted a hand to pull at her chemise, and it soon pooled at her feet.

With a groan, he took her into his arms and kissed her, putting all his desire into the moment. She responded move for move, caress for caress, until he could hardly bear it.

He ran his hand along the front of her thigh, then the flare of her hip before moving to her damp curls. His finger slid along her slick folds until her knees buckled.

He lifted her effortlessly and sat on the chair with her on his lap, legs on either side of him, his chausses still in place. He continued to touch her, the scent of her arousal increasing his own. Her breasts taunted him, and he licked first one tip and then the other.

"Arabela," he muttered, nearly out of his mind with need. "I want you desperately."

"Then take me," she whispered. She eased back to push at the top of his chausses. "Take me now."

"But—"

"Shh." She placed a finger over his lips. "Let us enjoy this moment."

He wanted to argue, to insist he wanted much more than a moment. But words were impossible. Logic and caution failed him, especially when she moved from him to allow him to stand and quickly unfasten his chausses and kick off his boots, shoving away the barriers between them.

He sat back, reaching for her, lifting her to place her back on his thighs.

"My goodness," she said with astonishment as she stared at his manhood. She took hold of him, her inexperienced grasp nearly sending him over the edge.

He placed a hand over hers to still her movements before his need overcame him. "Slower, my sweet. Your touch undoes me."

She appeared surprised at his words. "Truly?"

"Truly. Let us find pleasure with each other." He touched her again, bringing her to the brink before lifting her to ride him only to pause.

His gaze met hers. "Are you certain?" he asked, wanting her agreement before continuing.

"Aye," she said on a breath. With his assistance, she lowered herself onto his shaft.

"Hold tight, my sweet," he whispered, wishing he could further ease the pain that came with this first time.

"Oh." The catch in her voice paused his movements while she adjusted to the feel of him.

That pause nearly killed him. Yet he waited, pressing kisses along her neck, his hands caressing her body until at last, he felt her tenseness ease. He kissed her, hoping to convey how much this moment meant to him.

Then inch by marvelous inch, he fully sheathed himself inside her.

Her head fell back as her body arched, adding an extra layer of sensation.

With a growl, he lifted her only to fill her again, then again. She quickly caught on, mimicking his movements until her body shuddered. "Chanse? I—"

He thrust into her again as he reached to find her delicate nub. "Let go. I've got you."

She shuddered at his words as her body found release. The keening sound she made caused him to move quicker. He followed her a moment later, diving off the edge of the precipice to land with Arabela in his arms.

She collapsed against him, her breath coming in gasps as she wrapped her arms around him.

He held her tight, his face buried in her hair, wishing he never had to let her go.

"You're certain all is well?" Chanse asked as Arabela shifted in front of him on the horse as they rode toward St. Mary's late that afternoon once the rain had ceased.

She swallowed the truth. *Nay, she wanted to say. I'm in love with the knight who captured me body and soul. But I don't think he feels the same.*

But she said none of that. How could she when he hadn't offered any words of love nor any promises?

She appreciated it was better that way. If he uttered vows he didn't intend to keep, she would only be hurt more, and she hurt enough already.

Not for a moment did she regret what had happened. She couldn't have turned him away if her life had depended on it. He held her heart.

The problem was that he had yet to realize it.

Nor did she care to be the one who told him. He'd already saved her life. How could she possibly burden him with the full truth of the depth of her feelings?

She'd known what might happen—what she wanted to happen—the moment he'd suggested they wait out the storm in the cottage. But never could she have guessed how deeply their making love would affect her. 'Twas as if the physical joining of their bodies had released her heart and handed it to him.

Even as he'd withdrawn from her, she'd been certain he didn't feel the same as she. His thoughts moved quickly to the practicalities of their situation such as her comfort, the weather, and their safe return to St. Mary's.

But she refused to have second thoughts. Nay. He'd given her a gift beyond measure. Now she had a memory to hold on to, regardless of what her future might bring.

Then why did she want to cry?

She gathered her wits to push aside the urge. This was not the time. Not in front of Chanse. The idea of him being remorseful only made her hurt more.

His regret would be worse. His gentle touch offered comfort yet kept a distance between them that she already despised. She reminded herself this was exactly what she'd wanted—the freedom to choose. She'd chosen Chanse and held the joy of him tight to her heart. Or rather, where her heart used to be.

"Not much farther," he said even as his hand caressed her thigh.

She nodded, unable to answer. How could she possibly love a man when she knew so little about him? She didn't know where he lived or what his family was like, other than his brother. She didn't know why he wanted to help prevent England from attacking Scotland. She didn't know what his dreams were for his future or even if he had any.

But she knew his integrity, his honor, his skills, his determination in the face of danger. She knew all that was important and made him the man he was.

At this moment, that was enough. She could only hope she'd come to know the rest.

Did she dare tell him how she felt? Give him a hint of her

thoughts? The gates of St. Mary's came into view as she considered doing so. What awaited her within those walls she didn't know.

What did *she* want? Without any hesitation, an answer came to mind. *Chanse*. Though she doubted he was of like mind, how would she know if she didn't raise the subject? She was wasting an opportunity to speak with him that not might come again any time soon.

Chanse watched the road from the cover of the woods. With the road nearly empty, he urged his horse into a gallop and soon they were passing through the convent gate.

Gathering her courage, she turned to look over her shoulder. "Chanse."

Before she could say more, the pounding of hooves caught her notice. She turned to see Braden riding toward them from the stable.

"I have news," he said as he brought his horse alongside Chanse's. "The earl is meeting with the stranger on the morrow at midday at The Bull and Boar Tavern."

Arabela's heart dropped at the information. Never had she received a clearer sign from fate that her feelings were not meant to be revealed at this time. Besides, how could she ask Chanse to consider a future with her when all of this remained between them?

"Excellent news," Chanse said. "But how are we going to identify him?"

"My hope is that Matthew might recognize him," Braden said.

Before Chanse could agree, Arabela interrupted. "I'm more likely to know him than Matthew."

"Nay. 'Tis too dangerous," Chanse said.

But Braden regarded her thoughtfully. "Why do you think that?"

"He was at the garrison while I was in the great hall. While I rarely heard what my father and his guests spoke of, I knew who they were. I don't think Matthew can say the same."

"But that means they'd recognize you as well," Chanse argued.

"Not if I'm disguised. I could wear the squire's attire."

"Nay," Chanse protested. "That wouldn't pass close scrutiny."

"Then mayhap the prioress would allow me to borrow one of the sisters' gowns. Besides, I only need a glimpse of the person. They might not even see me." The more she considered the plan, the more she liked it. Actively helping to solve their problems seemed like a good idea. Once all of this was over, mayhap she'd have the opportunity to tell Chanse what was in her heart.

"I don't like it. We know you're safe here."

"But if the identities of the Sentinels and their plans aren't exposed then Arabela will never be safe." Braden looked at Arabela as he spoke.

"True," she agreed. "This is our best hope to put an end to the situation." *So you and Braden can return home*, she thought.

That would be a gift to you both for all you've done to aid me. While it seemed small in comparison to what they'd both risked for her, she wanted to do what she could even if it meant saying goodbye.

But she didn't say her worst fear. Now wasn't the time. Mayhap there a chance the brothers would remain in Berwick. Ilisa called the city home but from what little Chanse had told her, she knew they hadn't been in the area long.

"I disagree," Chanse said, his voice tight. "The chances of you gaining entrance to the city is slim even in disguise, let alone you identifying the man without him seeing you."

"I want to try." Though nerves pinched the pit of her stomach, she was certain this was the right thing to do.

"With proper planning, it might work," Braden said. Then he looked at his brother, waiting for his agreement. "Ilisa and Alec will be safer if Graham's plans are halted. 'Tis our best hope unless you have another idea."

Chanse shook his head. "I still don't like it."

"You don't have to like it," Braden said with a smile. "But you do have to help its success."

Chanse's gaze held hers. "Only if we can find a way for you to be unrecognizable."

If only that were truly possible, but Arabela knew it wasn't. However, she was willing to take this risk with the hope of being one step closer to putting an end to her father's plans. Then mayhap she could move forward with her life, whatever course that might take.

CHAPTER 20

Chanse paced the courtyard as the supper hour neared, something he seemed to be doing on a regular basis since their arrival. "There has to be another way."

Arabela had insisted on speaking with Prioress Matilda alone to discuss a disguise to gain her entrance to the city. Chanse didn't care for her request, but she stated that the prioress's opinion on the issue was the one that truly mattered. Why did he feel as if she were already stepping away from him?

Braden leaned against one of the columns that edged the courtyard, arms folded over his chest as he watched Chanse. "You're wearing a path in the ground."

"As would you if we were discussing Ilisa," Chanse shot back only to realize the risk both Braden and Ilisa had taken when they'd ventured to Graham's holding, posing as others. He paused, ran a hand through his hair and faced Braden. "My apologies."

"No need. I understand." The knowing glint in his eyes had Chanse turning away to resume his pacing.

He didn't care for that glint either. Nor did he have any intention of addressing the reason it lingered in Braden's eyes. Braden seemed to suspect what happened earlier in the day when he and Arabela had ridden to Graham's manor house.

"I'm surprised you weren't caught in the rain," Braden had said as he studied Chanse's attire while they'd seen to their horses upon entering the convent.

"We found shelter for a time and managed to dry." Chanse hadn't been able to meet Braden's gaze for fear his expression would reveal too much.

"Shelter? How fortunate." He should've known Braden wouldn't let it go so easily. "You must've had to remain in this...shelter for a time as the rain continued much of the afternoon."

"Aye." Chanse felt his face heat as his brother continued to stare.

"What sort of shelter was it?" Braden asked.

"We found one of the cottages on the edge of Graham's holding that you mentioned."

"Interesting."

Chanse had made an excuse and left his brother to his thoughts.

But now, he could feel Braden's steady regard once again.

"You've come to care for Arabela." Braden didn't form it as a question but as a statement of fact.

Which it was. Why Chanse bothered to try to hide anything from Braden remained a mystery. "Aye."

"How much?"

"What?" Chanse paused in his pacing to study him.

"How much do you care for her?"

"Does it matter?" How did one measure such things?

"Of course. But what matters even more is whether she knows how you feel."

It took all of Chanse's fortitude not to turn away from the question. "How can we discuss such things when far more pressing matters hang over our heads?"

Braden reached out and took Chanse's arm, the intensity in his face and his grip surprising. "That is all the more reason to share them when the opportunity arises. Because you may not get another."

"I'll keep that in mind." Chanse knew to what Braden referred. His brother had nearly lost Ilisa before he'd had a chance to tell her the depth of his feelings. "This situation isn't the same."

Chanse had been able to tell from the moment he'd seen Braden and Ilisa posing as husband and wife that more was between them than their mission. That wasn't the case with him and Arabela. They were in difficult circumstances with their lives in danger. Decisions about the future were impossible when they didn't know what the morrow would bring, let alone the coming sennight. Now was not the time to discuss their feelings, especially since he wasn't quite sure what they were. Of course, he cared for her, but—

"Take my advice and grasp the moment with both hands," Braden argued. "Before 'tis too late."

Before Chanse could say more, the prioress and Arabela joined them in the courtyard.

"We have a slight change in plans," Arabela announced, her voice low as though not wanting anyone to overhear.

"Dressing as one of the sisters will draw too much notice," Prioress Matilda said. "They're frequently in Berwick. The residents gather around them when they go for one reason or another. Most are well known by those who live here, so Arabela would be asked far too many questions if she dressed as a nun."

For a long moment, Chanse held hope that the idea of Arabela entering Berwick had been abandoned.

"Instead, I'm going to take a cart with dried herbs to sell," Arabela said.

"How will that disguise you?" Braden asked before Chanse could.

Arabela smiled, satisfaction evident in the tilt of her lips. "I'll wear simple clothing and have an entirely different purpose than the person they were told to watch for."

"And she'll have a reason to give the guards at the gate as to why she wants to enter," the prioress added. "They can look through the cart for themselves and won't find anything amiss."

While Chanse understood the logic of the prioress's argument, an uneasy feeling came over him. Then again, when it came to placing Arabela in danger, everything made him uneasy. Her very presence stole his logic and intuition. He was no longer certain what was a good idea and what wasn't. He looked at Braden, hoping he'd question the idea thoroughly.

Braden nodded in approval, much to his dismay. "That just might work. How soon can it be arranged?" he asked.

"The prioress has already requested the attire be brought to my chamber," Arabela said. "The cart is being prepared as we speak. We can enter the city well before midday on the morrow and be in place before Rothton and the other person arrive for the meeting."

Prioress Matilda turned to Arabela. "Sister Catherine will review the contents of the cart with you to make certain you can identify the herbs in case you're questioned."

"Mayhap she could tell me some of the prices for them as well," Arabela said. "I don't want to stumble over the answers if asked."

"Excellent idea," the prioress said.

"I'll be ready come the morn." Arabela's gaze lingered on Chanse before she looked away.

The prioress gestured for Arabela to precede her as they walked toward the area of Arabela's chamber, their conversation continuing.

Braden caught Chanse's gaze. "Don't say it."

But Chanse had to. "I don't like it."

"You're going to curse us if you keep stating that." Braden shook his head. "Instead of worrying over Arabela, you should determine how you're going to make it past the guards. I'll meet Arabela near the entrance and lead her toward the tavern. If all goes well, she'll be within sight of both of us at all times, and we'll be ready before midday. She'll identify the person with whom Rothton is meeting, and we'll know all the members of the Sentinels. We're close to meeting our objective and will soon be able to return home."

Chanse had a difficult time matching Braden's enthusiasm.

THE NEXT MORN, Chanse waited for Arabela to emerge from her chamber. He'd eaten supper alone as Arabela was busy with preparations. Or was she simply avoiding him?

His night had been a restless one, his dreams filled with memories of them making love scattered with nightmares of Lord Graham seizing Arabela at the city gate.

The sight of her dressed in the roughly woven brown kirtle and cloak had him shaking his head. The garments were much different than the fine ones he'd removed from her slim form the previous day but didn't hide her beauty or her noble bearing.

"You're going to have to walk differently," he advised.

She stilled. "How so?"

"You move like a lady." Her posture and elegant movements would gain notice even if her clothing didn't.

"What do you suggest?"

"Try hunching your shoulders slightly." She complied. "A little more."

At his nod, she walked toward him but still looked too much like a lady, at least to him.

"Shorten your stride."

She changed her steps to more of a shuffle but forgot to hunch.

They worked on it for a short while before he was satisfied. "Now we need to see what we can do about the way you speak."

"I dinna ken."

His eyes widened. "I'm impressed."

"Och, but I've lived in Scotland all me life. I've heard enough of thick brogues to make them sound convincin'." She kept the accent as she spoke.

Damn if it wasn't appealing. What else did he still have to learn about this woman?

Edith joined them to look over the details for herself. She seemed even more nervous than Chanse did.

"Are ye certain I can't go with ye?" the maidservant asked.

"I wish you could, but the guards might be searching for the two of us since my father knows we left together. The prioress thinks it best if I go alone."

"Take great care, milady," Edith said as she adjusted the hood of Arabela's cloak to better cover her hair.

"I'll return before you've had a chance to worry." Arabela hugged her.

"Remember," Chanse told Arabela, "I won't be far behind you, and Braden will be in front of you. You need only act as if you have nothing to hide."

All too soon, he watched as Arabela led the donkey pulling the small cart of herbs, worry already gnawing the pit of his stomach. A thin blanket lay over the cart to protect the dried herbs from dust.

He'd warned her to take every possible precaution as well as given her the basic directions from the gate to the tavern in case his arrival in Berwick was delayed for some reason.

Though he longed to ride beside her, he remained behind, waiting. When she neared the gate, he'd ride for the trees and approach Berwick from a different direction with the hope that no one would realize the two of them were together.

What if Arabela was recognized? Would the donkey behave itself? What if the animal bolted? What if she forgot to walk as they'd practiced? What if—

He stopped himself before he went mad, thinking of all that could go wrong. Instead, he tried to think of a solution to each of those possibilities. And waited.

When she neared the gate, he left the convent and rode into the woods for a distance so that he could approach the city from the south. Soon, he joined the line of travelers who wished to enter Berwick and tried to focus on his part of the plan.

He breathed a sigh of relief when those behind her shifted, giving him a glimpse of her. Well over a dozen people walked between them with wagons, carts, horses and all manner of goods, making it difficult to keep her in view. The guards would collect taxes from those intending to sell goods, which made the line move slowly, let alone when they were asking additional questions. He intended to tell the guard that he was visiting his brother. He hoped that would be enough to gain him entrance. His saddlebags contained a change of clothing to make it look as if he intended to stay for several days.

At last Arabela reached the guard. Though Chanse couldn't hear what either of them said, he watched as she gestured toward the cart and pulled back the blanket to reveal the bundles of herbs. The guard didn't seem satisfied by whatever she said. He walked around the cart, lifting the blanket on the opposite side to closely examine the contents.

Then the guard turned to look over Arabela from head to toe, shook his head, and waved for the other guard to join him.

Chanse's heart threatened to beat out of his chest, but he could only watch from afar and hope.

~

"How long do ye intend to remain in the city?" the guard asked.

"All the day, unless I sell me herbs afore that." Arabela swallowed against the panic that threatened. The man was questioning her far more than he had those who'd entered before her. Did he somehow sense her deception?

The man glanced at the other guard and again waved him over, but he looked over the cart and shook his head, continuing his conversation with one of the other people who waited in line.

The urge to release the reins of the donkey and run as fast as her legs could carry her nearly overwhelmed her. An image of Rory or her father coming through the gate to chase after her made her mouth go dry. Her gaze swept wildly over those nearby in search of them.

Then she squeezed her eyes shut, hoping to quell her panic. A deep breath helped as well. Chanse's voice echoed in her mind, telling her to remain calm no matter what happened. Thank goodness he'd prepared her for just such a thorough inspection.

With renewed determination, she hunched her shoulders further and tried to look at the guard as if he were nothing more than a bug on her shoe. She waited while he circled the cart once again as if he expected something to jump out at him.

"Do ye want to buy some lavender for yer woman?" she boldly asked, making her brogue as thick as possible. She reached into the cart and held up the sweetly fragranced stems with their purple buds. "'Twill make the stench leave ye and yer home. It makes a fine soap."

"Nay," the guard shouted as though offended by her remark. "Go on through."

Relief made her knees weak as she urged the donkey forward, holding tight to his bridle. The animal jerked his head at her tense grasp as though demanding she relax. She loosened her hold and ran a hand along its neck, pleased to have its assistance in getting into Berwick.

Though she wanted to risk looking back to see if Chanse was close behind, she kept moving forward. Two cobblestone streets fanned out from the gate, one in a northerly direction and the other to the east. Narrower streets crossed the main ones. Berwick was even larger than what she'd expected. But her view of the city was soon hidden by the three and four-story buildings that lined the street.

Many had a long horizontal shutter they'd opened to serve as a display table for their wares. Colorful signs stated the store's purpose. She'd never seen so many items offered for sale. How she wished she could browse through the products and haggle with the shopkeepers. Some watched those walking along while others worked in the back of their shops to produce more of whatever they sold.

The sheer number of people was shocking. She'd never been among so many. She paused alongside the street, searching for Braden whom she was supposed to follow to the tavern. But he was nowhere in sight. Though Chanse had told her the general direction of the tavern, the streets were more confusing than she'd expected. Had she already passed the street on which she was supposed to turn?

The panic she'd been so happy to leave behind seeped back in. Where was Braden? She risked a glance back at the gate, but she couldn't see any of those who waited in line from here. Surely she could simply wait until either Braden or Chanse arrived.

"Get on with you and that beast!" called the shopkeeper near where she stood. "You're blockin' customers."

She waved to acknowledge his request and reluctantly moved forward, uncertain what to do. The donkey didn't care for the people and horses and other carts moving past. His ears flicked back, and he shifted, signs that he might bolt.

"Easy," she said as she ran a hand over its nose. "Why don't we get through this together?"

With jerky steps, the donkey started forward again, but its gait was faster than she wanted.

Arabela reviewed Chanse's instructions. He'd said to turn left at the potter's. But which potter? She saw no fewer than three. After she'd walked past the first one, she realized too late there would be no turning around on the busy street.

She searched the crowd but still didn't see Braden. Another glance behind her showed several men on horseback, but none were Chanse. The terrible feeling of being lost and alone came over her, leaving her trembling. If she went too far or turned down the wrong street, how would they ever find her?

With slow steps, she guided the donkey left at the next corner, hoping she could circle back to find the correct street. The quiet here was most welcome. She paused again, thinking to wait here where she could watch the street that led from the gate.

"Lookin' fer the market square?" a man asked as he emerged from one of the buildings, wiping his hands on the leather apron he wore.

"I'm waitin' fer a friend first," she replied, realizing she'd nearly allowed her brogue to slip.

"Ye can't wait here with that donkey and cart," he replied with a shake of his bald head. "The guards won't allow anyone to linger in this area. They'll be on ye like flies on—er—honey."

She nodded, heart pounding at the idea of the guards approaching her.

"If ye're in the city to sell yer wares, the market square is where ye need to go." He pointed in the direction of the square. "Keep an eye on the church steeple and walk toward it. That'll tell ye if ye're in the right place." He watched her to make certain she followed his instructions, which forced her to turn right at the next street.

What more could she do but go to the square? She had no idea where the tavern was from here. She didn't know where to wait until Braden or Chanse found her without drawing unwanted attention.

With slow steps, she guided the donkey toward the center of town, continually watching for Braden or Chanse. Most of the traffic appeared to be going in that direction as well. Several people complained at her slow pace, but she waved them around her, unwilling to arrive at the square any quicker.

In truth, she had no idea what to do when she got there. People would expect her to set up her cart to sell the herbs, which she didn't want to do. Her best hope was that Chanse would find her before then. If not, she'd watch how the other vendors did their business and do the same. She could only hope it wouldn't come to that.

At last, she reached the market square. Some of her fear fell away as she looked in awe at the chaotic scene before her. So many people. So many wares. 'Twas like the market fair that had been held at home several years ago but even bigger. One side of the square had permanent wooden stalls while on the opposite side, carts of various sizes were lined up in rows.

"Those without stalls take yer carts to the north side of the square," a man called in a booming voice. He pointed to where he wanted the newcomers to go.

Arabela looked behind her to realize she wasn't the only one who seemed new to the experience. Several others stared at the confusion rather than following the man's order. The mix of shoppers and vendors made it difficult to comply with his request.

She couldn't shake her sense of foreboding. Mayhap she should return to the city gate and search for Chanse. With so many people milling about, they'd never find her here. While midday had not yet arrived, she had little time to waste.

As best she could, she wound her way through the crowd, hoping to find a place to turn around. A man strode past, jostling her and her hood fell back. She quickly pulled it up.

"Arabela?"

She turned at the sound of her name, the strong hand on her arm holding her still.

Rory.

CHAPTER 21

Arabela's heart thundered as she stared at her betrothed—nay, her nightmare—in disbelief.

His gaze swept over her from head to toe then to the donkey and cart. "What do you think you're about?"

Her thoughts slowed as fear took over. Words failed her.

"I knew I'd find you if I looked long enough." His satisfied smile brought a lump to her throat. "Your father will be most pleased."

Just as quickly as the smile came, it disappeared, anger hardening his coarse features. "You've led us on a merry chase. Edinburgh. Dunbar." He tightened his hold on her arm and jerked her close. "You'll pay for wasting my time." He raised his hand and she flinched, bringing back his smile, though there was nothing friendly about it. "That's right. You should be worried after what you put us through."

"Release me," she demanded and tried to wrench free. After all she and Chanse had endured, this couldn't be how it ended.

Rory laughed. "I'm not letting go. Where's the bastard who took you?" he demanded, his gaze searching the crowd.

"I don't know what you mean." Her gaze followed his, trying to gather her thoughts and think of some way to escape.

He leaned close, his face a foul breath away from hers, as he forced her back against the cart, the edge digging painfully into her hip. "Don't lie to me, you little bitch. We know you had help. Your father might choose to believe someone took you captive, but I know the truth. You left willingly with the bastard."

"Nay. I left of my own accord." How much did he know? Did he realize who she'd been with? She prayed he didn't. The idea of him harming Chanse made her ill.

"I know the truth. When I find him, I'm going to kill him," Rory said. "He can't have left you on your own for long. We'll wait right here until he shows up, shall we?"

Arabela's thoughts raced. Chanse might very well come to the market square looking for her when he didn't find her near the gate or at the tavern.

Chanse was skilled, something she'd witnessed with her own eyes when he'd competed in the tournament held to celebrate her birthday, but Rory was bigger. Meaner. The idea of the two men fighting was terrifying, for she feared Chanse might lose. He'd fight with honor while Rory had none.

Chanse had already sacrificed too much to save her. Dying in the market square at Berwick before her eyes? Nay. Not when she could do something to prevent it.

She might be nothing more than a pawn, but this time, she could choose how she was used. And for what cause. She chose Chanse. He was worth any sacrifice. She should've told him of her feelings when she had the opportunity.

"If I promise to go with you..." She swallowed hard at the thought then continued, "willingly, will you leave be the one who aided me?" she asked. With luck, she'd manage to find a way to escape once she knew Chanse was out of Rory's reach. If she could make it back to the convent, they could form a different plan.

He looked at her in surprise before a calculating look came over his expression. "Only if you agree to go through with the wedding."

Her heart dropped, a denial on her lips. Marry Rory? After all she'd done to escape him? Nay. Yet what choice did she have? Her thoughts flew, searching for another way. One that would keep Chanse from being hurt. She searched the crowd for the sight of his broad-shouldered form only to halt, lowering her gaze.

If she wanted to protect him, it was imperative that he didn't find her when Rory was at her side.

What should she do?

She closed her eyes, already knowing the answer. She'd do anything to save Chanse. He'd given her a taste of freedom. And hope, though that flame burned no longer.

She nodded, lips pressed tight to keep from crying.

"Say it," he demanded, leaning close.

"Aye, I'll marry you if you leave him alone." Though she gave her word, surely, she could find some way to make Rory change his mind about wanting to go through with the wedding. But how?

Only a moment passed before she realized that would prove impossible. If he wanted to be king, he had to marry her. She'd be wiser to focus her efforts on her father. He couldn't truly believe Rory with his brutish ways would make a good king. She was certain he'd stop listening to her father's advice soon after he was crowned. Her father wouldn't care for that.

The journey home would take nearly a sennight. By the time they arrived, she should be able to convince her father that Rory wasn't the right choice. She held tight to the idea, determined to find a way to make her father listen.

Rory's smirk was an unpleasant sight that chilled her blood. As though to test her word, he released his hold on her and eased back to offer her his arm.

She took it, careful to keep her eyes on the ground. If Chanse was coming, she didn't want to know. Nor did she want him to see her. Not now that she'd made that promise.

∽

CHANSE CLENCHED his teeth to keep from cursing at the guard who was searching his saddlebags. He'd even had to remove them from his horse for the guard. What did he suspect Chanse of taking into the city? Far too much time had passed while he'd waited for those in front of him to be searched as well.

"How long will ye be in Berwick?" the man asked.

With effort, Chanse mustered a smile—anything to appear disarming despite the sword strapped to his side. Odd how his attempt at a casual smile no longer felt as comfortable on his lips as it had before he'd begun this mission. "A few days. Long enough to visit my brother."

He wondered if they questioned everyone because Lord Graham realized someone had helped his daughter. He didn't believe the lord knew the identity of that person. What were the chances of keeping it that way?

A shout from a disgruntled person toward the back of the line sounded, followed by additional murmurs from others who waited.

The guard gave Chanse another long look before waving over the man who'd searched his saddlebags. "Return his bags. He can pass. The line is long enough."

Chanse soon rode through the gate, looking over the crowd for the donkey and cart, for Arabela. But she was nowhere to be found. He halted in the middle of the street to look all around him, certain he'd missed her, ignoring the shouts from those behind him.

Still nothing.

He wanted to call her name though that would serve no purpose. His blood thrummed in his ears, muffling the sounds around him. Where could she be? Nearly frantic, he rode up the street a short distance before returning to the city entrance.

Nothing.

The crowd made it difficult to maneuver without trampling someone, but he was almost beyond caring. He was desperate to find her. He rode down several of the streets, including the one that led to the tavern, then circled back to the main street.

Nothing.

Had Braden found her and taken her all the way to the tavern? He kneed his horse toward the place, searching for her as he went. The street near the meeting place held no donkey and cart.

And no Arabela.

Before he could decide whether to venture inside with the hope Braden was there, his brother strode out, a scowl upon his face.

"They've changed the location of the meeting," he said when he neared. His gaze swept the area. "Where is she?"

Chanse's stomach fell. "I was hoping she was with you."

Braden's gaze met his. "Nay. I haven't seen her. I couldn't leave to find her for fear I'd lose the chance of finding out where they moved the meeting."

Worry rushed through Chanse, clouding his thoughts. Emotions made clear thinking impossible, and he didn't care for it. He felt dull-witted, unable to decide on the next step.

"We'll find her," Braden said. "She can't have gone far."

That wasn't what Chanse feared. He felt down to his bones that something was wrong. Terribly wrong. "Where is the new location of the meeting?"

"Sir Gilbert invited them to the keep." Sharing the news brought back Braden's scowl.

Sir Gilbert de Umfraville served as governor of the city and had replaced Ilisa's brother after the siege. They'd had a few encounters with Gilbert, none of them pleasant. The idea of him becoming involved with the Sentinels was concerning.

"I'm surprised," Chanse managed.

"As am I. He has more ties to England than most. Why would the Sentinels want anything to do with him?"

Chanse couldn't determine a response. His thoughts were too full of worry for Arabela.

"Something's wrong." His gaze held Braden's, conveying what he couldn't with words.

Braden studied him a moment then nodded. "Aye. Ride to the market square and see if she's there. I'll meet you as soon as I retrieve my horse from the stable."

Chanse couldn't bring himself to ask if Braden felt the same. He didn't think he could take it if he did. He trusted his brother's instincts more than his own.

Instead, he turned his horse toward the center of the city, watching the crowd as he went, hoping to see her. The square was filled with people, some shopping, others selling. Riding gave him a better vantage point but also made it difficult to move through the crowd. He hoped remaining astride his horse would make it easier for her to see him.

The side of the square that held stalls for those who sold their wares on a regular basis was the most crowded. He focused on searching the other side of the square where carts were lined up in an orderly fashion.

The familiar donkey and cart stood toward the back. His heart surged at the sight.

But no Arabela.

He quickly dismounted, ignoring the weakness in his knees and the tightness in his chest. He led his horse toward the donkey. Its reins were looped over a pole placed there for that purpose. The cart was still covered.

An old man stood nearby, guarding a similar cart overflowing with bundles of aromatic rushes. "Is that yer cart?" he asked.

"Nay. Did you happen to see the woman who brought it here?"

"Aye, she left a short time ago with a man."

"What did he look like?"

"Big knight. Dark hair. Pock-marked face."

The pain in Chanse's chest heightened, making it difficult to breathe. That was an apt description of Sir Rory from what he'd been told. "Damn and blast." Thoughts reeling, he asked, "Did you see which way he took her?"

"He didn't take her. She went with him willingly enough, though she seemed surprised to see him."

"Willingly?"

"Aye. No doubt of it."

Chanse shook his head, unable to make sense of what the old man said. He couldn't imagine her going with Rory of her own accord no matter the reason. Not after all they'd been through to escape him.

"Was anyone else with them?"

"Not that I saw." The old man nodded toward the far side of the square. "They left the square in that direction. I was watching as I couldn't ken why she'd leave her donkey and cart unattended. Thieves are thick around here. You can't trust anyone."

Nay, agreed Chanse silently. You couldn't trust anyone. Not even beautiful ladies who'd stolen your heart. Why had she gone with Rory? Was she telling the knight and her father of his and Braden's efforts to halt the Sentinels? Nay. He halted his spiraling thoughts. He refused to believe that.

The woman he loved would never—

Loved? His mind poked at the description as though testing it to see if it were real. Aye. Love. No other word captured what he felt for Arabela. He loved her. She would never betray him.

Then why had she gone with Rory?

"What's happened?" Braden asked his hand on Chanse's shoulder.

"She's gone." He turned to look at his brother, still reeling from the news, fear for her safety churning his stomach. "She went with Rory."

CHAPTER 22

Arabela's breath hitched as Rory escorted her through the streets. She had to keep herself from running away as fast as her legs could carry her. Could she break free using one of the methods Chanse had taught her? Nay. She'd given her word and intended to keep it. For now.

But her hand curled into a fist where it rested on his arm.

"Where are we going?" She blinked back tears, uncertain if they were from the pain in her heart or the fear of what was to come.

"To your father."

"He's here? In Berwick?" Though she wasn't surprised, the news did nothing to calm her worry.

Rory didn't bother to answer.

"Are we going to the tavern?" she asked. What better way to keep Rory off balance than to make him realize their secret plans weren't so secret?

He halted abruptly to stare at her. "What do you know about a tavern?"

"I heard a rumor that an important meeting was to be held at a tavern at midday."

His eyes narrowed with suspicion before he continued forward, his long stride forcing her to nearly skip to keep pace with him. "Nay. We're going somewhere else." He led her to a stable where his horse waited.

He didn't bother to pay the lad who fetched his horse, but the boy wisely held his tongue. Rory mounted and reached down to take Arabela's hand and pull her up before him.

She couldn't help but note the difference of him behind her compared to Chanse. She despised Rory's touch, the feel of his body behind her, his foul breath on her neck, his arms around her, holding the reins—everything about him. She felt trapped with no hope of escape. Reminding herself that it was her own doing didn't help.

Had Chanse reached the market square? Did he have any idea what had happened to her? She hoped not. The idea of him coming after her caused her hands to tremble with fear for what Rory would do to him.

Rory kicked his horse, and the large animal surged forward, tipping her against Rory. He laughed in response and tightened his arms around her.

"Mayhap we should make a stop before we meet your father," he whispered in her ear. "You could show me how much you appreciate me not killing the bastard who helped you leave."

Her stomach clenched as disgust filled her at the thought of repeating the beautiful moments she and Chanse had shared with this man. But if she married Rory, that was exactly what she'd be doing. Such an idea was inconceivable. "I think not."

He drew back on the reins, slowing the steed. "I could return to the market square and find him this very moment. I have no doubt his reaction to seeing you in my arms would give him away."

"No need." She forced herself to pat Rory's forearm, hoping to appease him.

"Are ye certain?" His threat had her shifting her hand to his thigh.

"I'm certain." Would that be enough? Once they were farther away from the market square and the possibility of seeing Chanse, there'd be no need for such gestures.

The horse started forward, jerking its head to protest being held back. Rory loosened his hold on the reins, and the animal continued deep into the city.

He released a hand from the reins and squeezed her breast painfully. His thumb rubbed back and forth across the tip, and his hips shifted. The feel of his hardness against her bottom made her cringe. "You're mine now." He nuzzled her ear.

She bit her lip to keep from telling him that it was too late. She was already Chanse's, body and soul. Love bloomed inside her and with it came hope.

~

CHANSE WAITED outside the small hut in Berwick where Braden, Ilisa, and her young brother, Alec, stayed. Braden had paid the old man in the square to return the cart and donkey to the convent with a message to the prioress, advising her their plans had changed.

Braden and Chanse had an idea of how to save Arabela, but they needed Alec's assistance to implement it. Thank goodness one of the tavern serving maids had overheard the messenger who'd advised the Earl of Rothton of the change in the meeting place. She'd easily shared her knowledge in exchange for one of Braden's coins.

Chanse brushed his hand along his horse's neck, needing to do something to calm himself. Various possibilities ran through his mind as to why Arabela had gone willingly with Rory.

'Twas impossible to shut out the hurt and doubt of her actions. After all they'd shared, how could she? *Why* would she?

No matter how he viewed it, her decision made no sense. Not when he knew what he did of Arabela. She didn't care for Rory, and she realized the consequences of Rory being placed on the throne as much as anyone. Without her, Lord Graham had no reason to help make Rory king. And without Graham, Rory had no chance of reaching the throne.

Arabela was the key to all of their plans.

Including his own.

Guilt sprang forth, causing him to bow his head. He'd been determined to use her in his own way. Except he believed his purpose had been the best for the people of both England and Scotland. He thought Arabela agreed on that as well.

Was she planning something? Was that why she'd gone with Rory? His hand slowed its path along his horse's side. Or had she thought to protect him?

The memory of her in his arms, of all the moments they'd shared during their journey, and most especially those in the cottage during the rainstorm filled his mind. She meant so much more to him than the original purpose he'd intended. He wanted—needed—her in his life. In his arms. He wanted the chance to explain just what she meant to him, to tell her of his love.

He might not understand why she'd chosen to go with Rory, but he refused to believe the worst. Some other reason was afoot.

Determination sparked deep within him, and he held it tight. He was going to rescue her this time, whether she wanted to be rescued or not. She would not sacrifice herself to protect him.

Braden, Alec, and Ilisa emerged from the hut.

"Ready?" his brother asked.

"Aye," Chanse answered, feeling calmer now that he had his purpose firmly in mind. He placed a hand on the boy's shoulder. "'Tis good to see you, Alec. We're in need of your skills once again."

Alec grinned. "Braden mentioned that. I'd be pleased to assist you."

Ilisa wrapped an arm around Braden's waist. "Are you certain I can't go with you to help as well?"

Braden returned her embrace. "Nay. I need you free to advise Matthew of the situation when he returns. There's also the chance that Garrick and Sophia will arrive."

The idea of having their cousin's assistance was a welcome one, and Chanse missed Matthew's presence more than ever, but they couldn't wait for either of the men. Time was of the essence.

"I pray Garrick and Sophia come soon," Ilisa said. "I'm most anxious to see my sister." Her brow furrowed as she looked at them. "I expect each of you to take great care and avoid any unnecessary risks."

Braden nodded as did Chanse, both easily agreeing to her request.

But Chanse intended to do whatever it took to free Arabela as well as keep Braden and Alec safe.

Rory would be a formidable opponent if it came to a fight. Somehow, Chanse thought it would. After all, the throne was at stake for Rory. But Chanse had even more to fight for—love.

"Ready?" he asked, anxious to find Arabela. He remembered those bruises on her wrist from Rory all too well. She was in danger in more than one regard.

He mounted his horse, pulling Alec up behind him as Braden bid his wife goodbye. Watching the two kiss, their deep love for each other apparent, made Chanse realize even more what he might have with Arabela if given the opportunity. He should've told her what was in his heart in the cottage. Why had he thought it better to wait?

They rode through the streets, taking the long way around the city toward their destination. Berwick Castle, where the governor resided, was on the highest rise within the city walls and grew steadily closer.

"Nearly there," Alec said with a hint of apprehension in his tone.

As far as Chanse was concerned, they couldn't arrive soon enough.

～

ARABELA'S STOMACH churned as they rode through the gate and into the inner bailey. A flag danced in the breeze high above the keep, the white hawk on a blue background catching her eye. She doubted that Sir Gilbert de Umfraville, who served as governor of Berwick, would aid her. She tried to think of the keep as Ilisa's former home, but that did little to make it feel welcoming.

In truth, 'twas difficult to think of anything with Rory directly behind her. They continued until they reached the steps of the keep. Rory dismounted, and Arabela slid off the horse before he could aid her. His scowl suggested he didn't care for the small gesture of defiance. That only made her want to find another way to annoy him.

He took her arm and marched up the steps. The guard there held open the door, and within moments they were near the entrance of the great hall.

Rory jerked her to a halt. "You will behave yourself and remember your promise."

Arabela met his gaze, saying nothing. Chanse was not here so acting submissive was no longer required as far as she was concerned.

She heard her father's voice before she saw him, the sound making her stiffen. His anger would be equal to Rory's. But nothing she intended to say or do would please him.

Other men were in the hall with him, she realized as she listened to the voices echoing from the large chamber. Mayhap their presence would delay whatever punishment her father decided for her.

She and Rory rounded the corner and entered the hall. Her father, the Earl of Rothton, and a stranger sat at a trestle table with silver goblets before them. A fire burned in the massive hearth, but still the room felt cold.

The conversation halted at their approach.

Her father's eyes widened with surprise. "Rory, what have you found?"

"Your daughter has returned to us, my lord."

Arabela looked at Rory, his polite words so different than his normal tone. Who did he seek to impress?

"Arabela, my dear. We feared you were lost from us forever." Her father rose along with the other men. "How terrible that you were taken captive before the wedding."

She opened her mouth to correct him only to be pinched from behind by Rory. Apparently, she wasn't to speak the truth in front of the others.

Her father came around the table to embrace her. "You ungrateful girl. How dare you," he whispered. He drew back to look into her eyes, and she could clearly see rage burning there. "How do you fare?" he asked with a concerned tone which belied his anger.

"I'm well," she said then bent her head, pretending to be a dutiful daughter until she knew what was afoot.

"You must tell us what happened," he said. "Who took you?"

"I-I'd rather not speak of it." What purpose would be served in saying anything? She had no intention of revealing Chanse's identity or sharing any details of their journey.

Tears filled her eyes. She and Chanse had been so close to succeeding. The idea of being back with her father and Rory made the situation feel hopeless. She had to find a way to convince her father that Rory shouldn't be king before they reached her home.

"What a terrible ordeal you've endured," her father continued. "We'll speak more of it once you're feeling better." He patted her shoulder awkwardly. "Now that you've returned, we can proceed with our plans."

She lifted her head to study him, wondering how he could raise the subject when she'd only just arrived.

"You remember the Earl of Rothton?" he asked with a pointed look to prompt her response.

"Of course," she curtsied.

"This is Sir Gilbert de Umfraville, our host. He serves as governor of Berwick."

The tall, stocky man bowed, gray marking his beard and temples. He didn't appear particularly pleased with the situation based on his frown.

To her surprise, the Bishop of Moran entered the hall from a doorway and moved toward them. His sparse gray hair circled the back of his head. His brows were still black, giving him an odd appearance, as though different parts of people had been put together to make a whole.

"We also have the pleasure of another guest joining us," her father said as he smiled broadly at the bishop.

She'd met the man twice before at her father's keep. He must be one of the Sentinels. Disappointment filled her at the thought, even though she'd suspected that might be the case. Such men should hold themselves above political issues in her opinion, though she knew that wasn't the case.

The bishop greeted her, his smile more practiced than sincere.

"Dear Arabela, we've been so worried about you." But his dark eyes told her that was a lie. Her arrival simplified things for all of them. Now they didn't have to alter their plan—or so they thought.

"May I rest before we begin the journey home?" she asked. The more time she had to form a plan, the better. If her father had spent any time with Rory while they'd searched for her, he had to doubt Rory's ability to rule. She need only point that out as often as she could in the coming days—if she could convince him to listen.

"Of course, you may rest. You must be exhausted," her father said with false concern as his gaze swept over her. "We certainly need to find you something other than those rags to wear. The future queen cannot be seen in such attire."

She clenched her hand into a fist at the reminder of what would happen when she returned to her father's holding.

"You'll need to be dressed appropriately for the ceremony."

"Ceremony?" she asked, alarm filling her at his words.

"The bride and groom are here." Her father gestured toward the bishop. "The bishop would be pleased to marry you, wouldn't you?"

The bishop smiled broader. "I'd be honored to unite the future king and queen."

Nay, she wanted to cry out, but her breath caught in her throat.

"Excellent," her father said. "No more delays. The two of you will be married this very day."

"But the guests," she protested, trying to think of a reason to convince him to wait.

"The celebration will be held at your coronation." He glanced at Rory as if to seek his agreement.

"That will be an event worthy of a great feast," Rory said with a nod.

"I would prefer to be married at home." Her mind grasped any excuse to delay.

"This is an opportunity we cannot miss," her father said with a shake of his head. "The bishop is here and so are the two of you."

"Father—"

"Sir Gilbert," her father interrupted her as he turned to their host.

"Would it be possible to acquire more appropriate attire for Arabela? We don't want her married in rags."

The man hesitated for a long moment. "Of course, my lord. I'll have it seen to immediately."

"Mayhap you could also have someone show her to a chamber where she might rest and prepare herself?"

"My pleasure," the governor said though his expression suggested otherwise.

Before Arabela could think of an excuse, she'd been escorted up the stairs to a chamber with a guard posted outside the door. The stark room offered no comfort. She rushed to the window, hoping for a way to escape the madness of the situation. The drop to the ground made that impossible.

With a lump in her throat, she looked out over the city she'd so longed to see, but her tears made that impossible. She wiped them away, reminding herself that at least Chanse was safe. That was all that mattered.

A knock on the door had her turning in concern. Before she could answer, a maidservant holding a piece of clothing and a pitcher entered. The door closed behind her as she bobbed a curtsy.

Arabela stared at the finely embroidered kirtle the maidservant set on the bed. She couldn't—wouldn't—prepare for a wedding she didn't want. "Nay."

The maidservant didn't appear any happier than Arabela as she set the pitcher on the nearby table. "My apologies, my lady, but Lord Graham insists."

Arabela pressed a hand to her stomach. Marry Rory now? She felt ill at the thought. Her mind whirled, desperate to find a way out of this terrible situation.

The guard posted at the door prevented her from fleeing, and the window was too high to be of use. She could refuse to say her wedding vows but didn't think it would serve any purpose. Whether or not she agreed would make no difference. What other choice did she have?

The maidservant poured the water into the basin. "Here's some water to wash."

"To whom did the kirtle belong?"

"Sir Gilbert had it made for the woman he intended to make his next wife, but that didn't come to pass."

Had that woman been pleased to avoid the marriage or disappointed? Arabela closed her eyes. Whether they had anything in common didn't matter. Her thoughts were taking a wild turn in an effort to make her feel less hopeless. It wasn't working.

She turned to the maidservant. "I'm in need of assistance. Do you know of any way I might escape?"

Though sympathy filled her expression, she shook her head. "My apologies, my lady, but my orders from Sir Gilbert are clear. I cannot help you."

Desperation filled Arabela. "If you could merely suggest how—"

"So sorry," the maidservant muttered then hurried out, leaving Arabela alone.

She held a hand to her mouth and drew a shuddering breath. She had to remain calm and determine a way out of the situation. If only she'd found a way to wait for Chanse upon entering the city. She never would've gone to the market square or encountered Rory.

At least she knew Chanse was safe. The thought of making certain no harm came to him gave her strength. She'd gotten herself into this mess, and she needed to find a way out. Somehow.

All she knew was that if there was any chance of escape, it wasn't in this chamber.

Hands shaking, she removed the rough kirtle then splashed water on her face, hoping to remove the traces of her tears. The only way to leave this room was to pretend to go along with the marriage. She fixed her hair, replaiting it tightly as she knew Rory preferred it loose. After shaking out the kirtle to remove some of the wrinkles, she donned it over her chemise. The soft wine-colored wool was finely woven with a paler shade of embroidery along the neck and edge of the sleeves. The garment fit well enough, and she laced it with fingers that refused to fully cooperate.

Mayhap the guard posted outside the door would allow her to pass when he saw she was dressed for the wedding. Then she could find a way to leave before her father or Rory found her. She may have promised to go through with the wedding, but that had been with a threat hanging over her head. The time had come for action.

~

"Do you remember where it is, Alec?" Chanse asked as he followed the lad on foot toward the bushes and trees that covered the hillside below the side of the governor's holding. The horses remained tied at the base of the hill to draw less notice. The wooden wall that protected the keep was slowly being replaced with stone.

"Not far now," he said as he walked slowly forward, searching to and fro.

Chanse glanced at Braden, unable to hide his concern as to whether they could find the small wooden door that marked the tunnel entrance which led to the keep.

Alec, Ilisa, and Sophia had escaped the siege of Berwick two years ago by using this secret tunnel. Garrick, Braden, Chanse, and Alec had used it in the spring to rescue Sophia and Ilisa when they'd been lured there on Graham's order. But it was so well hidden with brush that Chanse didn't know if he could find it again without Alec's assistance.

Larger shrubbery now covered the area. Chanse knew they were near the entrance, but it had been well hidden.

Alec halted abruptly and turned with a frown then backtracked. Chanse's entire body stiffened, his concern growing.

Braden patted his shoulder in reassurance as he passed by then walked alongside Alec. "What do you think?"

"Right in here," the boy murmured as he turned in a slow circle.

Shaking off his worry, Chanse followed Alec's gaze, looking for a hint of the small opening.

"There!" Alec pointed to a bush that looked much like the others.

But if Alec said 'twas here, Chanse believed him.

He and Braden followed the lad who dropped to his knees and wiggled into the brush. "This is it," he declared triumphantly.

Chanse's knees weakened with relief as he pushed his way through the foliage, Braden directly behind him.

Alec pulled and pulled at the door to no avail. Chanse offered his assistance, and the two of them managed to open it.

Braden had brought a rushlight and within a few moments had it lit. Alec knew the tunnel the best, so he led the way with Braden behind him, holding the light aloft. The tunnel was longer than Chanse remembered, but he was pleased to see cobwebs, which suggested no one had passed this way since they'd used it in the spring.

He released a deep breath when they reached the stairs that led to the keep.

"What if she's already left?" Alec asked as he paused at the foot of the stairs. "We might've missed seeing them leave while we were searching for the entrance or in the tunnel."

"Then we'll discover that when we get into the keep." Braden's calm response eased Chanse's worry only slightly.

Alec's concern was a valid one. Surely Rory would leave as quickly as possible to return Arabela home for the wedding. If so, they were wasting time by taking this path. There was no way to know what Rory's plan was.

If he were Rory, he'd want to marry Arabela as quickly as possible. They hadn't seen any sign of Graham thus far. Where might he be?

The truth was that they didn't know. With so few of them, they couldn't keep watch over all the possibilities or people involved.

With a shake of his head, Chanse set aside those doubts. "We've come this far, and we'll know soon enough."

Braden nodded in agreement.

Chanse started up the stairs, motioning for Alec to remain at the foot of the steps.

"I'm not staying down here," the lad declared as he joined them. "I can aid in saving your lady."

Chanse glanced at Braden as he realized how much Alec had

matured since they'd first met him. The boy had endured much during the siege and wanted nothing to do with knights upon their arrival in Berwick.

"I'll not have you risk your neck, Alec," Braden warned. "Your sister will have my head if you return home with the smallest scratch."

"Humph." Alec scowled but continued with them to the top of the stairs.

Chanse closed his eyes for a moment, his heart pounding as he silently prayed that Arabela was unharmed. He reached for the door, only to realize it shuddered beneath his hand.

CHAPTER 23

Hope bubbled up inside Arabela. She swallowed it back, attempting to calm herself as she opened the chamber door and stepped out.

"Hold." The guard blocked her path.

"I'm going to the great hall to meet with my father and Sir Gilbert." Would mentioning the governor help convince him to allow her to leave?

"I'll escort you," he said as he stepped aside.

"No need. I can find the way."

"My orders were clear, my lady." He followed her down the stairs.

She refused to give up hope. Not when it was the only thing moving her forward. If she could reach the front door ahead of him or—

Or what?

Her choices were nil. Fear slowed her thoughts. Did she tell the guard she needed a breath of fresh air? Or pretend to enter the great hall only to find the kitchen and a rear door?

She risked a glance at the man to see how closely he followed.

"This way, my lady," he said with a gesture toward the great hall.

As though reading her thoughts, he shifted to block the path to the front entrance.

That left her with only one unlikely option, but she had to try. She dipped her head to acknowledge his request. Instead of entering the hall, she continued past it. Heart pounding, she didn't so much as glance into the room. The murmur of voices reached her ears, but she kept walking. She'd only managed a few steps before the guard grabbed her arm and drew her to a halt.

"I need to see to something in the kitchen first," she told him with as much confidence as she could muster.

He frowned at her statement, nearly releasing her arm only to tighten his grasp and shake his head as he reconsidered. "To the great hall." Then he pulled her toward the entrance.

"Arabela," her father said, rising from the table as he caught sight of her. "I was just going to send a servant to fetch you."

With the guard at her back, she had no choice but to move forward. Rory stood near the fire a short distance away. The Earl of Rothton remained sitting at the table, his expression unreadable. Neither the bishop nor Sir Gilbert was there.

"I'd prefer to return home before we wed," she said with a lift of her chin. "Mother should be in attendance."

Her father came nearer as if to greet her and leaned close. "Then you should've considered that more carefully before you left," he whispered.

"You cannot truly believe Rory will make a good king," she said quietly, certain Rory wasn't close enough to hear.

Her father looked at her in surprise, doubt forming a crease in his brow.

"Surely you know that once he is crowned, he won't heed your guidance."

His lips pressed tight, dashing her hopes. "I am not in need of your opinion. You will cooperate. Do I make myself clear?"

"Or?" she asked. What was left for him to threaten her with?

"We know who aided your escape."

Her heart sank at his words. Were they true? Had he somehow found Chanse?

"Do not make us punish him for your mistake." But when his gaze shifted to the side, avoiding hers, she realized he bluffed.

She didn't bother to respond to his empty threat. While pleased to think he couldn't harm Chanse, the information didn't help her current predicament.

"Father—"

"As soon as the bishop returns, we'll proceed with the wedding."

Before she could think of a way to use his absence to her advantage, Bishop Moran entered the great hall.

"Excellent," her father said. "Let us begin the ceremony." He moved away to speak with the bishop.

Rory drew nearer to take her hand. She pulled it back.

"What are you about?" he asked, his expression darkening.

"I don't wish to marry you," she said, no longer caring who heard her. "Surely that's clear by now."

He scoffed. "What you want doesn't matter. This is for the greater good."

"You must mean *your* greater good. If Father manages to put you on the throne, King Edward will not be pleased. He'll march on Scotland once again. Do you truly want to lead this country into war?" Her gaze swept over each of them, pinning them with her question.

Her father looked furious, the bishop uncomfortable, and the earl glanced away, refusing to meet her gaze.

"'Tis time Edward was shown a lesson," Rory said. "We can defeat him with the right person making the right decisions." His confidence astounded her. He truly believed his words. Or were those her father's?

"When the people of Scotland can't agree on who should be king, how do you intend to convince them to stand as one?" she asked.

"A war is exactly what we need to unite the country," Rory insisted. "We'll have a common enemy to fight instead of each other."

"How many will die in the process?" A sick feeling washed through her. "Do you remember how many were killed, including women and children, when he laid siege to this city? His wrath will be far worse if he comes to Scotland again."

He scowled. "Death marches alongside war. This will give us the chance to rid this country of the English once and for all."

"If you truly believe that, then there's no hope for our country. No hope for our people." Though she knew she'd never convince him, she had to try.

"You're only a woman," he said with a dismissive look. "I should've known you wouldn't understand." He shook his head as though disgusted with her. "But soon you'll see the truth."

"Arabela." Her father's sharp command had her turning to face him. "You must learn not to argue with your husband."

While she knew heeding her father's words might save her from harm, she couldn't hold her tongue. If they'd been alone, Rory would've already have struck her. Yet how could she remain silent when she knew this was wrong? Not just for her own sake but for Scotland. She wouldn't have any power as queen to stop Rory or her father. Instead, she'd be forced to watch as her country was torn apart.

"Let us proceed with the ceremony," the bishop said, his displeasure at their argument evident in his tight expression.

Rory squeezed her arm as he escorted her toward the bishop. She jerked it free only to have him take it once again.

"I do not wish to marry Rory," Arabela stated as soon as they stood before the bishop. "I do not consent to this."

"Ignore her," her father commanded. "She's not in her right mind after being held captive. She knows not of what she speaks."

The bishop frowned as he looked back and forth between her and her father. "Mayhap this isn't the right time to proceed."

Her father glared at the man, who shifted uneasily. "We must do this now, as we agreed."

"Very well," the bishop relented, much to Arabela's dismay.

"I will not agree to this," she insisted, hoping the bishop would consider her opinion, despite her father.

"Where is Sir Gilbert?" Rory asked. "He's to serve as a witness along with the earl."

"We've wasted enough time." Her father gestured to the bishop to continue. "No doubt he'll be along shortly."

The bishop cleared his throat, his expression smoothing, his body straightening as though he prepared for a performance. He held Rory's gaze for a long moment. "Do you promise to take this woman to wife, if the Holy Church consents?"

"I do," Rory responded, his oath echoing in the great hall.

Arabela swallowed against the lump in her throat as she realized no one was going to listen to her protests.

Rory held tight to her arm as though he believed she'd bolt if given half the chance. Her father kept his gaze on the bishop. The earl remained by the table as though wishing to distance himself from the proceedings.

Tears had her blinking. She'd been so close to achieving her dream of being more than a pawn. Marriage to Rory would be a trial each and every day—if she survived it. She regretted even more not telling Chanse of her love.

"Lady Arabela," the bishop continued. "Do you promise..."

She ignored his question since she had no intention of responding. Heart heavy, she closed her eyes and filled her mind with the image of Chanse, thankful for the time they'd had together and the sweet taste of what an ideal life could be like.

∽

CHANSE MOTIONED for Alec to step back as he braced a hand on the door to keep it from opening, prepared to do battle with whoever was on the other side. Braden handed the rushlight to Alec and moved beside Chanse. Both drew their swords.

At Braden's nod, Chanse took his hand off the door. It opened to reveal Sir Gilbert de Umfraville.

"Hold," Sir Gilbert whispered, raising a hand to stay their attack. He glanced behind him briefly. "I hoped one of you would make an appearance. Someone has to stop this madness, but I cannot do it alone."

Chanse could only stare at the knight who'd caused them so many problems in the past. The last time they'd used the tunnel was to free Ilisa and Sophia from his grasp, though he'd been tricked into holding them. He'd done little to help end the situation. "Why would you do so?"

"I don't wish to see Sir Rory crowned king any more than the English do. But I have to continue living here. 'Twould be much better if *you* halted Lord Graham and the bishop. I wish to remain innocent in all this if possible."

"The bishop?" Chanse repeated, his mind latching onto the term. "The Bishop of Moran?"

"Aye," Sir Gilbert confirmed.

Braden shifted to stand beside Chanse and held his gaze. "'Tis true then. Arabela was right. The bishop is the other Sentinel."

Sir Gilbert shook his head. "I don't know anything of the Sentinels."

Chanse didn't believe that for a moment.

"But I want this stopped and these men gone from my keep," the knight continued. "Lord Graham asked to hold a secret meeting here, but I only agreed to avoid angering him."

"Is Lady Arabela here?" Chanse asked.

"Aye," Sir Gilbert confirmed.

"How many are in the hall?" Braden asked.

"Graham, Sir Rory, the Earl of Rothton, the bishop and the lady. Is Sir Garrick here as well?"

"Nay. Only the two of us," Chanse said, deliberately not mentioning Alec, hoping the lad would remain hidden.

"Humph. The two of you will have to do. But don't count on me for assistance." He frowned for a moment. "In fact, I'll stand by the entrance to the great hall, and one of you can disable me first."

Chanse could only stare at the large knight certain he couldn't have heard him right. Then he looked at Braden, wondering if he could make sense of what Sir Gilbert said.

"We must hurry," Sir Gilbert said. "They're starting the wedding ceremony."

"Wedding?" Chanse's mind went numb. "You don't mean—"

"The bishop is marrying Sir Rory and Graham's daughter. Hurry." Again, he glanced back to make certain no one watched then motioned for them to follow. He paused just inside the great hall with his back to them.

Chanse remembered the layout of the keep, but the idea that Arabela was being married at this very moment caused his movements to slow.

Sir Gilbert folded his arms across his wide chest as though he'd been there the entire time. Another man, who stood just in front of the governor, watched as well.

"There you are, Sir Gilbert," Lord Graham's voice rang out. "I didn't think you'd want to miss this memorable event."

"Honored to be a witness to history," Sir Gilbert declared even as he dropped one hand to his side and motioned Chanse and Braden forward.

Chanse drew closer, still worried that Gilbert was leading them into an ambush. But he could just see Arabela and Rory standing before an older man dressed in a white vestment gathered at the waist by a cincture less than a stone's throw away.

Braden shifted closer, pointing to where a guard stood. How the man hadn't noticed their approach was a mystery. Perhaps he thought if Gilbert hadn't noticed there was nothing with which to be concerned.

With a nod at Braden, Chanse grabbed Gilbert loosely around the neck from behind, still half expecting the man to put up a fight. He did but with little effort. Chanse quickly disarmed him, tossing aside his sword while Braden did the same to the guard.

Though Gilbert held his silence, the guard cried out, drawing the attention of the rest of the occupants of the great hall. Gilbert sagged against the wall as though Chanse had knocked him out. He slid to the ground and lay still.

Braden struck the guard with the hilt of his sword, and he fell to the ground as well. But his motionless body wasn't an act.

"What is the meaning of this?" Graham called out. He studied Braden and Chanse, obviously recognizing them.

Chanse was pleased to note his face paled as his gaze latched onto Braden.

Arabela's eyes widened with surprise at the sight of him. Relief filled him at the realization that she appeared to be unharmed.

"Chanse." She took a step toward him.

He should've anticipated what happened next, but Rory was quicker than he'd expected. The knight grabbed Arabela, holding her before him like a shield, his arm wrapped about her throat.

"I'll break her neck," Rory threatened.

Cold rage ran through Chanse. The man had no honor if he hid behind a woman.

Graham glared at Rory before turning back to Chanse. "You'd better leave if you want her to remain unhurt."

Chanse knew how twisted Graham was, but he thought he'd be protective when it came to his daughter. Yet Graham stared at them as if he took no issue with Rory using his daughter.

"Release her," Chanse demanded as he moved closer. He kept his focus on Rory, leaving Graham to Braden. The bishop and the earl both backed away.

"Additional witnesses to the wedding are welcome," Graham said with a forced smile. "Especially *English* ones."

Arabela's eyes went wide at her father's announcement. "English?" she repeated, her hands pulling at Rory's arm.

Chanse cursed under his breath. He should've told her the truth. About him. About his purpose. About everything. She'd more than earned his trust—she'd earned his love. But he'd given her nothing in return.

Rory's gaze swung from Graham to Chanse and Braden. "English?"

"Aye. Both of them. They can give the news to King Edward of the marriage as well as the coronation. If they're still alive to do so."

Chanse ignored Graham in favor of watching Rory. "Arabela is not part of this. Release her."

"Not until the wedding is completed." Rory glanced at the bishop as Graham nodded in agreement. "Continue."

The bishop frowned, keeping his distance. "I don't think—"

"You are not here to think," Graham interrupted. "You are here to perform the ceremony."

"Being forced to do so will not make it binding," the bishop argued, though his tone lacked conviction.

"You have been nothing but a thorn in my side from the beginning," Graham said as he moved closer. "For once, do as you're told."

The bishop's mouth gaped. "I do not have to take orders from you."

Their argument dimmed in Chanse's ears as his focus sharpened on Rory. The man frowned, his attention shifting to Graham.

This was Chanse's opportunity. He glanced at Arabela. She ignored the men, her gaze remaining steadily on Chanse. No doubt lingered in her expression, despite the fact that she'd just learned he was English. She gave the slightest nod then went limp, causing Rory to struggle to keep her upright.

Chanse lunged forward and drove his fist into Rory's chin. The impact sent pain shooting up Chanse's arm. Chanse shook his hand even as he prepared to strike again.

Rory shouted in protest as he stumbled toward Arabela, who'd tried to crawl away. He grabbed her, but she rammed her elbow upward, catching him in the nose. The man roared then struck Arabela with the back of his hand.

Rage exploded in Chanse, and he hit Rory again, the blow driving the knight backward, but still he remained on his feet.

Rory caught his balance and plowed his fist into Chanse's jaw. Though larger than Chanse, he wasn't nearly as determined. Chanse quickly regained his balance and hit Rory again, wondering what it would take to force the man to stay down.

Arabela gasped and scrambled away as Rory lunged for her once again.

Chanse punched him, this time landing a blow that snapped his head back and took him to the floor where he remained, moaning.

Chest heaving, Chanse watched him for a moment to make certain he wasn't going to move. Then he turned to Arabela and assisted her to rise. With a gentle hand, he brushed the loose strands of hair from her face. "Did he hurt you?"

"Nay." Her gaze swept over his face, her dark eyes softening as she stared at his jaw. "This must be painful." She placed gentle fingers over the spot where Rory's fist had landed.

Chanse put his hand over hers. "I don't feel a thing."

Her soft smile made his words true.

"Hold." Braden's order had him turning to see his brother with his sword pointed at Graham and the bishop. The earl was nowhere to be seen.

"What is this about?" Sir Gilbert asked as he pretended to wake, though he still didn't rise to his feet.

Braden raised a brow, silently asking if Chanse was well.

Chanse nodded. Keeping one arm around Arabela, he played along with Sir Gilbert's question. "We've come to halt the wedding. These men are part of the Sentinels of Scotland and should be held until the proper authorities can decide their fate."

Graham glared at Braden. "You know not of what you speak. You have no say as to what happens here."

Sir Gilbert stepped forward, blustering as though he'd had no knowledge of their actions. He directed the guard who was slowly coming to his senses to restrain Rory while Braden kept his attention on Graham and the bishop, neither of whom protested overmuch.

Alec entered the great hall with two of Sir Gilbert's guards, taking in the occupants as he strode forward to aid Braden.

Chanse drew Arabela aside, relieved to allow Braden to handle the situation. There would be no easy solution to the situation. Some shared Graham's vision of what direction the country should take. Those supporters would want Graham free to continue his ideas. But few wanted to risk war with England.

None of that mattered to Chanse at the moment. His only concern was Arabela.

He turned her to face him. "Are you certain you're not injured?"

"Aye." But the caution in her eyes hurt, though he knew he had only himself to blame. How could he gain her trust?

"I owe you an explanation," he began.

She closed her eyes, hiding her thoughts from him.

His heart squeezed in response. "Arabela," he tried again. "I owe you an apology. I should've told you who I was and why I was here."

She opened her eyes but still didn't look at him, which made him realize he was speaking what was in his mind rather than what was in his heart. Yet he couldn't. Not here in the present company.

Frustration filled him. He refused to release her before he had his say, and she understood how he felt. He glanced at Braden with a raised brow. His brother nodded.

That was all the permission he needed. He took Arabela's hand in his and led her out of the great hall where they could have some privacy.

With both her hands in his, he faced her. "I love you. I don't know why I waited so long to tell you. Aye, I'm English, but I want to protect the people of this country as much as you. I may have taken you captive, but you've stolen my heart."

A smile tilted the corner of her lips, tightening his chest, even as she lifted a finger to press against his mouth. "I love you, as well, Chanse. I thought you charming but arrogant when I first met you. But I quickly learned the honorable man you are. I would keep your heart and cherish it always if you promise to do the same."

"I do," he vowed even as he drew her into his arms. "Will you share my life with me and be my wife?"

"I'd be honored."

He hesitated. "And if that life is in England?"

"My life is wherever you are," she answered readily.

He grinned, his happiness lifting him. He couldn't help but lift Arabela as well, spinning her in a circle. Then he set her down and kissed her, hoping she felt the same measure of the joy he did.

CHAPTER 24

Arabela leaned against Chanse as they rode toward St. Mary's. His arms were wrapped tightly around her and had never felt more secure.

Sir Gilbert was dealing with the Sentinels, who would have to explain themselves to John De Warenne, Earl of Surrey, the man appointed by King Edward to watch over Scotland. Her father had been enraged to have his plans questioned, but Sir Gilbert had shown surprising diplomacy in handling those involved.

Chanse had advised her that Matthew had delivered a message to their English contact with the information they'd discovered and was expected back soon. Neither Braden nor Chanse believed her father or the other Sentinels would be punished. Instead, they'd be forced to report to the Earl of Surrey on a regular basis. Arabela was relieved and hoped the earl could find a way to bring Scotland together in a peaceful manner, her father included.

She wanted nothing more than to set all of that aside and bask in the moment. She'd been given an opportunity for her dreams to come true, and she didn't intend to waste it.

Chanse rested his cheek against her hair briefly. "When I couldn't find you near the gate or the tavern, I was beside myself with worry."

"I must've turned at the wrong street. I tried to wait for you but was told I couldn't block the street." She stiffened. "We need to go back for the donkey and the cart."

"Braden arranged to have it returned to the convent earlier. He should arrive with Ilisa and Alec soon."

She leaned against him once again only to turn her head and look back at him. "English? I wondered but thought you most likely lived near the border."

Chanse tightened his arms around her. "We live in the heart of England. I should've told you earlier. I'm sorry for that. I convinced myself that the less you knew, the better. If we were caught, you'd have little to tell them." He shook his head as though his reasoning no longer made sense. "There are many things I should've told you. I confess that trust is slow to come to me."

She patted his arm. "I kept a secret or two of my own as well, joining the convent being one of them. Why don't we agree to treat each other honestly from this day forward?"

"Agreed." He sighed. "My family is...unique. We have many secrets. Revealing them to the wrong person could cost us everything, so we have learned to be careful. I hope you'll be patient with me as I learn to share with you."

Arabela shifted in the saddle to place a quick kiss on his lips. The weight of his tone spoke of how important this was to him. "We'll learn to trust together."

The love shining in his eyes warmed her heart. "I know I ask much, but I'd be pleased if you'd consider holding our wedding at home with my family. Would you be willing—"

"Aye," she agreed before he could finish. "I would." His body relaxed, making her realize how concerned he'd been about her agreement. The idea of leaving Scotland was both exciting and frightening. But in truth, she'd already left her home and everything familiar. She didn't want to remain within reach where her father could use her again in some way if he determined a new plan.

"You'll love my mother and father, and they'll love you."

"Truly?" She couldn't quite imagine such a family.

"As I said, my family is like no other in more ways than one." He chuckled, making her wonder what was behind his statement.

"I look forward to meeting them."

"There are quite a few de Bremonts. Many live near my holding. You'll soon grow weary of them."

"I cannot imagine such a thing." She hesitated a moment, but reminded herself of their agreement to speak honestly. "Why does my father fear your brother?"

Chanse hesitated only a moment. "The reason is something I should've told you earlier as well."

"Does it have to do with Ilisa's miraculous recovery and my own?" She hadn't been able to reconcile the fall her friend had taken with her lack of injuries. Not when she'd been walking normally within a few days. Added to that was her own unexplained recovery. She shifted her shoulder at the thought.

"Indeed." He drew a deep breath. "Braden has a special gift."

"A healing one?" She'd heard rumor of such things but never believed. Not until now. Yet there was no other possible explanation for Ilisa's quick recovery.

"Aye." He sounded both relieved and surprised at her guess. "As I said, my family is special."

She frowned, uncertain of his meaning. "All of them?"

"Not all."

"And not you?"

"Nay." Before he could say more, Edith waved from the convent gate.

"Thank heaven ye've returned," she said, wiping her eyes.

Arabela smiled as she slid off the horse to hug the maidservant. "I have much to share with you."

"Chanse?"

Arabela turned at the call to see a tall knight striding toward them from the convent grounds.

"Garrick?" The excitement in Chanse's voice matched his expression. He swung his leg over the horse to drop to the ground, striding forward. "'Tis good to see you."

The two men embraced, slapping each other on the back as men so often did. Arabela smiled as she watched them.

Garrick's gaze shifted to her then back to Chanse, a brow lifted in question.

Chanse held out his hand, and she placed hers in it. "Lady Arabela Graham, this is my cousin, Sir Garrick de Bremont."

Curiosity followed Garrick's surprise. "Graham? Surely not—"

"Daughter to Lord James Graham?" she asked, amused at his reaction. "'Tis true."

Garrick stared at Chanse in consternation.

Chanse grinned. "We have much to tell you. But most important is that Arabela will soon be my wife."

Edith gasped at the news, her smile causing Arabela to do the same.

"I saw something, but I didn't realize..." Garrick shook his head, not finishing the thought. "Congratulations are in order." He turned to her and smiled, holding out his hand. "Welcome to our family."

Her heart filled at his sincerity as he clasped her hand in both of his.

"What are we celebrating?" asked an attractive woman near Arabela's age as she joined them, a slight lilt to her tone that spoke of Scotland.

"Sophia," Garrick said as he placed an arm around her, "Chanse is to be married soon to Lady Arabela."

"Oh!" Sophia's eyes widened. "How exciting." She hugged Arabela then Chanse, causing happiness to overflow in Arabela.

The sound of someone approaching the gate had them all turning to see Braden, Ilisa, and Alec arrive. Alec swung his leg over his horse and dropped to the ground to rush into Sophia's arms.

"Alec!" Sophia cried, her tears causing Arabela to sniff in response, especially when Ilisa hurried to join her sister and brother.

"You are both well?" Sophia asked as she leaned back to study each of them as if to make certain for herself.

The three spoke all at once, their joy at being reunited lifting the hearts of those who watched.

Chanse placed a comforting arm around Arabela. "Wait until you meet the rest of my family. My mother will cry for certain."

"With happiness, I hope," Arabela said.

"She won't allow either you or Ilisa out of her sight for a time, I'm afraid," Braden added, his gaze on his wife's happy reunion. "Prepare to be smothered with love by both her and our father."

Chanse chuckled even as he nodded in agreement. "'Tis true."

The idea was inconceivable to Arabela, but she eagerly anticipated such an experience. She leaned into Chanse. "Have I told you how much I love you?"

"Why don't you say it again," he said as he drew her into his arms. "I will never grow weary of hearing it."

Aware of Braden's regard, she lifted onto her toes to whisper in Chanse's ear. "I love you, Sir Chanse de Bremont."

He turned his head to kiss first one cheek and then the other. "And I love you, Lady Arabela. I vow to keep you, forever and always."

EPILOGUE

TWO MONTHS LATER

Chanse raised his sword, leveling it at Matthew as they stood in the inner bailey of his holding on the fine autumn afternoon. *Home.* There had been days when he hadn't been certain he'd see it again. Yet here he was, blessed as never before.

His homecoming had been made even sweeter by the addition of Arabela. When he'd left England with Braden two seasons ago to follow Garrick to Scotland, he would've never guessed what they'd endure, nor the outcome—that he, his brother, and his cousin would return with Scottish brides.

Matthew laughed. "Marriage suits you, my friend. But you are in far too high of spirits to spar." He shook his head. "Your heart's not in it."

Chanse chuckled as he lowered his sword and rubbed his chest. Matthew was right—Arabela held his heart. The feeling was inexplicable. His joy indescribable. He loved her more than he'd thought possible.

He and Arabela had been married at his mother and father's holding on the rise two valleys to the west of his. But soon after the ceremony, they'd ventured here, both anxious to settle in at their keep and start their new life together. The past fortnight had been filled with more special moments than he could count. Nights of making love and days of conversation that had brought them even closer.

Already, Arabela had made their keep more of a home than he could've guessed. Her touch was everywhere, from their chamber to the great hall to the kitchen. The servants adored her as did the men in the garrison. A letter had arrived from her mother, advising Arabela that she'd chosen to stay at St. Mary's for the foreseeable future with Prioress Matilda. Arabela had been pleased at the news, and the last of her lingering worry had eased.

Matthew's arrival the previous day had been surprising but welcome. His friend seemed unsettled, but Chanse had yet to discover the cause. The knight surely missed Scotland but couldn't remain there without living in fear of retaliation from Graham. England was a safer place but hadn't yet provided happiness. Chanse knew that would take time.

Matthew playfully struck his blade against Chanse's, the sound ringing in the air.

They exchanged several practice blows until a call from the portcullis paused their efforts.

"Your mother and father have arrived?" Matthew asked as if uncertain he'd heard the shout correctly.

"It appears so. I'll advise Arabela." He strode across the bailey and up the steps of the keep. In truth, he was surprised they'd waited this long to visit.

His wife was coming down the tower steps with Edith behind her as he entered. "Done with sparring already?"

"Momentarily. My parents are here."

The delight in her expression pleased him more than he could say.

She clapped her hands together. "How wonderful."

"I'll see to some food and drink," Edith said then hurried toward the kitchen.

Chanse reached for Arabela's hand, and they walked out to greet them. Their horses along with two soldiers driving an ox and cart entered the bailey, Matthew at their side.

"Lady Cristiana," Arabela said and hurried down the steps to hug her then turned to Chanse's father. "Sir William."

His father gathered her into his embrace as though she were his own daughter. "We hope we're not intruding."

"Not at all," Chanse replied as he kissed his mother's cheek and clasped his father's shoulder.

"We have something for Arabela that your mother insisted we bring," his father said, a twinkle in his eyes.

"You do? How thoughtful," Arabela said, her excitement causing Chanse to smile.

"Wait until you see it before you make such statements," his father warned.

His mother playfully slapped his father's arm. "She's going to love it. Trust me."

His father grinned. "I do. You know best."

"Aye," his mother said with confidence. She looped her arm through Arabela's. "Come. Let us have a look and see if I'm right."

His mother pulled off the blanket in the cart, revealing three wooden frames of different sizes then turned to watch Arabela.

Arabela's mouth dropped open. "Are these looms for spranging?"

"Aye." His mother grinned. "You took such an interest in it that I thought you might like looms of your own."

Arabela's eyes filled with tears as she hugged his mother again. "That is the most thoughtful gift. I don't know what to say."

"Spranging?" Chanse asked.

"'Tis a type of weaving using only warp threads," his mother explained. "A lost art for which your lovely wife has shown talent. She picked it up so quickly when you were staying with us that I had some looms built for her."

Arabela turned to him. "The interlinking of the threads allows it to stretch to hold whatever is placed in it. Like a net of sorts but better. 'Tis amazing."

"I brought a selection of thread as well," his mother said, patting the wooden chest next to the looms.

Arabela opened the chest, chatting with his mother as she explored the variety of colors and sizes.

Her pleasure at the gift had Chanse placing a hand on his father's shoulder. "I believe Mother was right. She loves them."

His father shook his head. "'Tis good that I didn't wager with your Uncle Nicholas on it. His daughter enjoys this type weaving as well." He waved a hand toward the looms.

Matthew cleared his throat. "Lady Rihann weaves?"

Chanse turned to his friend, noting the hint of red in his cheeks. Did Matthew carry affection for his cousin?

"Her tapestries are exceptional, but she also enjoys sprang," his mother said.

To Chanse's surprise, Matthew appeared fascinated by this information. Before he could question him, Arabela asked, "Will you stay for the evening meal? We'd be so pleased to have you."

"We were hoping you would ask," his mother said with a smile. "Weren't we, dear?"

"Aye." His father whispered to Chanse, "I hope your kitchen has improved since Arabela's arrival."

Chanse smiled. "Everything has improved with her arrival."

His father chuckled as the men followed the ladies up the stairs. "Have I ever told you about your mother's first sennight at our keep?"

Chanse laughed. "I believe I've heard the tale." His father frowned, as though disappointed. "But Arabela hasn't."

A smile lit his father's face as he hurried forward to walk beside Arabela. "I find myself quite parched."

"You're in luck, for we've just finished a fine batch of ale from the apples in the orchard. Would you care to try some?"

"I'd be delighted," his father said then leaned forward to look at his wife. "Did you hear that, dear? She's newly married and already seen to the brewing of ale."

His mother only shook her head. "You only say that because I failed at doing so when we first wed."

"Do you remember the time..."

Arabela glanced back at Chanse as his father began his tale and gestured for Chanse to catch up, wrapping her arm through his as he did so.

"Walk with us, *husband*," she whispered with a smile.

"My pleasure, *wife*." Chanse held her gaze, his love for her blooming, a sensation to which he knew he'd never become accustomed.

～

Read the beginning of the de Bremont family story in A VOW TO KEEP, Book 1 of the Vengeance Trilogy. My Book

Revenge was all *he lived for...until he met her.*

Sir Royce de Bremont has spent his entire life plotting revenge against his traitorous uncle. Kidnapping the man's bride-to-be brings Royce one step closer to fulfilling his vow of vengeance.

Lady Alyna of Montvue has no desire to marry nor to become a pawn in a game of vengeance. Her only wish is to find a safe place to raise the orphan gifted with second sight she vowed to protect.

The beautiful lady and her precocious son make Royce long for a family of his own, yet until he reclaims his birthright, he has little to offer them. Alyna soon realizes this bold knight has captured her heart but fears she's merely part of his plan for revenge. As passions rise, Royce must choose vengeance or love.

Buy it today!

ALSO BY LANA WILLIAMS

Medieval Romances:

Falling for a Knight Series

A Knight's Christmas Wish, a Novella, Book .5

A Knight's Quest, Book 1

A Knight's Temptation, Book 2

A Knight's Captive, Book 3

The Vengeance Trilogy

A Vow To Keep, Book I

A Knight's Kiss, a Novella, Book 1.5

Trust In Me, Book II

Believe In Me, Book III

Victorian Romances:

The Seven Curses of London Series

Trusting the Wolfe, a Novella, Book .5

Loving the Hawke, Book 1

Charming the Scholar, Book 2

Rescuing the Earl, Book 3

Dancing Under the Mistletoe, a Christmas Novella, Book 4

Tempting the Scoundrel, a Novella, Book 5

Falling for the Viscount, Book 6

Daring the Duke, Book 7

Wishing Upon a Christmas Star, A Christmas Novella, Book VIII

The Secret Trilogy

Unraveling Secrets, Book I

Passionate Secrets, Book II

Shattered Secrets, Book III

Contemporary Romance:

Yours for the Weekend, a novella

If you liked this book, I invite you to sign up to my newsletter to find out when the next one is released: https://lanawilliams.net/

If you enjoyed this story, please consider writing a review!

AUTHOR'S NOTE

Thank you for reading A Knight's Captive, the third full-length book in the Falling For A Knight series, which follows the next generation of the de Bremonts. The series begins with Rylan's story, A Knight's Christmas Wish, a novella. If you're interested in reading Chanse's parents' story, check out Believe In Me.

The sack of Berwick, Scotland, in 1296 was a dark point in the country's history and was the first battle in the First War of Scottish Independence. King Edward I, angered by Scotland's alliance with France, marched on the city with 30,000 infantry and 5,000 cavalry, according to some accounts. The death toll ranges from 7,500 to 13,000, and included men, women, and children. If the king of England's goal truly was to make the mills "flow with their blood," he succeeded. And so began a bloody era for Scotland's independence.

While most of the characters in this series are fictional, the backdrop of the events are true. Sir William Douglas was governor up until the siege and was held in England afterward for several years. He was eventually released after agreeing to accept the English King Edward I as overlord of Scotland. However, he later fought alongside William Wallace. Sir Gilbert de Umfraville was his sworn enemy and took his place as governor. The Guardians of Scotland truly did exist,

AUTHOR'S NOTE

and in my fictional world, a competing group formed called The Sentinels.

Reading about the tumultuous events of this period is fascinating. I hope you enjoy the story and that it catches your imagination, as it did mine.

If you'd like to know when my next book becomes available, I invite you to sign up for my email newsletter, follow me on Facebook, or on Twitter.

Reviews help authors tremendously and also help other readers find books, so please consider leaving a review. It would be much appreciated.

Thank you, dear readers. I couldn't do this without you!

Happy Reading!
Lana

Made in the USA
San Bernardino, CA
19 January 2019